PLAYING WITH TROUBLE

MCKENZIE BROTHERS #5

LEXI BUCHANAN

HFCA Publishing House
Ireland

www.lexibuchanan.net

First Published 2014
This Edition 2024

Cover Design: Alison Chaffin Higson
Editor: Sirena Van Schaik
BETA Readers: Emma Clifton, Heidy Bendana, Kristy Louise Garbutt, Jamie Grant and Nadine Winningham

SYNOPSIS

Lucien McKenzie has lived alone for six years after being severely injured in a car fire. He has shut out everyone but his family. Despite his initial reservations, Lucien finds himself drawn to Lily's friend Sabrina and the way she challenges him emotionally. As they spend more time together, he begins to open up and considers letting Sabrina into his life on a more permanent basis.

Sabrina feels like she is on a roller coaster with Lucien. One minute he needs to be close, the next he pushes her away. He's tormented by his demons, and all she wants to do is be the person he turns to when he's in pain.

Can a man who struggles and hides his true nature from the world keep the love of a good woman? Or will he push her so far that she walks away from him forever?

PROLOGUE

Lucien

I LET THE WHISKEY SLOWLY WORK ITS MAGIC AS I WATCH the woman dance with someone else. The burn numbs me from the inside out. She's never far from my thoughts. Her body is enveloped by another man, making me wish the whiskey would work faster. That someone should be me. Things changed six years ago, though, and that someone would have been me.

That was years before she returned home from London and started spending time with Lily. At first, I thought my preoccupation with her was due to my lack of female companionship since the fire—it had been years since I'd been with a woman. But that wasn't it— my obsession with her is getting out of hand. Gritting my teeth, I nod for the glass to be filled. I don't want or need a woman in my life. I can't have a woman in my life, least of all her.

It isn't that I don't have material things to offer because I do. It's the physical aspect of relationships that I haven't been able to offer anyone in years. Or at least, I thought I couldn't offer that until Sabrina showed up. Now, my libido is awake, but only when Sabrina is around.

My body hums, but it isn't because of the whiskey. It's because of her and the way her hips move when the guy holds her tight. It's driving me crazy. I take a sip of my fourth drink and tear my eyes from her for a moment to scan the room. This wouldn't be so hard if Sebastian and Carla showed up with Ruben and Rosie. At least then I'd have a distraction. I need some conversation to still the thoughts running through my head.

Where are they? I'm starting to think that getting Sabrina and me here alone was perhaps the plan all along. I wouldn't put it past the women to get together and plan this.

Even Ramon showed up with his newly cropped hair and stayed for about thirty minutes before disappearing with Sylvia. I wish he would make up his mind about whom he wants.

I should have left when he did, instead of sitting here punishing myself with visions of Sabrina writhing around with someone else.

My hand tightens around the glass as the guy slides

his hands onto Sabrina's bottom and pulls her tightly against him. I see her stiffen before she glares in my direction. Distaste is clear in her frown, yet she lets the guy continue kneading her ass.

As I hold her gaze, fire ignites through me, and my pants become uncomfortable. If she weren't arousing me so damn much, I'd laugh. My first full-fledged erection in years occurs in Ruben's club, Kenza, and the woman who caused it is in someone else's arms.

The question is, what should I do about it? She can't just be a quick fuck. She's a family friend. Something tells me I should run in the opposite direction because I don't think one, two, or a thousand fucks will get her out of my system. As I watch her leave the dance floor and head toward the restrooms, I realize that I need her. I need her so much that if I don't get inside her soon, I'm going to ejaculate in my pants right here. Nearly six years is a long time to go without an orgasm.

I don't have the strength to walk away from her anymore—not now, not when my body has chosen her.

Sabrina

I escape to the restroom and slip into the largest stall, closing the door and locking myself away from the outside world. Tears burn my eyes, but I hold back my sobs until I hear the room empty out. I need complete privacy, so that no one can witness my total meltdown.

When I agreed to come here tonight, I certainly didn't expect to be stood up by my girlfriends—let alone be left alone with brooding Lucien. The same guy who can never say a nice word to me. He gave me smoldering looks the whole time I was dancing with some nameless guy.

Tears slip from my eyes, a strange mixture of lust and pain, mirroring all the feelings I have for Lucien. There's no doubt that I lust after the man. He is handsome and charming—to everyone but me. He has a loving and caring attitude toward his family. But my feelings aren't just about the way he looks. Part of me wants to erase the pain in his eyes. My heart aches for all that Lucien thinks he has lost because of what happened to him.

Lily told me how lonely she thinks he is. Despite how his family has tried to set him up, he refuses to have female company. He has a will of steel and refuses to budge on the matter. I've suspected for some time that he has cut himself off because of what happened to him. Maybe he has an injury to his groin area. But maybe I'm wrong. If that were the case, surely he wouldn't be looking at me with heat in his eyes, fists clenched tightly around his glass. He wouldn't be looking as though he were trying to keep himself grounded at the bar, away from me.

Leaning against the wall, I rest my hand between my breasts, inhaling deeply and willing myself to calm down as I feel my chest rise and fall with each breath. All I need to do is pull myself together, forget the passion in his eyes, and forget how my body and heart reacted to him. Even now, despite being tied up in knots, I can feel the trail his gaze burned into me.

How could such a scorching look make me so aroused? I silently moan when I move my hand to my right breast and come into contact with my aroused nipple. Shards of pleasure ripple down between my legs.

As I start to lift my short skirt to reach my panties, there's a thump on the door.

I jump, straighten up, and listen.

Another thump. "Sabrina, open up."

Lucien!

Without thinking, I quickly open the door. My mouth twists into a surprised "O" as the hottest guy I've ever seen barrels toward me. He wraps me in his arms and seals his lips to mine, his touch demanding. Somewhere in my befuddled brain, I hear a door slam, and a second later, I feel a lock slip into place.

"Sabrina," Lucien groaned, running his mouth along my jaw and neck. "I need you," he says, his voice thick with lust.

"Yes."

I'm sick of pretending. I want the real man.

Lucien turns and pins me against the door with his hips. I feel his arousal, thick and long, against me.

My tank top flies through the air, followed quickly by my bra.

He growls before ducking his head toward my breasts. I jolt against him as he feasts on each breast in turn, the throbbing between my legs growing more intense.

"Oh God, Lucien," I moan, threading my fingers through his hair and holding him to me.

His hands reach beneath my skirt, and then I feel my panties rip. His fingers slip inside me.

I'm a hot, quivering mess in his arms. From the way he's shaking, I'd say he's the same.

"Help me," he begs, trying to undo his zipper.

I remove one hand from his hair, reach down, and manage to open the denim. I can't resist reaching inside to bare his throbbing cock and rub my thumb over the weeping head. One side feels slightly rougher than the other—maybe burned?

"Enough." He knocks my hand away, aligns himself, and enters me in one powerful thrust. "Jesus," he curses. "It's been years."

My eyes widen in shock. I open my mouth to question him, but he seals our lips together. We both let our bodies do the talking for us.

1

Sabrina

Two nights ago, Lucien was buried deep inside me. He felt amazing, just as I had dreamed he would. At the time, we simply reacted to each other. We didn't think or worry. We just allowed our lust to sweep us away. But afterwards, it felt weird. I don't usually have one-night stands, but I didn't give it a second thought when Lucien followed me into the restroom at Kenza. I wanted him so much that I forgot everything the minute he touched me. However, as we dressed, I tried to slip out the door before he could say something I wouldn't like. His arm snaked around my waist, and he pulled me back to him. He whispered, "Spend the night," and I did.

We made love all night in the pitch dark. Lucien being in control the whole time was a huge turn-on for me. It kept me on the brink of orgasm. He was amazing, but morning soon arrived. When I woke up, I found him fully showered and dressed, sitting solemnly in a chair in the corner of his room. I knew then that he would be my first one-night stand.

After that, I couldn't wait to leave his apartment. All I wanted to do was get back to my place and drown my sorrows alone. He made it worse by following me around his bedroom, acting like he wanted to say something but didn't know how.

We had a connection from the minute we met, and it only grew stronger after the night we spent together. At least, I feel as though it has. I'm sure Lucien feels it as well. However, from what I've heard, he's been alone for so long. This tells me that he isn't ready to have his life disrupted by me dropping into it.

At least, that's what I thought until he called me about thirty minutes ago, asking if we could talk. I shake the worry from my thoughts and set my phone down.

As I slip on my nice red jeans, which show off the curve of my ass nicely, and a sheer white blouse, I can't help but wonder how the night will end. Part of me wonders if he's coming here because he has an itch that needs scratching. But a huge part of me hopes he wants to date me exclusively and have some fun.

I know it's early, and there's a difference in age, but we're both consenting adults, so I don't see how age has anything to do with it if we both want it.

I glance in the mirror one last time as the doorbell chimes. Fear races up and down my spine, and my hands begin to shake with nervousness.

I quickly fluff my long, mahogany curls, take a deep breath, open the door, and meet Lucien's gaze. He's a handsome man with short, dark hair that occasionally falls into his eyes and a strong, chiseled jaw that is currently sporting a five o'clock shadow. His deep blue eyes bore into mine as I stand unmoving in the doorway. "Are you planning on making me stay outside all night?"

"Oh, God. Sorry. Come in."

I shuffle backward and out of the way so he can enter. His scent wraps around me as he enters, causing my knees to weaken. Everything about him is delicious, making my panties wet with just one look in my direction.

I've been slowly combusting ever since I first met him, when he turned that smile on me before it became a frown.

Watching him walk around my apartment only adds to my discomfort, and my nerves dance on the edge. I feel like my body is ready to fight or flee. He looms large and always makes my heart flutter.

"Can I get you a drink or something?" I ask, swallowing the nerves plaguing me.

He turns, giving me his full attention.

"You make me nervous," I admit, as he observes me

silently. I offer up a nervous laugh and fidget. "You don't really. Okay, maybe you do." After pausing to avoid making a fool of myself, I continue, "You do make me nervous because I don't know what you want with me. The other morning, I had the feeling that you couldn't wait to get me out of there, but at the same time, you didn't want me to leave," I tell him honestly. I start to relax, if only a little.

His gaze stays hot on me as he prowls toward me like a lion free of its cage for the first time. I've probably just described Lucien perfectly—at least for right now.

"I don't know what the hell to do with you," he whispers when he reaches me, just before his mouth descends on my neck.

My arms reach for him, and my fingers slide into his hair to keep him close.

"Kiss me, Lucien."

He does as I beg. His tongue assaults my mouth, making my pussy clench with need. I can't get enough of this man.

I whimper when I feel his fingers on my zipper, and I sigh as he slides my jeans and underwear down my legs. I try to kick them off, but they get caught around my knees. Before I can free myself, Lucien's hand cups my wet pussy. His fingers stroke me and seek entrance to my core, which they find, plunging inside.

My whole body is awash with pleasure. Reaching for his zipper, I yank it down and shove my hand inside.

Lucien hisses when my fingers wrap around his cock. I pull his cock out and rub the crown, which is slick with excitement.

Wanting to be free of my jeans and panties, I wiggle them down my legs, but that only increases the pressure building inside me as Lucien's fingers match my movements. He drives his fingers deeper while I rock my hips against his hand.

"Help me. I want to feel you inside me."

"Fuck, yes."

He withdraws his fingers, grabs my hips, and swings me around. My hands fly out to brace myself as he shoves me face-first over the back of the sofa.

Christ!

I can't breathe, the lust coursing through my body overwhelming me. No one has ever treated me like they can't wait to be inside me. Lucien may deny that he wants me and that we have a connection, but our bodies know what we want.

And that's each other.

Lucien

If I don't get inside her soon, I'm going to blow my load in my pants. Now that my dick has come back to life, I have six years of fucking to get out of my system.

I just wish it had taken a liking to someone else and not to someone I can't get out of my head. I close my eyes, and she's there—her delicate face twisting in passion, her hazel-colored eyes filling with desire for me. Her mouth is red, plump, and kiss-bruised from the force of my passion. The thought of her sweet pussy almost makes me come on the spot. I only have to think about going down on her—which is pretty much all the time—to taste her on my tongue.

I'm losing my fucking mind.

"Lucien. God. I need you."

"Fuck!"

"Don't move."

I bend over and wince when my dick scrapes against my zipper. I quickly kick off my shoes, yank off my pants, and toss them over a chair. Bending again, I pull her jeans and panties off her legs and toss them behind me. Spreading her thighs open, I expose her hidden treasure, open her lips, and dive in with my mouth. I feel on top of the world when she comes on my tongue.

My balls pull tight against my body. I have seconds before I explode.

Growling, I jump to my feet and stroke Sabrina between her thighs. I can't get enough of touching her, but I have to wait until I've finished to love her slowly with my mouth again.

I fist my dripping dick and guide it slowly into her tight sheath. My legs quiver as she grips and releases me, sucking me further into her body.

Holding her hips, I slowly withdraw, feeling her wet walls grasp my cock as if trying to keep me from leaving.

Slowly retreating again, I pause with the head of my shaft surrounded by her clenching entrance. The length of my cock is a live wire leading straight to my balls. One more stroke, and I'll be in heaven.

She shoves herself back onto me and starts coming. This sets the fuse alight, which travels the length of my cock to my balls before they explode.

I close my eyes tightly, trying to breathe through the pleasure she's wringing out of me. Her tight pussy doesn't let up, continuing to flutter up and down my length and milk me. I'm surprised she hasn't broken me in two given how strong her spasms are. But fuck, I've lost all sense of everything right now except for what her pussy is doing to my cock.

HAVING SABRINA SNUGGLED UP TO ME IN THE BIG BED makes my heart flutter, but fear washes over me with how I crave her.

Because of the scarring on my body, I keep my long-sleeved T-shirt, which I always wear under my shirts, on at all times. Half of my closet is full of them.

I came here tonight to talk to her, hoping it would lead to us fucking each other's brains out. But I never expected to develop real feelings for her. Those feelings are urging me to run and never look back.

If I thought running would make her stop occupying my thoughts, I would do it in a heartbeat.

As my hand caresses her naked body, I realize that I'm not ready to walk away yet. That's where my proposal comes in. Nobody can get hurt with a proposal, right?

"Hey," she mumbles, bringing my gaze up from her hip to her sleepy eyes.

I'm tempted to bend down and kiss her on the nose because she looks so cute snuggled against me.

I quickly untangle myself from her before I can follow through with my plan. She frowns and reaches for the covers.

I don't stop her.

"Can you put something on? I want to talk to you."

"Okay."

I walk into the living room and briefly sit on the cream-colored sofa before standing up and looking out the window. The dark night sparkles with streetlights, but it seems empty outside. I watch a lone car navigate the streets below. It rounds a corner and fades out of sight. I hear her walk into the room behind me. She didn't make me wait long.

"What's wrong?"

Why do I suddenly feel like the biggest bastard in history?

I rake my hands through my hair and turn to stare at her for a moment, deciding if this is the right thing to ask. It was the reason I came over here, but now I wonder if she'll be insulted.

"Lucien?"

What the hell!

"I want you." I laughed. "Okay, I guess that's obvious by now, but what I'm trying to say is that I don't do relationships. If you agree to be with me, I'm not going to offer you marital bliss. It's just going to be about our wants. Mine—yours—the hot way that we connect." I gesture toward the sofa where I'd taken her earlier, and I feel a thrill of triumph as passion fills her gaze.

"It's just two adults coming together for mutual pleasure." I pause and take a deep breath, knowing this is going to be the kicker. "I need you to keep it quiet from our families." My fists clench. "We're also exclusive. I don't want you going from me to someone else or from them to me."

Fuck. Why did I say that out loud? The thought of her with anyone else makes me see red. There's no chance of my being with anyone else because the only woman I want is standing in front of me, fighting to keep a neutral expression on her face. She's the only one who can give me a hard-on. If I weren't so damaged, she'd be the woman I'd want in my life permanently. It wasn't just her body that grabbed my attention from the beginning, it was the whole package.

Her eyes darken with hidden emotion as she tightens her mouth in thought. When she finally speaks, her voice is cordial—friendly, but lacking the usual spark of passion.

"Okay. No-strings sex." Her eyes searched mine, and I nodded, even though it wasn't a question, as she continued, "Exclusive to each other—I can do that. Give me a call tomorrow. I need sleep."

With that, she turns on her heel, disappears back into the bedroom, and closes the door behind her.

Fuck! Why do I feel like I've just broken her heart?

2

THREE MONTHS LATER...

Sabrina

THE BLANKET BUNCHES UP UNDER MY HANDS, AND I FEEL an ache in my knees when I'm thrust forward. Lucien grips my hips tightly as he fucks me from behind, and I feel tears welling up in my eyes. This should turn me on, but I just want to cry. Since the night he came to my apartment, we've been seeing each other—but only after Lucien made it clear that it was strictly for sex, nothing more. I still can't believe I agreed to it. We don't talk much. In fact, we don't do much of anything unless we're both naked.

Lucien won't let me touch him. He insists on having the room pitch black while he strips, keeping his T-shirt on. This makes me nervous every time until he cups my face in his hands and kisses me. As soon as our lips meet, I forget everything. He arouses me like no one ever has before. He touches a part of me that I didn't even know existed. A lump catches in my throat because, as much as this means to me, it means nothing to him. This thing between us is just us letting off steam and giving each other a mutual release. For me, though, it's so much more because my heart is involved. That's why I feel close to tears.

Over the past couple of weeks, I've sensed a change in Lucien. He still kisses me with as much passion as always, but when we come together, he makes me face away from him. It's as though he can't bear to look at me, and it hurts. It hurts a lot. I'm really not sure I can go on like this anymore.

I love him, and walking away from him would break my heart, but being with him like this is making me sick. I've been a complete mess lately. I've lost weight. I've been avoiding my friends because I know they'll find out what's going on. My best friend, Lily—the very woman I should confide in—has Lucien's heart. I'm positive she has it, which is why he warned me that it could never be anything else.

Today, however, I'm not sure I'll be able to hold back my tears.

Lucien continues to thrust into me as his hands roam up my body and cup my breasts. When he pinches my nipples, he shifts his position, causing him to slip deeper inside me. I'd usually explode with pleasure at this point, but my lust for him has disappeared today. For the first time.

Tears seep from the corners of my eyes as he rubs my clitoris, but my body is unable to react to his touch the way it usually does. I feel empty, devoid of passion and lust for the only man I have ever loved.

"Fuck!" he growls, gripping my hips again. He thrusts a couple more times before I feel him come inside me. He whispers my name when he does.

After having the protection talk at the beginning, we don't use anything—I'm on the pill, and he's clean and hasn't had sex for years. I was incredulous at first, but given how he uses my body, making up for lost time, I believe him.

There's nothing like feeling him slide inside me bareback. He usually makes my toes tingle with pleasure.

Lucien collapses on top of me, pushing me into the quilt. Then, he rolls onto his side and slips free of my body. He doesn't touch me while he catches his breath.

Feeling lost and neglected, I curl into the fetal position, away from him, and let my tears fall. I won't do this again. I can't do this to myself anymore.

"Sabrina?"

"What?" I can't keep the tears out of my voice.

"You usually come first. I'm sorry. I'll make it up to you next time."

If he cared, he'd say he'd make it up to me now, not next time.

Without looking in his direction, I roll from the bed and quickly dash toward the bathroom. Once inside, I lock the door and turn on the shower. I climb in, sink to the floor, and let the tears stream down my face. My body starts shaking as wracking sobs take over. This is what he's done to me. I should have said no when he asked me for sex. But I didn't, and now I'm paying the price with a broken heart.

What's wrong with me? Why do guys think I'm good for sex? Before I met Lucien, I was very naive.

I need to find the strength to tell him I'm not coming back. How will I do it? How can I walk away knowing that if I'm not here for his needs, he'll find someone else? It will make me sick to see him with someone else. But being with him is slowly making me sick.

I push my tears away and try to pull myself back together. I quickly finish washing up in the shower and turn it off. I dry myself with the blue, fluffy towel and pull on my clothes, which I left hanging in the bath-room. I usually stay naked and let him look, but not today.

I open the door and walk out into the lit bedroom. Lucien is dressed and sitting on the edge of the unmade bed, his elbows resting on his knees. He turns his head to look at me, watching as I try to ignore him while shoving my feet into my boots.

Seeing my purse on the table by the door, I don't

bother fishing out my makeup bag. Instead, I gather my things and turn to face him.

He doesn't look happy, his jaw tightening. He's angry. Well, so am I.

Unable to stand the silence any longer, I blurt out, "This is it. I won't be coming back."

He doesn't react except for a twitch at the corner of his left eye, which tells me he isn't as calm as he wants me to believe.

"Is this because I took pleasure without giving you anything?" He looks embarrassed. "I said I was sorry. You're usually there with me."

"So it's my fault?"

He shrugs.

Bastard!

"This has nothing to do with you fucking me earlier." I can't bring myself to call it anything else.

"Then why? You usually enjoy yourself."

He makes me so sad and angry! "This whole arrangement with you is making me sick. This isn't me. I don't know who I am anymore. I've lost weight. I can't sleep." I edge toward the door, and when I turn back to him, tears are flowing down my face again. "I'm sorry, but I can't do this with you again. Please don't ask me."

I dash out of his apartment and practically fall into the elevator.

What have I done?

Lucien

Watching her leave stabs me with a pain I don't want to think about. I've wanted her to leave me alone for weeks, but she kept coming back. That's why I acted like a bastard today.

I like rough sex as much as the next guy, but I've never left a woman unsatisfied like I just did. The only way I could stay hard and finish inside her was by thinking about the sex we had in the restroom at Kenza. It hurt me just as much as I knew it hurt her, and I wouldn't have been able to stay hard otherwise. I couldn't enjoy having her on the bed knowing she wasn't enjoying it. I forced the pleasure with images of her writhing under me. I needed her to be the one to walk away.

She's the only woman since the fire to give me an erection. So it was only natural that I'd want her in my bed. I had years of pent-up aggression that needed to be released. The only drawback was my fucking heart. I never expected to feel real emotions for her. I couldn't have something like this. I didn't want or need it. Yet there she was, slowly sinking under my skin and igniting feelings that started as tiny sparks when we met into a raging inferno. I couldn't even be in the same room with her without feeling burned by the sparks flying between us.

We spent months dancing around those sparks and quickly stamping out any fire they caused until that night at Kenza changed everything. I couldn't stay away, like a dog scenting a female in heat. Or maybe I was the one in heat. Six years...

Six years of thinking I would never be intimate with a woman again. Then Sabrina walked in and chased away every doubt I had about intimacy. My body started to come back to life, slowly at first, then quickly. That night at Ruben's club, I had the hardest erection I could ever remember.

It wanted Sabrina's warmth. After getting dressed, I couldn't bring myself to leave her, so I took her back to my place, where I fucked her all night. Two nights later, our no-strings-attached sex started. She surprised the hell out of me when she accepted my offer. I think she surprised herself as well.

I knew it hurt her when I wouldn't have sex facing her, but I couldn't risk her touching me. I couldn't risk seeing the repulsed look on her face when she felt my damaged skin. That is why I had to make her leave me. I needed her to hate me enough that she wouldn't want me again. I know myself. If I'd been the one to stop this, I probably would've lasted two days before breaking down her door to get to her. This way, she hates me.

I rub a hand over the pain in my chest at what I've done to her and to myself.

I'm not a bad person. As far as I know, I've never hurt anyone the way I just did. I have no problem admitting that I love my parents and family. My brothers and I might piss each other off, but we're always there for each other. Carla and Rosie have Sebastian and Ruben so tied up in knots that I find their interactions hilarious. They're both pussy-whipped. They don't have a problem admitting that, either.

Then there's Lily, Michael's wife and my best friend. I even admit that it's a strange relationship I have with her. I understand why people think there's more going on than there ever has been or ever will be, but I can't explain our connection without mentioning other things.

When I first met Lily, she was the first woman in a long time not to flinch when I shook her hand. She held her own with me and didn't treat me with kid gloves. I immediately felt a connection to her that had nothing to do with sex, though it took Michael and my brothers a while to realize this.

Lily just saw me for who I am, and for reasons I can't decipher, she became my best friend. I'd be lying if I said I didn't hope for more, but that feeling only lasted thirty seconds. She's a beautiful woman who has my brother wrapped around her little finger, just like my niece and nephew do. Michael has no chance.

I used to think I'd have everything Michael has now, but everything changed the night of the accident. Once I was on the road to recovery, I realized that wasn't in my future anymore. I mean, who would want to wake up next to me for the rest of their life?

My brothers know I'm alone by choice, even though we haven't discussed it for a while. They seem to have given up trying to get me to start dating again. I'm just not interested. I couldn't say whether or not my impotence had anything to do with that. I just wasn't interested until Sabrina came along.

She knows about my injuries and doesn't seem bothered by them—for now. She's reached for me so many times while we've been naked that I've nearly given in to her. To be honest, I crave her touch more than anything else. In the end, though, I just couldn't do it. I wouldn't be able to bear the disgust in her eyes when she touched the scars and realized how deep they were. So I stopped her. I know I hurt her every time, but I don't think I could've survived if she'd turned away from me in disgust.

I've been there before. I watched a woman who was supposed to love me turn away in disgust. It was hard, but I survived when Alyssa, my girlfriend at the time, walked away from me because of my damaged body. I don't think I could survive the same treatment from Sabrina. She's unlike anyone I've ever known, and that scares me. So I made her leave of her own free will.

She was my weakness.

Fuck!

My hands are itching to grab my phone and check up on her. I can't do that. I needed her to leave and never look back, to let her anger keep me away. But damn, she was upset.

I grab my phone and dial Ramon, frustration and impatience building as I wait for him to answer.

"What?"

"Well, you sound the way I feel," I grumbled. "I need you to do me a favor without asking questions. Can you do that?"

After a moment of silence, he clears his throat. "As long as it won't land me in jail. I kind of like my freedom right now."

"Don't be a dick. Can you check on Sabrina?" I cringe, knowing what's coming.

"What the hell have you done to Sabrina? She's one of Lily's best friends, for God's sake!"

"We had an argument, and she left upset. I can't go check on her, and if I ask one of the other girls to, they'll be too nosy. Look, just go check on her, okay? Just don't mention me."

"What am I supposed to say for being there? I've never shown up unannounced at her place before. I've never even been to her place before," Ramon snarls, his agitation clear through the connection.

I sigh and run my hand through my already messy

hair. "Look, if you have to, say I was concerned about the way she left, but only say something if she asks."

"You owe me big time," Ramon says a second before the line goes dead. I glance at the phone before my hand moves, almost of its own volition, and sends it crashing against the wall on the opposite side of the room. I watch it shatter, but I don't care.

I turn and head toward the bathroom, flinging my clothes off as I go. I'm about to step into the shower when I catch a glimpse of my back and freeze. The weight of what happened to me hits me in the chest like an arrow.

With legs that feel ready to give out from under me, I finish stepping into the shower and lean against the wall to stay upright. I clench my fists and breathe through my nose to ward off the frustration I feel in my body.

The once smooth skin on my body is gone, leaving me scarred for life. Not my entire body—my chest and abs are relatively free of scars—but my right side, including my arm, back, buttocks, groin, and leg, took the brunt of the injuries.

My brother, Michael, once asked me if I would do it all again knowing I would be left the way I am. I didn't need to think about it because my answer was yes. A mother and child are alive because of me, so how could I ever answer no?

As my breathing evens out, I think about the two people who are alive because I climbed into their vehicle at the scene of the accident to rescue them. Samantha is now thirteen and won a bronze medal at the horse show here in Lexington over the weekend. I don't have contact with them, but every now and then, I check up on Samantha to make sure she's doing well. She appears to be.

With a heavy heart, I push the past from my mind, hoping that Sabrina is all right and that I have the strength to stay away from her. I have a feeling she's going to be the only woman I ever crave.

3

Sabrina

"I'M STILL NOT SURE ABOUT THIS, RAMON," I SAY, grasping my seatbelt and trying not to jump from the moving car.

"You can't hide forever," he replies, glancing at me quickly before turning his attention back to the road.

It's been five and a half weeks since I last saw Lucien and since my friendship with Ramon started. I even missed the twins' birthday during this time because my heart was too raw. I just couldn't bring myself to be around the McKenzies. I'm sure Lily saw through my excuse about having the flu.

I glance at Ramon from the corner of my eye, but his eyes are staring straight ahead. He has saved me in more ways than just giving me a ride. The day Lucien shattered my heart, Ramon came to check on me. I hadn't heard him come in, and I have no idea how he managed it, but he found me naked and in a heap on the floor of my shower. I didn't care and didn't try to cover myself. Instead, I just cried as he lifted me from the floor and took care of me.

I didn't become embarrassed by it all until later, but he sheepishly admitted to me that although he's been with a few women, he actually prefers guys. It took me a few minutes to realize what he meant, and then I started laughing.

Since then, we've spent more time together. I like Ramon and have enjoyed spending time with him, even if he is the wrong McKenzie. Before my meltdown, we hadn't spoken much, but now I have his number on speed dial. He confused me a bit with his comment about preferring guys, though, because I've caught him eyeing Sylvia more than once.

Despite my promise not to tell Lucien's family, Ramon knows all about the arrangement I had with his brother. I haven't gone into detail about what we did or how it ended, though. No doubt he put his own spin on my words and probably came to the right conclusion. I just told him that I needed more than Lucien was willing to offer, which is basically the truth.

I sigh and glance out the window. I've had a lot of time to think about our time together. First the fire, then the way Lucien started pulling away. Although I was the one who ended it, I realize now that he was pushing me away. Ramon knows how I feel about this, but he avoids the subject whenever I try to pin him down. He finally admitted that he agreed with me and that he didn't know how to bring his brother out of his self-imposed exile.

The only advice he gave me was to keep showing up wherever Lucien is. That is why I'm in the car with Ramon, on my way to his parents' house for Sunday lunch. I'm trying to stay calm as we approach their house, but I'm not sure anything can keep me calm. Especially since I'm about to come face-to-face with the man who has my heart—the man who pushed me away rather painfully—the man who needs to know...

"You have about two minutes to pull yourself together," Ramon says, breaking into my thoughts.

My heart thuds in my chest. I shouldn't be so nervous, right?

"Sabrina?" I feel Ramon glance in my direction. "You really need to calm down." He takes my hand and squeezes it reassuringly. "I know my brother, okay? There isn't any way he'll acknowledge what happened between you two. God, Lily would kill him if she found out, not to mention what my mom would do to him."

"I know. It's just that it's the first time I've seen him since last week." I pause and glance out the window before looking back at Ramon. "I don't really know what to expect. The fact that he probably won't acknowledge me hurts." I try to shrug off my depression about the whole situation.

As the ranch house comes into view, I tell myself it's natural to be nervous about facing an ex and that I'll get over it. But I'm not sure I will. Lucien is different from anyone I've ever known. The thought of him not wanting me anymore tears me in two. I know he wanted me. He was hungry for me. That wasn't hidden—only his emotions were. Someone must have hurt him in the past, and badly. I couldn't imagine what made him so protective of his heart and body. Thinking about it too long makes me want to cry. He deserves someone to come home to. Someone to kiss the pain away. I wish he knew how much I want to be that person for him.

As Ramon cuts the engine outside his family's home, my heart does somersaults in my chest when I spot Lucien. Our eyes lock for a second before anger fills his, and my heart drops when he turns and heads inside without saying hello.

He couldn't even be bothered to say hello.

I vaguely hear Ramon cuss as he climbs out. Walking around his SUV, he opens the door for me. He takes my hand, pulls me out, and pulls me into his arms for a hug.

"He cares more than he'll ever let you know," Ramon whispers in my ear before pulling back and grinning. "He'll be pissed if he's watching from the window."

Managing a small chuckle, I pushed him away. He

grabs my hand and slides his fingers between mine. With a slight tug, he starts walking toward the house. It looks like it has a fresh coat of yellow paint on the porch, which makes Pippa's colorful flowers in the flowerbed stand out. They certainly are in abundance. I guess it's a good thing no one in the family suffers from allergies because they certainly would with the amount of flowers around here.

"You ready for this?" Ramon asks, concern clear on his face.

"As ready as I'll ever be." I squeeze his hand. "Best get it over with."

Ramon gives me a once-over and opens the door, pulling me inside.

My eyes immediately find Lucien, who is standing by one of the front windows, frowning. He really can't say anything if he saw Ramon and me outside, considering he threw me away and told his brother to check on me.

"Sabrina, you look lovely," Pippa gushes.

I plaster a smile on my face and turn away from Lucien. I feel close to tears when Pippa pulls me into her arms. She nearly squeezes the life out of me.

"Thank you, and so do you. It's great to see everyone again," I say, avoiding looking into her eyes.

I decide it's best to avoid meeting Lucien's gaze and keep my back to him, sliding my hand back into Ramon's. He's my strength right now, and I'm not sure

I'll be able to cope with being here around Lucien and his family without him.

Ramon smiles and kisses me on the cheek. As he pulls away, his family watches us closely. I blush, and he shrugs as he pulls me to the sofa. He sits down and pulls me into his chest. His eyes look defiantly toward Lucien. I catch him grinning at Lucien, who looks like a thundercloud.

Seeing Lucien like this makes me think that he's affected by our breakup as much as I am, if you can call it that. Unable to take my eyes off him, I notice that he looks like he's lost weight—his face is leaner, and his cheekbones are more pronounced on his handsome face. My heart aches, and I want nothing more than to wrap him in my arms and never let go. However, I know that I'll only ever feel rejection from him.

I feel Ramon squeeze my hip and realize that Lucien has been holding my gaze. Before he turns his head and continues to look outside, I catch a look of regret on his face. This makes me snuggle closer to Ramon for comfort.

Pippa is telling everyone a story about her twin grandchildren, most of which I've missed thanks to the stubborn man across the room. She stops mid-story when Michael and Lily arrive with Charlotte and Jr., who appear ready for fun with their uncles.

After the greetings are over and we're back on the sofa, Sebastian strolls in alone. He sits on the coffee table facing me and asks, "Are you seriously dating Ramon? I thought," he says, looking between Lucien and me. "Well, you know?"

He's always blunt and to the point. His and everyone else's gaze makes me want to squirm in my seat, but luckily, Pippa comes to my rescue and smacks him on the head.

"Ouch... Jeez, Mom. I'm only asking a question."

"Hmmm. Yes, well… Where's Carla? I haven't seen her for a couple of weeks."

Sebastian laughed. "No, I haven't screwed up. She's been sick with the flu. She's here with me, but she came in through the back door to use the bathroom first." He winks at me, grinning. "Sorry, Sabrina."

"Thank you, but it's okay."

"So, if it's okay, are you going to answer my question?"

"No, she isn't," Ramon interrupts. "Stop acting like you're five, and go annoy someone else."

"You're no fun, brother," Sebastian adds, jumping up from the coffee table when Carla enters the room.

This family has come to mean a lot to me. After my father died and I moved back to the States with my mother, I realized that I didn't really have anyone. My mother is more interested in having the perfect daughter, which I am not—especially now. When she hears what I have to tell her, she isn't going to be happy. Even though part of me hopes she will surprise me, I know this might be the thing that causes her to say goodbye to me. She's never been a real mom to me. She's always made sure I had clothes and food, but nothing else.

Pippa is a real mom, and I love her. She doesn't have a bad bone in her body, and neither do her sons. I find them amusing when they tease each other, which they do even more when they are all together. Sebastian seems to be the one who starts it every time, as though he senses when his brothers or the mood needs lightening up.

Today, my eyes have a mind of their own, and I find myself gazing into Lucien's. With every look, my heart thuds in my chest, hoping he'll change his mind.

It isn't going to happen, but I can dream. After all, that's what I've been doing these past few weeks—dreaming. Dreaming of Lucien coming to his senses and coming after me. I dream of him telling me he's sorry and that he'd rather be with me than apart. In this case, dreams are so much better than reality.

"Sabrina," Ramon whispers. "You with me?"

I try to shake my thoughts as Ramon gets to his feet and pulls me with him.

"Sorry. I tuned out."

"I figured." He grinned and explained, "Mom wants us all to go sit out back. She's planning on taking a family picture."

"But—"

"You're family, Sabrina." He wraps his arm around

my shoulders and leads me outside, where his family has started to take seats.

Ramon walks around the table and stops at the seat beside Lucien. He pulls out the chair and helps me into it. I feel like refusing, but that would look childish. So, I let Ramon seat me and glare at him as he walks to the opposite side of the table. He winks at me, his mouth twisted in a smug grin, and sits facing me. Beside me, I hear Lucien curse under his breath.

Enough is enough! I'm starting to get angry. We're adults and need to move past whatever it was we had together. Taking a deep breath for courage, I try to keep my nerves at bay and turn to look at him. I intend to speak, but the words freeze in my throat when I realize he's already watching me from beneath his heavy eyelids.

He's resting his arms on the table in front of him, head bent, but face turned toward me. My heart jumps in my chest at his proximity and the look—full of need —that he's giving me. Time stands still, as neither of us is willing to break the connection we've just formed.

Lucien

As my brother pulls out a chair for Sabrina, part of me wants to kiss him, while the other part wants to punch him. If anyone knows about Sabrina and me and everything going on between us, it's Ramon. Now he's trying to play matchmaker.

As much as I love my family, it's sometimes a pain having siblings because they think they know better. In this case, they probably do, because I feel like a fish out of water around Sabrina. I want one thing, but my head's telling me that I'll get my heart broken if I go after her. Holding the gaze of the only woman I've ever let get close to my heart—romantically speaking—cuts deep. The pain in my chest every time I think about her, which is often, is unlike anything I've ever felt. My heart and body tell me I'm an idiot for pushing her away and treating her the way I did toward the end. However, my head tells me it's the only move I can make.

Sabrina has no idea how beautiful I think she is or that I'll use any excuse to be near her. She makes me feel so damn confused, as though I don't know which way is up or down. One thing I do know is that I can't handle the way she looks at me anymore, as if I broke her heart, which is impossible. Right?

"Sorry we're late," Ruben says, bringing me back to the present as he pulls Rosie down onto his lap for the family photograph Mom wants.

Sabrina greets the latecomers, but I can't take my eyes off her. I'm afraid that if I turn away, she'll be gone, and I'll be left to feel her absence. It's the same way I feel after every encounter I have with her. I know I'm confusing her with my mixed signals, especially when I forget why I need to keep her away from me.

I rub my temples, trying to work out the slight throbbing pain that has started there.

With a heavy sigh, I move my mouth closer to Sabrina's ear, taking in a deep breath of her heady scent. She senses my movement, turns toward me, and her lips brush against mine, sending a bolt of longing through me. She sucks in a small breath of shock, and a shiver runs down my spine straight to my dick. Whenever she's close, I spend most of my time trying to stay flaccid because she quickly does things to my body that I haven't felt in a long time.

Before I can respond, she pushes her chair back with a tight frown on her lips, her eyes darting around for an escape. She turns back to look at me, and I see a mixture of anger and sadness in her eyes.

"I can't do this, Lucien," she whispers, her voice tight and withdrawn. "You didn't want me, so leave me alone."

I watch her walk quickly back into the house and feel someone come up behind me.

"Don't be a complete bastard," Ramon tells me. "She's hurting, and you need to make things right before you lose her to Gavin."

What the fuck!

I turn around to face my brother. "Who the hell is Gavin?"

Ramon smirks. "He's been asking her out for a while now. He's a doctor at the hospital and on the fundraising board that Lily got involved in."

Over my dead fucking body.

I get to my feet, ignoring the stares from my family, and kiss my mom on the forehead. "I need to talk to Sabrina. We'll be back soon for your picture. I promise."

I let Mom go and follow the path Sabrina took to the house, my thoughts racing as I walk. I really have no clue what to say to her, but I know I need to say something.

The kitchen and family room are empty when I reach the house, so I head toward the guest bathroom, knowing that's where she's hiding from me.

I run my hand through my hair before knocking on the door and hear something clatter into the sink.

"Sabrina? Please let me in."

Nothing.

"Sabrina?"

Still nothing. I rested my forehead against the door and tried one last time. "Sabrina, please. I'm not leaving until you open this door and I say what I need to say."

The door is yanked open, and I practically fall into the room. Sabrina grabs my arm, stopping me from falling flat on my face.

"Sorry," she mumbles. "Are you okay?"

"I'm fine."

I turn away from her, distracting myself by closing the door to catch my breath. Falling into the room hadn't been on the agenda.

"What do you want, Lucien?"

I turn to face her, which is a mistake. Having her so close in this small space is wreaking havoc on my libido.

What do I want?

If I lie, I'll see the hurt I cause her. But if I answer honestly, will I set myself up for more heartache? I don't want to suffer either.

She steps right into my space, bringing with her the scent of summer—sunshine and wildflowers—her scent. She's so close. I only need to lean in to touch her, which I do. Her breasts rest against my chest, and I crave the feel of her naked body against mine. I have only allowed myself to be chest-to-chest with her once before, when we were both naked. She was holding onto the headboard, and the sensation was like nothing else. Needless to say, her touch alone brought me to the brink of orgasm.

"Lucien."

I meet her eyes.

Of its own accord, my hand reaches up and caresses her smooth cheek. Her eyes closed as she leaned into my touch.

"I don't think you realize what you do to me," I blurted out before I could stop myself.

"You said you don't want me." Her voice breaks as she tries to move away.

I wrap my arm around her waist and pull her close. With her so close, my dick thickens and lengthens, leaving her with little doubt about what she does to my body.

She presses her pelvis against me and rubs, causing her to gasp when I grow hard.

"You're playing with fire," I growl against her lips, pushing her up against the wall. One hand cradles her face while the other grips her hip as though it's my lifeline.

Our breathing deepens, and I want nothing more than to dip my head and taste her. My cock jerks behind my zipper, obviously liking the idea. However, I'm still not sure it's such a good idea.

Kiss her. Kiss her. Kiss her.

"Lucien," she says, almost breathless, "kiss me."

She's going to be the death of me. Without further thought, I kiss her, and all the reasons why I shouldn't fly straight out the window.

Her tongue dips into my mouth, and I'm lost. My passion for this woman overrides all the reasons why this isn't a good idea.

I wrap my hand in her silky hair and hold her against

me as I ravish her mouth and take everything she's willing to give. Her taste is unique. Like an aphrodisiac.

My tongue spears into her mouth, just as my cock wants to spear her pussy. I bet she's already soaked her panties with desire.

Her hands slide into my hair, and the small tug she gives sets my blood from burning to inferno. Growling, I grab her bottom, squeeze, and lift her up until she's perched on the vanity. We continue to kiss—no, consume—each other as I hold her there. Her legs wrap around my waist, pinning me against her. My dick is nearly as out of control as I am. It jerks and leaks with every moan she lets out, and it's only gotten worse since it's pressing tightly against her pussy.

My hands are all over her. I need to get to her breasts and her large, dark nipples, which I can never get enough of. Even before, when I had her on her hands and knees to fuck her from behind, I played with her nipples. She can bring us both to orgasm through nipple stimulation alone.

But damn, we can't do this!

"No!"

She isn't hearing me. "Sabrina, we can't."

I see my words starting to sink in when the look in her eyes slowly shifts from passion to hurt.

I take a step back and unwrap her long legs from around me. I follow her gaze as it travels down to my hard dick, and I groan mentally as she licks her lips. Fuck! She's going to kill me.

I turn my back to her, cursing under my breath. "I want you." I laugh and turn back to face her. "I can't exactly deny that, but I followed you in here to talk. I hate seeing you upset. Knowing that I'm the cause is tearing me up."

She shakes her head. "You already made your point about not wanting us to be together. I know you think I'm going to wake up one morning and hurt you. If you think I'm capable of that, then you don't deserve me in your life."

How can she be so accurate in her description of me? I ignore her words. My voice is filled with the cold tone I use as my defense. "I never said that." Mentally kicking myself, I look down at the floor. It's such a lame thing to say, but I can't think of anything else.

"You don't need to. It's obvious, plus Ramon has hinted as much."

"Why can't my brother stay out of my life?" I run my hands through my hair, knowing it isn't really my brother's fault. It's mine.

"One of these days, when I'm with someone else, you're going to wake up and realize that I really did care for you—scars and all—but it will be too late."

The challenge in her eyes causes me to move back into her space. She slides backward on the vanity, trying to get away, but I wrap my hands around her hips and secure her. Our noses touch as I lean in, my eyes searching hers for something other than the anger simmering just below the surface. What can I say to her? That I'll kill anyone who looks at her twice? How fair would that be to her? She's young—around thirteen years younger than me—and she needs someone to love and cherish her. She needs...

I FLED THE MOMENT I THOUGHT, "SHE NEEDS ME." IT WAS a gut reaction—a way to escape before I blurted it out and staked my claim on her. Fuck! I lose all sense of self-preservation when she's around, which is not in my best interest. Ten minutes after leaving her in the bathroom, I sat back at the outdoor table and had my picture taken with my arm around Sabrina. All kinds of thoughts whirled around in my head.

Throughout the meal, I managed to avoid having a full-blown conversation with her, although we were both part of the conversation around the table. That brings me to another woman in my life—Lily.

She hasn't looked well for a few days, which worries me. When I mentioned this to Michael the other day, he brushed me off. Today, she does seem to have color back in her face, but she can't sit still. If I know Lily, she has a secret, and keeping it to herself is killing her.

I catch her eye and smile. She's beautiful, and I love her like a sister. Not only that, but she's also turned my brother's life around, and I'm grateful for that. She's also become an amazing, loyal friend to me. I'd be lost without her. Without her, I'd still be stuck in a hole. My brothers listen occasionally, but I suppose they're tired of hearing about my problems.

I see her smile slip into a frown and look beside me to see Sabrina glaring at Lily. What the hell now? They're friends, or at least they were.

"What are you doing?"

She breaks her stare and faces me. "What do you mean?"

"Don't act stupid. Stop glaring at Lily. She hasn't done anything to you," I point out.

She opens her mouth to respond, but no sound comes out. Her eyes fill with tears. Just as I start to panic at the thought of comforting a crying Sabrina, she stands up, throws her napkin on the table, and hisses, "Well, you got your wish. Don't ever come near me again because I'm done. That's it. No more. Go to hell."

As I watch her run off toward the barn, I vaguely hear murmurs around the table, which I ignore, wondering what brought on that outburst.

I'm going to have to go make sure she's okay. Women!

As I climb to my feet, Ruben puts his hand on my shoulder, trying to make me stay put. "I'll go. I'm kind of fond of you. With the mood Sabrina seems to be in, it might be safer if you stay here."

4

Sabrina

Don't be stupid. Don't act stupid.

I'm so angry with him right now that I can't breathe. My lungs feel starved of oxygen, and the only thing keeping Lucien safe from me and my temper is the fact that his parents are sitting with him outside.

Lily is my best friend, and ever since I first started hanging out with Lucien at Kenza, I've had a hard time being around her. It's no secret that Lucien is best friends with her and cares for her. No matter how many times I'm told there's nothing between them other than friendship, I can't help but wonder. Hearing him practically tell me off like I'm five made me lose it.

The creak of the barn door makes me turn around, and I nearly lose my balance in my haste. Unfortunately, it's Ruben instead of Lucien, who I wouldn't mind impaling on a pitchfork!

"Do I need to wave a white flag?" he asks, which makes me laugh as he enters the barn.

I think this is me finally losing it, because I can't stop laughing. The more I laugh, the more tears stream down my face. Ruben waits patiently by the door until my laughter fades and the tears turn to heartache. Then he pulls me into his arms and lets me wrap my arms around his waist. He lets my tears fall all over him. The realization that Lucien will always belong to Lily and not me hurts so badly. No matter what our future together might have been like, if Lucien had gotten with the program, Lily would always come first.

"Hey, come on, Sabrina. What did my brother do?" Ruben asks, lifting my head so he can look into my eyes. "Here. It's clean." He hands me a handkerchief and takes a step back.

I wipe my eyes and blow my nose, trying to get myself together. I know he's waiting for an answer, but what do I say? No one other than Ramon is supposed to know what Lucien and I have been doing, so I'm not about to tell Ruben. I need to talk, though—badly.

"Look, if it helps, I know you and my brother have been sleeping together, but what I don't know is what he's done to mess things up."

"How do you know?" I counter.

Ruben looks taken aback for a minute before

laughing and saying, "Because I'm right. I'm always right."

I roll my eyes and mutter, "Typical man."

"Nothing typical about me, babe. Now, quit stalling and tell me what my dick of a brother has done, so I can go punish him."

I can't let him do that. Much as I want to skewer the man, I believe Lucien is punishing himself more than anyone else ever could. "Leave him be, Ruben. I'll get over him."

"Bullshit!"

I'm startled by his response.

"You're just as likely to get over him as he is to get over you. You can tell yourself whatever you want, but you two belong together. If I had to guess, I'd say it has more to do with Lucien and his hang-up about the car fire than with you. He was obviously affected by what happened, but he was coping just fine until *she* walked out on him. He never said why, but it doesn't take a genius to figure it out. As far as I was concerned, it was good riddance. I never liked her much and always thought she was with him for his money. But who knows?"

My eyes fill with tears, partly because of Ruben's words, and partly because of Lucien's history. How could someone who supposedly loved him walk away when he needed them the most?

Ruben steps toward me, places his hands on my

shoulders, and rubs them. "You are nothing like her, and I hope he realizes that before it's too late."

"I can't do this anymore, Ruben. It's making me sick. There is definitely a pull between us, but never mind. I need a distraction." I sniffle into a tissue. "We better get back before they send out a search party for us."

I wipe my eyes and try to calm down. I feel like a child who cries at the slightest thing, and that needs to change.

I shove the handkerchief into my purse, quickly reapply some lip gloss, and then turn and grin at Ruben. "Okay, I'm ready."

"Oh boy. I'm sure as hell glad I'm not my brother right now." Ruben laughs. "Because you're going to give him a lot of sleepless nights."

"Good," I smirk.

After one last look around the quiet barn, I let Ruben lead me back to the porch.

I'm not sure whether to say anything to his family—or even apologize—for running out the way I did. I know they must be curious, even though they're hiding it well. The glares Pippa keeps throwing at Lucien tell me she knows where my heartache lies.

Pippa gives my hand a quick squeeze. "Everything will work itself out. I promise."

As soon as she lets go of my hand, Ramon engulfs it in his as he pulls me into his arms. "Are you okay?" he whispers.

"I'm fine, but I wouldn't mind leaving early. If you don't mind?" I admit, pulling away from him.

"I have something to do, so it's no problem," Ramon replies, pulling me down onto his lap. "Have I told you how much I love snuggling with you in my arms?"

"No, but you better not let that get back to Sylvia." I smile, keeping my face averted. I don't think he realizes how obvious his feelings are whenever Sylvia is around.

He's the youngest McKenzie, and I've come to the conclusion over these past few weeks that he's just as troubled as his brother Lucien. I have no idea how to help him. I've tried to get him to open up, but he always changes the subject, saying there isn't anything to worry about. I'm not sure I believe him.

While sitting and feeling secure in Ramon's arms, I watch the McKenzies interact with each other. They are all handsome men. Michael and Sebastian have wives. Ruben has a fiancée, and we'll leave Ramon for now. They're not just attractive on the outside. The inside is beautiful, too. I've missed this while wallowing in my heartache.

Michael leans down and kisses Lily full on the mouth. Before I can stop myself, I glance at Lucien to see his reaction. He isn't looking at Lily and Michael. His attention is completely on Ramon and me. He doesn't look happy.

"Can I have everyone's attention?" Michael stands and taps his wine glass with a spoon. "Please."

Now, all of our attention is on Michael and Lily. Lily is watching her husband with so much love on her face.

I'm watching Lucien now, without his scorching gaze on me.

"Um, okay. Lily and I thought it was a good time to announce that baby number three will be here in about six months."

The noise fades into the background as I see the shock on Lucien's face, which he quickly hides. He stands and hugs both Michael and Lily before excusing himself.

I place my hand protectively over my stomach.

Lucien

As I walk into my downtown Lexington apartment, I can't stop thinking about what I'll never have. Learning that Lily was pregnant with Charlotte and Jr. didn't affect me nearly as much as today's announcement did. Hearing my brother announce that he's going to become a father for the third time is painful. Until he said it, I hadn't realized how badly I wanted what he has.

Growing up in a close-knit family who prioritized spending time together made me want a family of my own. However, I buried those feelings the day Alyssa made it clear how she really felt about someone like me. Of course, what she meant was someone with a badly scarred body. I've never struck a woman, but I came close while Alyssa was ranting.

I throw my jacket off and kick my boots in the general direction of the door. Then, I walk over to the floor-to-ceiling window. I spend more time than I care to admit standing here, gazing out at the skyline. It has become a constant habit these past few weeks.

Pouring myself a large scotch, I see Sabrina's face clearly in my mind. I may have been looking at my brother and Lily when Michael made their announcement, but I caught the distress on Sabrina's face before leaving. She looked hurt beyond belief.

Why do I keep hurting her? I deserve to have her fall for someone else. Someone who can give her everything I can't. I was hurt and angry when Alyssa left, but if Sabrina were to walk away from me for the same reasons, it would surely kill me.

I take a good drink from the glass and continue watching the skyline as the lights begin to glimmer in the darkening sky. The lights are like a million stars below. I can't help but wonder if one of them is Sabrina's. Or maybe she's with my brother, being comforted by him. At the thought of her with my brother—or any man, for that matter—the glass in my hand goes flying and smashes to pieces against the wet bar. I'm so fucked!

I ignore the knocking on my door, unable to move.

The careful, safe life I've worked hard to build is slowly unraveling, and I don't know how to get it back now that Sabrina has stepped into it.

"Lucien?"

Bang. Bang.

"Lucien? Open this fucking door before I break it down!"

Ruben!

Hearing his voice and the force of his knock gets me moving toward the door before he follows through on his threat. I open the door just as he's about to pound on it again.

"About fucking time, you asshole," he shouts as he pushes his way past me into my apartment. On his way to get a drink, he stops and points to the shattered glass. "You having a party without me?"

"Fuck you."

His eyes narrow at my response. He walks back to me, stands practically nose-to-nose with me, and asks, "What the hell is going on with you?"

I open my mouth to answer, but he silences me with a wave of his hand. "I want the truth, not Lucien's version of the truth. I want to know what the hell is going on with Sabrina and why the hell you had to hurt her the way you did."

If he didn't already have my attention, he does now.

"All this time, you've said that Lily is like the sister we never had. But anyone watching you receive

Michael's news could see that Lily means a lot more to you. Your jealousy was written all over your face. Even Sabrina noticed. She shut down after you left, and Ramon took her home."

I ran my hands through my hair and ignored my brother as I walked around him and dropped onto the sofa. I rest my head against the back of the sofa and gaze up at the ceiling, feeling drained. I'm forty-one, but right now, I feel like I'm ninety.

"Talk to me." I hear him pop the cap on a beer bottle. "What's really going on in that head of yours?"

I sense Ruben getting comfortable in one of the recliners opposite me.

Where do I start?

"I've never lied about Lily. She's an amazing woman, and I'd be lost without her. But she's Michael's wife—the mother of my niece and nephew. Maybe when I first saw her, I felt a twinge of attraction, but it only lasted seconds." I run my hand over my face and stare at Ruben from under my eyelids. He's probably going to regret asking me to open up to him by the time I'm finished.

"I wasn't jealous of Lily and Michael...or rather, I was, but not in the way you're thinking." I sigh. "I always wanted a family." I sit forward, resting my elbows on my knees. With my head feeling too heavy to be on my shoulders, I drop my face to stare at my feet. "After Alyssa, I gave up on wanting anything like the family we were raised in. I buried all those feelings until Sabrina.

When I heard Michael announce that they were going to have another baby, I realized that I wanted that with Sabrina. But I'll never get the chance. She deserves so much more than I can give her."

"Why?"

"What?" I asked incredulously. "I would have thought it was obvious."

"You heard me. Why does Sabrina deserve so much more than you? What can another guy offer her that you can't? I don't want to hear anything about the fire. It happened six years ago. It's time for you to let it go and start living again. These past years, you haven't been living. You've been existing." He takes a drink of his beer, but his eyes never leave mine as though he's trying to make his words sink in. "I'm not trying to make light of what happened to you, but you're hurting more than just yourself and us. You're also hurting a woman who would love you for who you are today, scars and all, if only you'd give her a chance. You could have everything Michael has with Lily. Relationships aren't easy." He laughs. "Look at Rosie and me. I love that girl. Even though her age was a big thing for me at first, I couldn't walk away from her. Don't leave it until it's too late. I'd hate for you to lose her."

I'm supposed to be the oldest brother, the one who gives out advice and looks out for them. It's not supposed to be the other way around. I shake my head. How things have changed.

"I hear you. I just don't think it's going to be easy."

Nothing worth having is easy." Ruben sighs before continuing, "Look. I don't expect you to wake up a new man tomorrow over what happened, but I do think you need to try with Sabrina. She'll help you. You know that, right? I've seen the way she looks at you. We all have. I think she'll do anything to be in your life." He starts grinning. "Shit! If anyone could hear me giving you advice now, they'd piss themselves laughing."

I laugh with him, but my heart isn't really in it tonight.

"Now that I've set you on the course of discovery, I'm going to go keep my woman warm."

"Did I really need to know that?"

"Yep, maybe it'll help tip the scales."

As I watch Ruben leave, I realize all I want is for him to stay. But it isn't Ruben I want here with me.

Sabrina

AFTER MY WARM SHOWER, I PUT ON A PAIR OF YOGA PANTS and a soft, long-sleeved, dark plum-colored knit tee shirt. Since arriving home about an hour ago, I've been hiding in my room, trying to avoid the discussion I know Ramon is waiting to have with me.

Lost in my own thoughts, I didn't notice Ramon's shock when I placed my hand on my stomach after Lily's announcement. I know he's going to have questions once I show myself. I'm just not sure I'm ready to answer them.

I gently caress my stomach, knowing there are a few hurdles to cross before I can think about what to do in six months. Being almost three months pregnant with Lucien's child wasn't something I expected to happen while I was single and not with the father. It was a hell of a shock, too. My periods have always been irregular, even when I was taking the pill. So, yeah, the idea of me being pregnant hadn't entered my head until I spent a few mornings praying to the porcelain gods. Now, I have to figure out how to tell Lucien that the pill wasn't effective.

Although I'm happy to be pregnant with his child, I know he'll want to do the right thing because of the way he was raised. And that, right there, is the problem. I'm torn. Do I tell him and spend a lifetime wondering if he loves me or if he's just doing right by his child and me? I know there's a connection between us. Sure, Lucien is ignoring it, but is it enough? Sooner or later, Lucien has to deal with that connection instead of pushing me away, but I want him to do it without a baby being the catalyst. With a heavy sigh, I open my bedroom door and walk into the family room, where I see that Ramon looks to be asleep on my sofa. He makes me smile. The sofa wasn't designed with a McKenzie in mind, as Ramon proves with one foot hanging off the end and the other curved under him.

"Are you going to stand there all night? Or are you going to come sit down and tell me what's going on with you?" he asks, stretching.

"You move any further, and you'll be on the floor," I point out as I move closer and take a seat in the recliner across from him.

"If you had a longer sofa, I wouldn't have that trouble." He grins but doesn't open his eyes.

I shake my head, return his smile, and remain silent. Instead, I stare at the dark television as the seconds slide by.

Ramon's deep breathing fills the room, and I find myself hoping he's gone back to sleep. Suddenly, his eyes pop open. "Spill it."

"You really are how I'd imagine an annoying brother would be."

"I am your annoying brother right now." He says. "Look, Sabrina. I'm guessing you're pregnant, just like Lily. Am I right?"

I nod, refusing to let tears appear. I've cried enough over the past few weeks and today, so I'm not going there anymore. For starters, it can't be good for the baby.

"I'm nearly three months pregnant. It obviously wasn't planned, but it's happened. Although it was a shock at first, I'm really happy. I just need to figure out how to tell your brother." Realizing that I'm biting my lip, I release it from between my teeth and smooth it out with my tongue—a nervous habit of mine.

"I don't know how my brother will react. He's been difficult to read for a while, but I know how much he loves children. I think that, although it will be a shock, he'll be happy in the long run." Ramon pushes himself up into a more comfortable position and looks a bit apprehensive.

He's worried about something, which tells me he isn't all that sure of his brother.

"What?"

He sighs. "With how much Lucien's been pushing you away, I'm a little worried. Don't get me wrong," he says quickly when he notices the panic on my face. "I stand by what I said about children, but you need to be prepared for him to accuse you of trapping him into being with you."

He isn't telling me anything I haven't already thought. I guess that's why I've tried not to think about it and put off seeing him again. He's also been causing me plenty of sleepless nights.

"I guess I need to talk to him so it's out in the open. My jeans are already uncomfortable, so it won't be long before my pregnancy starts to show." I groan, burying my face in my hands, and mumble, "I have to tell my mom. She isn't going to be happy. Her single daughter is pregnant."

"Isn't it her job to support you?"

"Um, you've met my mother. How can you ask me that?"

He shakes his head. "Okay, I guess, but I'm sure you'll be sick of mine within a month. She's crazy about grandbabies." He laughs. "But at least you'll take the pressure off me. I can't talk to her these days without her going on at me about marriage and babies."

Ramon leans back on the sofa, puts his feet up on the coffee table, and crosses his ankles.

"She just wants to see you as happy as your brothers are...well, most of your brothers."

"I know. I'm not as straightforward as they are," he says, looking sad.

I move from the recliner and sit down beside him on the sofa. I hesitate, unsure of how to comfort him, but then I think, "To hell with it," and cuddle into him. After a minute, I feel his arm come around me. I always feel like I can talk to him about anything without being judged or made to feel ridiculous. Now it's my turn to be here for him. I ask, "Why aren't you getting it on with Sylvia?"

Chuckling, he repeats, "Getting it on? Well, that's one way of putting it, I guess. The truth is, I'm not sure what I want. I'm attracted to her, but my heart belongs to someone else."

I try to sit up, but he holds me against him.

"I don't know what I'm doing anymore. I guess you could say I'm floundering. I've gotten to the point where I don't care who knows I'm gay."

I smile against him.

"I know you're gay, but I've seen you watching Sylvia. I thought you wanted her. You confuse me."

"I'd rather not go there because I confuse myself."

"So, the person who has your heart is a guy?"

"Yeah, Noah. Carla's missing brother."

Oh boy!

"Does anyone else in your family know?" I asked, knowing there was no way his parents knew—at least his mom didn't, since she kept pressuring him to get married and have children. I've caught his father looking at Ramon a few times, deep in thought. I hadn't thought much about it until now.

"I'm not sure about Michael, but I'm going to talk to my parents sometime soon. In fact, if Mom keeps at it, it'll probably be sooner rather than later."

"Your parents love you unconditionally, Ramon. They'll accept you no matter how you choose to live your life. I envy the love they offer you. I've only really had that from my father." Feeling close to tears again, I snuggle closer to him. "My baby will know love from its mother."

He kisses the top of my head and runs his hand up and down my back. "You're going to be a marvelous mother. All I ask is that you don't rule out Lucien. He's going to love being a father. It might just take him a while to get with the program. Just promise me you'll stick with him. He needs you, Sabrina. I have every faith that he'll realize that eventually. It might be a bumpy road until then, though."

Even though the thought of being constantly pushed away and hurt by Lucien frightens me, I know I wouldn't be able to do anything else, so I say, "I promise."

I feel him smile against my head. "So you're going to give me a niece or nephew. I think Ramon's a good name."

I pinch him on the stomach. "It's a great name. We'll see."

"You need to get some sleep."

"Will you stay with me? I don't want to be alone."

"I guess it's a good thing that I'm gay. It'll stop you from having your wicked way with me."

I roll my eyes, even though he can't see, and swat him on the hip. "In your dreams," I tell him.

Chuckling, he gets up from the sofa with me in his arms and heads toward the bedroom.

"If I'm staying, then I need a bed. That sofa of yours was made for a midget."

"That sofa is made for sitting on, not sleeping on."

He gives me a sleepy smile and carries me into my room. He places me on my side of the bed and helps me get under the covers before turning the lights out.

I hear the rustling of his clothes as he takes off his jeans and shirt, and then I feel the bed dip.

"I should have asked first, but are you okay with me sharing your bed?"

"I'm good."

"Then come over here and let me hold you until you fall asleep."

I do as he asks. I really do love him like a brother.

Lucien

I wouldn't recommend waking up to the shrill ringing of my phone after drinking close to a bottle of scotch the night before. My head feels like it's being pounded by a sledgehammer. I don't remember the last time I had a hangover like this, but it was probably in college.

I'm still trying to blindly grab my phone when I finally get it in my hand and hit one of the keys, stopping the damn noise. Now, all I can hear is Sabrina in my head. It takes a few seconds for my brain to realize the sound is coming from my phone. I obviously hit "answer."

I lift my phone to my ear and mumble, "Yeah," while staying stretched out on my stomach. I'm too sensitive to move an inch right now.

"Lucien?"

"Sabrina, are you all right?"

She sounds breathless. She certainly wakes me up anyway.

"I'm good, um, Could you meet me near the gazebo at Woodland Park? I need to talk to you, and it's important."

I can hear the nervousness in her voice, and I'll admit that, even though she always has my interest, I'm now more than curious.

"I can do that. Can you give me an hour?"

"That's fine. I'll see you then." She hangs up without saying goodbye, and I realize she's still mad at me.

I let my phone drop to the floor, wondering how I'm going to get up and look human in an hour.

AFTER PARKING, I CLIMB OUT OF MY SUV AND ADJUST MY sunglasses. It's sweltering outside today, which isn't helping the pounding in my head. I suppose it could be worse. Thanks to a concoction Ruben invented, I feel a lot better than when I woke up. The park is busy with families enjoying the sun and the area's facilities.

As I walk over the grass toward the gazebo, I can't help but glance over at the skate park. My brothers and I used to spend many a Sunday afternoon there with our skateboards, which we'd received for Christmas. In fact, if I remember correctly, Sebastian broke his wrist not long after that. He was showing off to some girls with a stunt he'd only seen on TV. Regardless, we'd had fun here in the past.

My mind wanders back to my woman. My woman. I clench my fists, wishing I'd been dealt a different set of cards—ones that didn't include the car bursting into flames.

With a heavy sigh, I look toward the gazebo, and there she is. She's standing in the shade of a large maple tree, looking as beautiful as ever. She takes my breath away, as she always has since the first time I saw her.

As I observe her now, she looks nervous. Her fingers reveal her nerves, first brushing her hair back and then fidgeting with her white cardigan. What could she be nervous about? I sigh. I'm an idiot. She's obviously nervous about meeting me. Every time we've been together, I end up hurting her somehow, whether intentionally or not. So it's no wonder she looks ready to run.

I pause to take her in, and then I start walking forward. The space between us seems larger than it is, but I take my time to drink her in. She looks breathtaking in a light pink sundress that caresses her breasts and flares at the hips. The soft fabric stops just above her knees, giving me a view of her deliciously tanned legs that go on for miles. My breath catches.

A few feet away, she turns and freezes. "Lucien," she whispers.

"Sabrina."

Will I always want to touch this woman?

I clear my throat and invite her to sit down as I move and park my ass on the bench a few feet away from where she's standing.

I give her a quizzical look and pat the seat beside me

when I notice that she hasn't moved from her spot under the tree.

"Sabrina, please come sit with me and tell me what you need to. You'll feel better once you've gotten it out."

At least, I hope she will.

She moves and sits beside me, but not as close as I would have liked. I guess that's to be expected.

She doesn't stop fidgeting.

After letting the silence settle around us, I ask, "What's going on with you? I know I've hurt you, Sabrina, but you don't need to be nervous about telling me anything. Anything at all."

"I'm nearly three months pregnant," she blurts out.

I laugh. "Is it mine?"

The minute the words leave my mouth, I realize that I've never wanted anything to be unsaid more than I do at that moment.

What the hell was I thinking, asking her that? Of course the baby is mine!

Baby! I'm going to be a dad!

I stand and look anywhere but at Sabrina. I don't want her to see how her words have affected me. I can't think straight. I've always wanted children of my own, but I imagined having their mother by my side back then. Now, I'm not so sure that's going to happen.

A baby.

Swallowing the lump in my throat, I try to pull myself together before turning back to Sabrina. That's when I realize my careless words have crushed her. She's now standing and slowly moving to the back of the bench. Her eyes are glazed, and her mouth hangs open as though she's in shock. I reach out to her, but she flinches away.

"Sabrina, I'm sorry. I didn't mean those words. It was a shock. I never expected you to say that. Please stay and talk to me. I'm begging you." I need Sabrina to know that I believe her, that the baby is mine, and that I want to be involved every step of the way. I could also use some time to breathe. I need time to process the bombshell she dropped on me. I'm not going to walk away from her now. Now, part of me is growing inside her.

"I can't. Not right now. I'm sorry, but I can't be with you right now." She turns and starts walking away, back toward the parking lot, leaving me standing here. I'm still numb from what she told me as I watch her go.

I yank the sunglasses off my face and continue watching her, wondering how I'm going to convince her. I want her to believe me when I say that I want to be part of the baby's life and hers.

Ramon must know about her condition. I'd bet anything he knows. I need to talk to him and get him on my side. Thanks to me involving Ramon a few weeks ago, she's obviously become friends with him. In fact, he's always at her apartment. If I didn't know Ramon's sexual orientation, I would have interfered by now.

I frown as I watch her. She seems to be leaning

slightly. Her right hand comes out as though she needs to lean against something. And then it happens.

I suddenly start running toward her as I watch her fall to the grass in slow motion.

Skidding to a halt, I drop to my knees beside her. I check her pulse and sigh with relief when I feel it, although it's a bit erratic.

I cradle her face in my hands and kiss her cold lips. "Sabrina," I whisper against her lips. "Please, baby. You have to be all right. I'm sorry for everything. Just please be okay."

"Mmm," she mumbles, starting to come around.

"Sabrina, baby. Open your eyes."

They flutter but stay closed.

"Sabrina, I need to see your eyes."

They flutter a few times before she stares at me. After blinking a few times, she struggles to sit up.

"No." I stand up and pick her up. "I'm taking you to the hospital to get checked out."

She doesn't say anything, but gazes up at me for what feels like hours before saying, "Okay," closing her eyes, and snuggling into my chest.

6

Sabrina

WAITING FOR THE DOCTOR TO COME IN WITH MY TEST results is excruciating. Not only am I lying in a hospital bed after Lucien insisted on bringing me in to get checked out, but he also insisted on staying and announced that he's my fiancé. That sure opened my eyes. Fiancé! A few weeks ago, I would have loved nothing more than to call him my fiancé. Even now, my heart flutters when I think about it, but I know the truth. He's only throwing that word around so he can stay with me when the hospital has a family-only policy.

I think he's trying to be supportive, but he's only making me feel uneasy. I'd ask him to leave, but I can't bring myself to do it when I see how concerned he is about the baby and perhaps me. I can dream.

When I hear someone at the door, I glance at Lucien, who is already watching me, before turning toward the door. I see the doctor coming in, followed by a nurse.

"Hello, Sabrina and Lucien. I'm sorry to have kept you waiting." He walks further into the room and sits beside Lucien. "Let me put both your minds at rest. Your baby is doing as expected. Sabrina, however, you need to take better care of yourself. I can see that you're not sleeping well, and the tests show that you aren't getting enough nutrients. When did you last eat a proper meal? I don't mean a meal where you spent the entire time picking at it."

I have no idea when that was. I usually have fruit for breakfast to settle my stomach, then maybe half a sandwich for lunch, and bits and pieces in the evening, but I've had trouble getting those down lately. I finally admit, "I'm not sure," and catch the frown that crosses Lucien's handsome face before I notice the matching one on the doctor's.

"Young lady, you need to take better care of yourself. Not just to make sure your growing baby is getting all the nutrients it needs, but also to keep you strong and healthy." My cheeks redden under the chastisement I just received as the doctor turns toward the tablet in his hand and starts typing. "I want you to stay in the hospital tonight just to keep an eye on you. If all is well tomorrow, I'll release you in the afternoon, but only if you have a place to go where you will be looked after. I want you off your feet for a few days."

"That won't be a problem," Lucien says for the first time since the doctor walked in. "She's going to be moving in with me, so I'll make sure she gets plenty of rest and is well taken care of."

I am?

The doctor nods with a hint of mischief in his eyes. "That's a wonderful idea. I'll leave you to get some rest. I'll be back to check on you in the morning. If you need me before then, ask one of the nurses to call me."

"We will. Thank you, Doctor," Lucien says, shaking his hand.

I'm still too stunned to say anything as the doctor leaves. I knew my life was about to change when I confessed to Lucien that I was pregnant with his baby. However, I had no idea that I would be moving in with him. I suppose it was a foregone conclusion, really. No matter how he thinks his life should be lived, Lucien is a family man. I suppose I've taken the decision to stay away from me before I could hurt him out of his hands. I just hope he doesn't hate me for it because I couldn't live with his hatred. It would destroy me.

"You're quiet," Lucien observes.

He dips his head slightly, his hands in his pockets, and watches me from beneath hooded eyes. I've seen him like this before. It's his way of defending himself against something he isn't going to like. Is he expecting an argument from me? My refusal to move in with him?

I'd love to move in with him under different circumstances, but I'm not going to turn down this opportunity. If we live together, it'll give me the chance to show him that I want to be with him and that his scars don't bother me.

"Sabrina, please. We need to talk before you decide that you don't need help and refuse to move in with me. I want you there, damn it!" He paces the floor in front of the hospital bed.

My silence is obviously killing him, which isn't my intention.

"Lucien, I'm not sure what's going on in your head, but I'll do whatever the doctor says to ensure a healthy baby." I place my hand over my stomach and caress the spot where I imagine the baby is lying. Lucien watches me like a starving man.

"Can you feel the baby?"

"Not yet."

Disappointment flickers in his eyes.

"It's too soon, but my stomach feels harder to the touch." I hold my hand out to him. After a few seconds, he comes back and sits beside my hip on the bed, placing his hand in mine.

Tingles of pleasure shoot through my body at his touch. I drop my head and look at my stomach, hoping he doesn't notice the blush on my face.

His hand tightens in mine, reminding me that I'm holding his. With a nervous smile, I push the covers down, lift my hospital gown, and offer him a view of my stomach.

The bedding pools in my lap as I bring his hand and place it on my stomach.

He inhales.

Our eyes meet.

His eyes move to my stomach in wonder as he begins to caress my skin where our baby is growing. My heart feels heavy in my chest as I watch him.

He has no idea how handsome he is. When he walks into a room, my panties practically melt away. He's not only sexy, but also so damn lovable. All I have to do is watch him with his family to see how much he loves them, and my heart falls deeper for him. Yes, I want to be the woman who gets to keep him—to love, honor, and cherish him. However, I'm just not sure that it's going to work out for us. I know he desires me and perhaps cares for me, but not in the way I want. Not in the way that I care for him—love him, even.

"Our baby, Sabrina," he whispers. "I can't believe it. I never thought—" He clears his throat. "I don't just want you to move in with me. I want you to marry me before our baby arrives. I want her to have the McKenzie name."

I stare at him, thinking he's saying one thing but dreaming he's saying something else. "What? I'm not sure I follow. You pushed me away. You hurt me more than anyone ever has. I'll move in with you while I'm pregnant, and you'll always have access to your child, but I'm not sure I want that kind of commitment from you, knowing it isn't what you want. I know you're only here with me because of the baby, not because you want to be with me."

My heart tightens as if a fist were squeezing it, but I push down the pain and longing. I'm not ready to marry him just because of the baby I'm carrying. I want him to realize that he can't live without me. I want him to propose because he loves me. A girl can dream.

He doesn't say anything but instead lifts his hand from my stomach and moves to the chair beside me.

I decide to say everything I want to say while I can. "I'm guessing you'd expect sex while we live together, whether as we are now or as husband and wife. If so, I should tell you that finding out you were with someone else would be a deal breaker. We wouldn't recover from it. I don't share." I took a deep breath, knowing he really wasn't going to like what I had to say next. "You also need to talk to someone. It could be me, one of your brothers, or a therapist because you can't keep thinking the way you do about your body. It isn't healthy. I'm not like your ex. The only thing that bothers me about your scars is that you were badly hurt and in pain, and that you're still suffering. I've repeatedly told you that I care too much about you to let the scars bother me or affect our relationship, but you won't listen or trust me."

I gaze long and hard into his eyes before they slide away to look at anything but me. I know he's still listening and weighing my words, so I continue, "During the time we were together, I kept trying to touch you, to hold you, but you always knocked my hand away. You ended up fucking me from behind as though you didn't care about me. I can't do that again. If we are going to do this, then we are going to take it slow and have a healthy relationship. If you can agree to give me a chance without anyone or anything getting in the way, then I'll agree to be engaged to you for now. As for marriage, we'll see how it goes."

Lucien

Well, she certainly told me. Until I heard her words, I had no idea just how badly I'd hurt her. Toward the end of our time together, I acted the way I did to push her away because I wasn't sure I could stay away otherwise. Look where that got us!

She's gotten under my skin and into my heart—the last places I wanted her to be. But what am I supposed to do now?

My life was so much easier before Sabrina returned to Lexington. Ever since then, I've been on a roller coaster.

She's going to be the mother of my child, which means I have to give something. I was raised to take responsibility for my actions, not ignore them.

But what am I going to do with her? How do I make things right between us? How do I make her feel comfortable being with me again? I have a feeling that once I get her inside my apartment, I won't be able to let her leave. Considering I said I only wanted to have sex with her, my current feelings make a liar out of me.

"Lucien?"

I drag my eyes from her stomach and meet her worried gaze.

She really doesn't need my crap right now. She needs reassurance more than anything.

"I heard everything you said, Sabrina, and I'm sorry I hurt you. I wish I could say it wasn't my intention, but that would be a lie. I wanted to push you away so you'd hate me enough to reject me when I came after you again. I'm completely messed up and I don't know what I want anymore. I thought I knew. But then you arrived in town, and ever since the first day I met you, every-thing has been turned upside down. I can't promise that I won't mess up again, but I can promise you that as long as we live together—whether as friends or as husband and wife—there will never be anyone else. In that, you have my word."

I take her hand, sighing with relief when she slides her fingers through mine. As she holds on tight, she caresses my thumb with hers.

"As for touching," I gulp, "I'll try. For you, I'll try. My back, hip, and buttock are the worst, and they aren't pretty." I can't meet her eyes now that I've admitted that.

I feel a slight tug on my hand and look up to meet her gaze.

"I'm not oblivious. I know you were badly burned, and I need you to believe that I have no intention of running away because of that. I like you. In fact, while we're being honest, I'll even say that I like you more than that. You make me feel good," she says, blushing. "When we first started hanging out, I really felt like you were my friend. I've missed you."

I'm guessing that was difficult for her to admit, because I'm not sure I can find the words to tell her that I missed her as well.

I clear my throat and change the subject slightly. "On the way to my apartment, we'll stop by your place. You can lounge on your bed while you give me packing instructions. Also, do I need to let your mom or the doorman know your forwarding address?"

She groans. "I forgot all about my mom. She isn't going to be happy about this whole situation. She's not really the most understanding person."

From what I've heard, that's an understatement. But I'll be damned if I let anyone upset her. "Don't worry about your mom. I'll be with you when you see her, and I'll put her in her place if necessary. As far as I'm concerned, you're my responsibility now, which means I'll protect you."

She rolls her eyes.

"Lucien, I like the idea of you protecting me, but I'm not sure I need protection from my own mother. She can be difficult, for want of a better word. I just don't want to upset her more than I already will when I tell her I'm pregnant."

Is she for real?

I stand and loom over her, placing my hands on either side of her head. "She's your mother and should be happy to be a grandmother. If she's not, then I'm not going to stay quiet."

She reaches out and places her hands on either side of my face. I have to fight the urge to move out of her reach. I promised to try, and if this is how she wants to start, then I'm going to hold still. It might be different when she tries to touch me anywhere else on my marked skin.

"I'm not going to hurt you," she whispers. "I wish you would believe me."

I close the gap between us and tenderly kiss her lips. "I'm trying, okay? I wish it was easy, but it isn't. I've been like this for a long time, so I'm not sure I'll suddenly wake up one morning and be back to the way I was before the fire."

"I don't expect that." She brushes the hair from my forehead. "We'll take it slow, but you have to let me try to help you."

"I will."

I kiss her again to show her that I really will try.

"It's about time you got your act together," Ramon announces.

By the look on Sabrina's face, she's just as surprised to see him in the room as I am. I certainly didn't hear the door open. I was lost in the woman currently holding my hand and caressing my scarred thumb.

Ramon notices this, although he tries to hide it.

I kiss Sabrina on the knuckles before sitting in the chair beside her bed, not wanting to let go of her hand.

Ramon stands on the other side of the bed. Leaning over, he kisses her on the cheek and asks, "Are you really okay?"

"I'm okay. Just tired."

"Do I need to move in with you?" Ramon asks Sabrina, smoothing the blanket over her.

"I'm good, Ramon. Thanks."

"She's moving in with me."

Two pairs of eyes focus on me.

Forcing myself not to fidget under my brother's stare, I add, "She needs looking after, and we're getting engaged."

Ramon starts laughing. "You, my brother, were looking for any excuse to keep her in your life. Now that she's given you one, you're jumping at the chance. I honestly thought it would take longer for you to come around, but I guess I was wrong."

I see the curiosity in Sabrina's eyes, but I ignore it. I'm not going there, and I wish my brother had kept his big mouth shut. He knows what he's doing. Although his heart is in the right place, I wish he would keep his thoughts to himself instead of blurting them out in front of Sabrina. God knows what he's been telling her behind my back.

"So, you're going to live in sin?" Ramon asks. He drags a chair over, sits in it, and faces me. "I mean, Mom isn't exactly going to be happy with that situation, especially since Sabrina's pregnant."

"Christ, Ramon," I splutter.

"What?" he asks, looking innocent.

My eyes narrow. "You know what? Don't you have something better to do than piss me off?"

"Actually, I do. I came to visit this beautiful woman, not you."

"Lucien, don't say anything else," Sabrina says, tightening her grip on my hand in warning. "And you," she says, pointing at Ramon, "stop trying to rile him up."

"It's working."

"I need to rest and stay calm, which won't happen if you two keep winding each other up. So please stop."

"Okay, truce," Ramon says. He gets to his feet, walks around the bed, and comes to a stop in front of me. He holds out his hand, which I take. He hauls me to my feet and tugs me into a hug. "Congratulations. If anyone deserves Sabrina and this baby, it's you." He pats me on the back before taking his seat again, leaving me shaken.

That's the closest he's ever come to expressing how he feels about what happened to me.

I need to get out of here.

"I'm going to give you a few minutes," I say gruffly.

I see surprise on Sabrina's face and understanding on Ramon's.

I quickly kiss Sabrina on the forehead and whisper, "I won't be long," to reassure her that I'll be back.

I exit Sabrina's room and make my way out of the hospital for some much-needed fresh air.

It hadn't really hit me until Ramon spoke, reminding me that I'm about to have one of the things I've always wanted—a child—something I thought I'd never have.

My chest feels tight, as if the feelings inside me want to burst free. I've kept them buried for years out of self-preservation, but now they're all coming to the surface. I have no fucking clue how to deal with them without running. Running is something I've become good at, especially since I met Sabrina.

I drop onto a bench outside the hospital and rest my elbows on my knees, dropping my head into my hands. I try to breathe through the panic taking hold of my body.

If I'm like this now, how the hell am I going to manage later on?

"Here."

A bottle of water is shoved in my face.

Ramon has caught me off guard again. "Thanks." I sit up straighter. "Why aren't you with Sabrina?"

"She sent me after you."

"Fuck!" The last thing I need is for her to worry about my reaction to everything. I don't want her to doubt my commitment to her and the baby. That's the last thing either of us needs.

Sabrina

LIVING WITH LUCIEN IS SWEET TORTURE. SINCE I WAS released from the hospital three days ago, he has been so tentative that I'm really going to miss him when he finally decides that he's had enough of me invading his space. He's been alone for so long that I know he'll eventually get frustrated with his space being invaded.

It doesn't stop there. In Lucien's apartment, there are only two bedrooms, one of which is unfurnished. Once he'd gotten me here, Lucien informed me that he had no intention of furnishing the spare room with a bed. Instead, he plans on turning it into a nursery for our unborn child. He went on to inform me that, as the mother of the unborn child, I was to share his bed. He promised not to touch me unless I asked him to. He has kept that promise for three nights, but I wish he hadn't made it because I crave his touch more than ever. I'm blaming it on my pregnancy hormones, even though I suspect it's my heart and soul that craves him.

While resting on the sofa with my Kindle in hand, I much prefer the view of the dining table, where Lucien is working.

He has no idea how attractive he is sitting there in a pair of well-worn jeans, a long-sleeve T-shirt, and bare feet. His hair is messy, and he looks so damn hot. I want to go over there and run my hands through his hair. I want to feel his arms come around me as he pulls me onto his lap. But I don't know how to ask for what I want, as fear of rejection sits heavily in my chest. I wonder if Lucien feels the same way, fearing that I'll reject him because of his body. His way of thinking makes me angry because he is so caring. I wish I knew who his ex was so I could give her a piece of my mind. It just pisses me off.

I'm startled out of my dark thoughts when Lucien sits on the coffee table in front of me. He leans forward and traces my eyebrows with his finger. "What's causing these?" he asks, worry clear on his face. "Or should I be asking who?" He pulls his hand away, but I catch it in mine.

"I was feeling rather violent toward your ex, if you must know."

His eyes widen in surprise.

"My ex?"

"I blame what she did to you for your difficulty believing that anyone would want you." I swipe a tear from the corner of my eye as he watches. "It breaks my heart. I wish you could see inside me, because then you'd never doubt my feelings for you."

He caresses my face and wipes away another tear. "It's going to take time. I can't promise I'll always be so willing, but until four days ago, I hadn't let anyone touch my face the way you did. It's a start." He smiles.

"Will you hold me?"

He pauses while my words sink in. Then, he picks me up, sits back down, and pulls me onto his lap. I rest my head against his shoulder, the most natural thing in the world. When he's like this, not pushing me away, it makes me feel like I'm truly his woman. The woman he can love and never live without.

"We fit well together," he whispers against my forehead.

That's the truth.

Feeling warm and secure in his arms, I ask, "Will you come to my OB appointment with me tomorrow? She said she'd perform an ultrasound."

He kisses my cheek. "I'd love to," he says, sounding emotional.

I try to lift my face to look at him, but he stops me by resting his head on top of mine.

"Thank you. It's at four. I've arranged to meet Rosie for lunch, so would you mind meeting me there?"

"No, that's fine. Just text me the address, and I'll be there."

He stays quiet, and I can't help but wonder if he thought I wouldn't want him to come. Have I not made it clear enough?

"Lucien," I say, tightening my grip on his hand against my stomach. "We're doing this together. Don't ever feel like you have to tiptoe around me when it comes to the baby. If you have an opinion or want to discuss something, please tell me. Don't keep it inside. If you promise to do that, then I will too," I smile. "Even if it's something the other person isn't going to like."

He chuckles. "I've been making a lot of promises where you're concerned lately." He kisses me again. "But I promise."

"Thank you."

I could stay in his arms like this forever. He relaxes me, and right now, I'm fighting to keep my eyelids open.

"Come on, you're going to ache if you fall asleep here."

Lucien holds me in his arms and carries me toward our bedroom, a place I really don't want to go. If he puts me on the bed, he'll let me go, and I don't want him to.

"I'll stay until you're asleep."

Or maybe not?

He kneels on the bed and gently places me on the

mattress. I'm tempted to grab his T-shirt to keep him with me, but he moves away and grabs a throw blanket from the back of the chair to cover me up. Lucien stands and looks down at me before climbing on the bed and spooning me.

"Is this all right?" he asks, sounding hesitant.

"It's more than all right."

He caresses my arm and hand before landing his hand on my stomach. With such care, he cradles our baby. My stomach hasn't started to expand yet. It feels rock hard to the touch, and my skinny jeans feel uncomfortable, but there is no visible evidence that I'm pregnant. Having Lucien act the way he does fills me with hope. I hope that we will make it past the remaining six months of my pregnancy.

Taking more initiative, I turn in his arms, coming face-to-face with him. Before I lose my courage—which surprises me as much as it appears to surprise Lucien—I wiggle closer and hook one leg over his hip. I wrap my arm around his waist and snuggle closer as I watch his eyes darken.

"What are you doing?" he asks in a strangled voice as I wiggle against him, starting to feel his reaction to my closeness.

"What do you think I'm doing?" I counter.

"I think you're looking to get into trouble."

"Hmm, the dirty kind of trouble."

He groans. "You're really testing my control right

now. You know that?" His hand lands on my bottom and squeezes, pulling me in closer to his straining erection.

I move my hips, desperate for him in a way that I've only ever been for him.

"Sabrina, we can't," he says, struggling for breath. "I want you." He laughs. "I think that's obvious. But I want to take things slow. We need to get to know each other without sex blurring the lines. Do you hear what I'm saying? I'm trying something with you that I gave up on years ago, and I don't want to mess it up. I want a fresh start. Before, our relationship was purely about sex. Although I want you, I don't want that to be the focus this time around. He moves his hand and holds me tight. "I want it to be more about us and our growing child."

Wow!

That certainly puts an end to any thoughts I was having.

I really have no words. His words have left me stunned. Just a few days ago, he was pushing me away, even though he couldn't keep his hands off me at his parents' house. Now, he wants everything he was trying to protect himself from.

Even though my heart loves this man, body and soul, I'm still afraid that my happiness isn't going to last.

Lucien

It's becoming harder for me to stick to my good intentions. More than anything, I want to have her under me and love her with my body. This morning, I woke up with Sabrina in my arms, my dick hard as a spike, knowing exactly what it wanted. But I meant every word I said to her yesterday evening. I really do want to get to know her—her likes, her fears, and what makes her tick. I want her to rely on me as if we were married. It would kill me if she turned to someone else for anything. At least I know she's safe with Ramon. He prefers guys, but I've noticed his eyes wandering to Sylvia a few times, so I'm not sure what's going on with him.

I desperately wanted to make love to Sabrina yesterday, but my fear of rejection was at the forefront of my mind. Next time I make love to her, it's going to be different. Not just a fuck to release our lust for each other, but sweet lovin'. I just need to accept that she isn't going to panic when she sees me.

Once we know each other better, I hope to feel more secure in our relationship before the big reveal. I don't want to frighten her or have a panic attack. No matter how many times I tell myself she's different, whenever I consider showing her my back, I see Alyssa's reaction when I worked up the courage to show her mine. It was a nightmare, and I sure as hell don't want to experience that again. A reaction like that from Sabrina would kill me. She means more to me than Alyssa ever did. My ex actually did me a favor by leaving. It's just my bad luck that she left the way she did.

The only other person who has seen my scars is my mom. She has rubbed ointment on them more often than not to ease the pain I sometimes feel. That was hard. Letting her see me like that. Even though she tried to hide it, I could tell she was upset. I could feel her distress in the slight tremor of her hands and in the way she averted her gaze once she'd finished. The first time she helped me, I took hold of her and made her look at me. What I saw was crushing—she looked heartbroken. That's the only time I've ever let my emotions get the better of me. I cried all over my mom. We've never discussed that day, and I'm relieved about that.

I know Lily has caught glimpses when I've changed shirts here and at her and Michael's place. Although I've talked to her about the fire and why I ended up in the car, we've skirted the full extent of my injuries.

With Lily, it's like having a nosy sister who won't leave things alone. I'm just glad my brothers, especially Michael, have accepted her as my friend. She was a breath of fresh air in my lonely existence, and I value her opinion more than anyone will ever know. She encouraged me to keep going when I wanted to quit.

It's my affection for Lily that has me lying on the floor in the family room while my niece and nephew crawl all over me. Both Charlotte and Jr. are teething and want to bite anything in sight, including me. Those little rascals know damn well that it hurts like hell to have their sharp teeth clamp down on my hand.

They're like piranhas.

Charlotte tries again to get to my fingers, which is how Lily finds us. She scoops Charlotte up and out of my way.

I sit up and make a grab for Jr., following Lily through to the kitchen, where I set him down in his high chair and strap him in. It's the safest place for him...and me!

"You looked so cute with these two all over you," Lily comments happily.

"Hmm."

I wish Sabrina looked as happy as Lily instead of like she has the weight of the world on her shoulders.

"Never mind," Lily says, placing chopped banana in front of the twins. She turns her gaze on me. "I want to know what's going on between you and my friend. I keep getting the feeling that all isn't well between you two, but I have no idea why." She frowns.

I'd love to confide in Lily about Sabrina being pregnant with my child, but I don't want to say anything until I've discussed it with Sabrina and decided how to tell my family. To be honest, I want her beside me when we make the announcement.

"Lucien? Where'd you go?"

"Sorry."

I run my hands through my hair and watch as Lily takes a seat opposite me with a curious look on her face.

"Sabrina's moved in with me," I blurt out, leaving Lily stunned.

"As in, you're both living together? I mean— I don't know what I mean. I know you two have been avoiding each other since Sabrina first came back to Lexington, but I had no idea you were actually together." She laughs. "Wow, where have I been?"

"We weren't sure if we were going anywhere, but she's been living with me for a few days, and she isn't going anywhere if I have anything to do with it."

"I'm surprised. Happy. But surprised. Not that long ago, you wouldn't listen to me when I told you that not everyone is like your horrible ex. Now, you've moved Sabrina in with you. Total turnaround."

I sigh. "Yeah, well, things change and take priority."

"What'd I miss?" Michael asks, joining us just as Lily is about to comment. The last thing I need right now is more questions about my relationship with Sabrina.

As Michael pulls Lily onto his lap, I glance at my watch to check the time so I won't be late to meet Sabrina.

Today, we're going to see our baby for the first time during the ultrasound, and I'm really looking forward to it. It was embarrassing how my heart swelled when Sabrina asked me to go. I was hoping she would include me in everything related to our baby, and she seems to want that just as much as I do. Now, it all depends on my ability to show her just how committed I am to her and our growing child. I sure as hell don't want to mess things up.

"You fuckin' with my wife?" Michael asks, scowling.

My eyes widen in surprise, and then I start laughing. Lily gives me a mischievous look. She must have told Michael about Sabrina and me while I was dreaming about seeing my child later today.

"Ask Ramon if you don't believe me," I grin, leaving him speechless.

"We're both thrilled for you, Lucien. It's about time you started living again," Lily adds.

She stands up and removes the empty bowls from in front of the twins, who have stayed surprisingly quiet.

"I'm still struggling to get my head around this. You've spent years alone. You spent years telling us that you didn't want or need any complications, and now this. Why? What's different?"

I knew Michael would want answers. Although I know Lily won't stop until she's satisfied, I knew it would be Michael who would ask me the question I don't want to answer. I'm not sure my reasons for staying alone have changed. I'm still afraid, and if I really stop to think about Sabrina and our child, I know it will send me into a panic.

It would be easier to get everything out in the open

and let Sabrina see me without my clothes, but right now, it feels like it would take more courage than I have. While Michael sits patiently waiting for me to get my head together, I'm not sure what to say to him other than the truth, which I can't tell him yet. So, I opt for a partial truth and say, "Things change. I'm sick of being alone. I'd rather have her with me than with someone else. We'll see how it goes."

I glance at Michael to see his reaction and notice a smile spreading across his face. "Does Mom know yet?" He laughs before I can answer. "Of course she doesn't. We would have already known if she had."

I know my mom is going to be beside herself with excitement when she hears about Sabrina, and even more so when she hears about her growing grandbaby. Over the years, it has hurt seeing the look on my mom's face when she looks at me. Knowing her heart was broken because of me has added to my list of regrets. I've hated knowing how much she's hurt because of me. Now, I can't wait to see the relief on her face when I tell her how my future is looking thanks to Sabrina.

"I'm going to take Sabrina to our parents' house tomorrow," I say, glancing at my watch. "But right now, I need to leave before I'm late meeting her."

I get up from the chair and quickly kiss the twins before walking around Michael to hug his wife.

"I'm really happy for you," she whispers in my ear.

"Thank you." I kiss her on the cheek, then Michael

grabs me, gives me a hug, and shoves me away with a grin splitting his face.

"Go get your woman, and you better not screw this up."

"I'm going to try not to."

8

Sabrina

THE CLOCK ON THE WALL TICKS SLOWLY, SECONDS slipping away, then minutes, and I can't help but watch. Where is Lucien? Lucien was supposed to be here fifteen minutes ago, yet there's still no sign of him. He promised he would be here, so I'm not giving up on him yet. He's really happy about becoming a father, so I don't believe he would miss this appointment unless he couldn't physically get here. The thought has me biting my lip.

I hope he's okay.

"Sabrina, are you ready?" Crystal, my doctor's nurse, asks.

I told them to see the woman who arrived at the same time as me because Lucien hadn't shown up. Now,

103

I am the only one left. I can't keep putting them off, or they'll schedule another appointment for me. I've been looking forward to seeing my baby today, so I don't want that. With a heavy heart, I follow Crystal to a room with subdued lighting and an ultrasound machine.

"Make yourself comfortable on the examination table. The doctor will be in soon."

Left alone, I feel as though someone else has taken over my body. It's as if I'm floating above the room, watching someone else carefully place her purse on the chair beside the table. I watch someone else climb onto the examination table and lie down, her long fingers fidgeting with the buttons on her blouse. I shake my head, trying to clear the feeling from my brain, and close my eyes. If I can't regain control, these thoughts are going to cause me to panic. Lucien should be here. He promised he would be, but he isn't here. I need to remember to bring my cell phone with me so I can call him or check if he's tried to get in touch with me. What if something happened to him? Leaving my phone at home is a habit of mine that I need to break.

"Hello, Sabrina," says my OB, India Simone, walking into the room and bringing me back to earth. "How have you been? Has the morning sickness started to subside?"

"I haven't been sick for over a week now."

She nods at my response.

"I received a message that you'd been admitted for an overnight stay in the hospital. What happened?"

She sits beside me and waits.

"I wasn't in a good place. I guess I forgot to eat every once in a while, but I'm all right now. I've moved in with the father of my child, and he's been making sure I eat small meals throughout the day."

"Good. It sounds like you need someone to help you. Is he going to join us today?" she asks. I have to fight back tears.

"He was supposed to be. I don't know where he is. He promised me, and breaking his promises isn't something Lucien would do. I just don't know."

"Well, how about we record the scan so you can take the DVD home and show it to him?"

I nod, unable to speak.

The doctor pushes my shirt up to my ribs, pulls my yoga pants down around my hips, and helps me settle back down. She shoves paper towels into the top of my yoga pants and warns, "This is going to be cold," as she squirts some liquid onto my stomach.

"Okay, you ready to see your baby?"

"Yes," I whisper.

I'm excited, but the fact that Lucien isn't here with me has kind of taken some of the enjoyment out of this moment because I wanted to share it with him.

Then, the door opens.

I turn around and feel my eyes fill with tears of relief when he appears.

"God, I'm sorry I'm so late. Did I miss it?" he asks, sounding panicked.

"No, I take it you're the missing father? You'll be happy to know I'm just about to start."

"Thank God."

He seems to sag with relief before quickly coming to stand beside me. I notice that he's disheveled and looks hot and bothered, with his hair half plastered to his head.

"What happened to you?"

"There was an accident a few blocks away. I was stuck between two intersections, so I couldn't turn or take a different route. I tried calling you, but you didn't answer. It kept going to voicemail. God, Sabrina," he says, dropping into the chair behind him. "I thought I wouldn't make it here. I thought I would miss..."

"Shush. You're here with me now, and you haven't missed anything. I wasn't ignoring you. I left my phone in the bedroom."

Seeing how hard he's trying to hide his distress at being late is endearing, and it makes me want to wrap him up in my arms. Times like these make me wish nothing would ever change, but I know better. Part of me expects him to go back to how he was before I told him I was pregnant. Then, he'll push me away again. I'm not expecting him to change overnight. I know it's going to take time. That's why I'm having a hard time trusting that he'll always be here for me, given how he's been in the past. But he's here with me now.

"If you're both ready."

I meet Lucien's eyes and smile.

He takes my hand and says, "We're ready," without breaking our eye contact.

We hear the beep of the machine and turn to see the grainy image of our twelve-week-old baby. It has just become real. I'm not really listening to the doctor explain vital details because I'm thinking about nothing but seeing Lucien holding our son or daughter. I want that so badly that I don't realize I have tears pouring down my face until I feel Lucien mopping them up with a tissue.

"Baby, stop. I can't keep up."

I finally get a clear view of my handsome guy hovering over me. He looks slightly damp.

"I'm good."

"You sure?"

"Yeah." I smile to reassure him and turn back to the monitor to watch our baby as Lucien takes my hand. I can't even form the questions I want to ask. They've flown the coop.

Luckily, Lucien's brain is still working, and he asks a question of his own.

"Can you tell how far along Sabrina is?"

"She's twelve weeks and two days," she says. "I'm going off the answers Sabrina wrote down on the questionnaire all newly pregnant ladies are asked to fill out, and her answers match what the ultrasound is telling me." She looks to me. "Everything seems to be going as planned, but after the scare you've had, I want to see you twice a week for the next three weeks, and then we'll reevaluate."

What isn't she telling me?

"I can see the wheels turning, Sabrina. I'm not concerned about anything. You were admitted to the hospital, though, so to be on the safe side, I want to keep a close eye on you for a few weeks. That's all, I promise."

"I'll make sure she's here."

"I'm sure you will." She grinned at Lucien. "Please make the appointments on your way out. For now, let me clean you up and sort out your photographs and DVDs."

She starts to wipe my stomach clean while I gaze at Lucien. I've never seen that look on his face before, and my brow wrinkles in confusion until I realize what it is—wonder.

"Are you okay?" I ask him as the doctor moves to the other side of the room.

He takes a deep breath before standing and bringing his forehead to mine. "Yeah," he says, his voice breaking. "It's amazing seeing our baby. It's just become real. We're going to be parents." He kisses me on the lips. "Thank you." He kisses me again, hovering above me with mere centimeters between us. "You and this baby will always come first, Sabrina. It won't be easy for me. No one changes that quickly."

I cover his mouth with mine.

Pulling away, I say, "The past is what it is. Although I'm not making light of what happened to you, we need to start living for our future." I kiss him again, pull back, and smile. "I can't wait to tell your parents. Your mom is going to freak out."

He moves away and helps me sit up on the table, laughing. "That she is."

"We'll leave my mom for now."

"I think it might be better if we tell her first, just to get it out of the way, and then we can go tell your folks." He puts my shoes back on and helps me stand, then adjusts the top of my yoga pants.

"I've told you how she's likely to react. I'm not sure I can handle her negativity right now."

Lucien leans into me, his warmth making me feel safe as he gently brushes my hair from my face. "My mom will pull you out of whatever your mom does to you. Just remember that I'll be with you. Don't let her play on your mind. You need to stay stress-free."

"I know you're having a private conversation, but I have to agree with your boyfriend. The sooner you tell her, the sooner you can move forward and enjoy being pregnant." The doctor hands me the pictures and DVD, then starts showing us out of the room. Suddenly, she says, "Oh, and in case you're wondering, there isn't any reason why you can't continue having a normal sex life."

As soon as the words leave her mouth, I feel my face heat up, and I feel Lucien's hands tighten on me as he pulls me slightly closer to him.

"That's good to know," he responds.

He ushers me out of the office and into the elevator without speaking.

He presses the button for the underground parking and stands opposite me with his ankles crossed and his back leaning against the elevator wall. The look on his face is so heated that I'm sure my panties have melted right off.

"Sex, hmm."

Lucien

Ever since the doctor brought up sex, I haven't been able to stop thinking about it. Up until a few months ago, I hadn't had sex in almost six years because my penis refused to become erect. Then Sabrina appeared, and I had a permanent erection. Now, the doctor has given us permission to have sex again—not that we needed permission—but ever since she mentioned it, my dick has sprung to life and wants to be buried in Sabrina's warmth.

From Sabrina's fidgeting, I'm guessing she's aroused, which is why I'm driving back to our apartment instead of her mother's. I want to show Sabrina what she means to me with my body. I'm not sure I'll be able to give her what she wants—me fully naked—but I can worship her body and give her pleasure like no one else ever will, because she's not going anywhere. That's just unthinkable.

I refrain from touching her as I pull into my parking space at our apartment building. Otherwise, we won't make it out of the car.

I jump out and run around to open the door for Sabrina. I take her hand and pull her out of her seat. She comes up against me, causing a groan to burst from my lips. I feel like my body is about to combust from the lust running through me.

"I want you," I say.

She replies, "I'm not complaining," and that gets me moving.

I take her hand and practically pull her toward the elevator. Once inside, I wrap my arms around her, bury my face in her neck, and hold her close. Her hands land on my backside, pulling me toward her, leaving little doubt about how much I want her.

My heart beats to the rhythm of what's going on in my pants.

When I hear the elevator ping, I take a deep breath and turn Sabrina around to face me. I slide my hands against her stomach and pull her flush against my body.

She presses her ass against my hardening length and gently rotates her hips.

I can't look at the couple who just entered the elevator because the lust on my face would be clear to anyone, even a stranger. I'm too far gone to hide what she makes me feel.

Sabrina reaches back with one hand—the one hidden from view—and caresses my ass again.

The elevator opens on our floor, so I push her out in front of me, keeping her trapped in my arms as we make our way to our apartment. As soon as the door opens, I push her inside and press her up against the wall, holding her in place with my body.

"Tell me if you don't want this. If you don't want me inside you."

I need to hear her say that she wants me as much as I want her. I don't want either of us to have any doubt.

"I want you, Lucien. I want you so much that I constantly ache for you."

I'm not sure I'm going to be able to keep myself in check after hearing her words. Feeling her against me does things to me that haven't happened before.

"We need a bed."

I grab her ass, hearing her gasp as I lift her. "Wrap your legs around me."

She does as I ask. Her arms go around my neck, and her fingers snake into my hair, sending goose bumps down my spine.

If she's not careful, I'm going to take her on the floor. As it is, my legs feel like Jell-O, and I barely make it to the bed before dropping her on it. She bounces slightly and laughs.

She falls silent as she watches me unfasten my belt and pants. I let them fall to my ankles and kick them off with my shoes. I'm not ready to take off my T-shirt yet. Small steps.

Sabrina sits up on the bed and kicks off her shoes. She quickly removes her clothes and reaches out to trace my length through my boxers. My shaft twitches and leaks with excitement. It's not just her touch. It's also the sight of her sitting naked in front of me—her breasts and nipples swollen with arousal. Her trimmed pubic hair leads to her wet heat, making my mouth water.

"Let me see you, Lucien," she says, stroking me. "Please."

I look up at the ceiling to catch my breath, but nothing works. I feel like she's taking the very breath out of me.

There is slight scarring on my hip and groin, with puckered skin around the base of my dick and along one side. I guess I should be thankful it stopped there. I would have had a lot more problems if it hadn't.

I can show her my skin because trust has to start somewhere.

With her watching, I shove my shorts down my legs, then catch my breath when her hand closes around my erection. I feel like a teenager, reacting to her touch as if I'm seconds from coming. I haven't let anyone touch me here since the fire. When I was with Sabrina, I pushed her away whenever she tried to touch me. Now that I've finally let her touch me there, my body is gearing up for release.

She strokes down to my balls and massages them between her fingers. My legs shake like a newborn colt.

"Lucien, you're beautiful," she whispers against the tip of my cock. Her breath caresses me like a breath of fresh air. I watch her tongue appear from between her pink lips. Our eyes meet as I watch her lick around the head and trace the slit where pre-cum is leaking out. If she's not careful, I'm going to come on her tongue.

"You like that."

I have no idea if she expects an answer, but I'm too far gone to think about opening my mouth.

She licks all around the base of my shaft, tracing her tongue over the puckered skin without hesitation.

"How long has it been since you've been touched like this?" she purrs, her tongue darting out again to lick the precum leaking from my tip.

I groan and force my hips to stay still. All I want to do is thrust toward her.

"Hell...six years."

"No one's touched you for all that time?"

It does sound odd for a full-blooded guy, but it's the truth.

"That's right. Fuck!" I curse as her mouth finds my balls.

"Come in my mouth."

"What?"

"I want you to come in my mouth."

Her hand grips my shaft more firmly as she massages my nuts with her tongue. Her thumb plays with the tip as her wet tongue works its way back up, sucking me in.

"I want to pleasure you," I hiss between my teeth.

"You can. After I've given you this."

Her free hand slides against my bare ass, pulling me closer so that I'm standing between her legs. She caresses me while her mouth and tongue work their magic along my length. The tightening in my balls is almost unbearable. I hold her against me, my hands tangling in her hair.

I look down and watch myself slide in and out of her wet mouth. Our eyes meet, and I watch her swirl her tongue around me, curling my toes in pleasure, before she sucks me down her throat. My balls feel heavy, like they're ready to explode like a Fourth of July rocket. Nothing is going to stop me.

"I'm coming..."

My eyes roll back in my head as she sucks harder,

and her little moans of pleasure are the final stroke I need.

Holy fuck!

Sabrina removes her mouth and uses her hand to finish me off.

She wipes her mouth with her shirt and grins at me as I continue to spill over her hand.

"No more," I croak, dropping to the bed.

I feel her wipe my cock clean before she snuggles in beside me.

"You needed that," she says, and I hear a smirk in her voice.

"Hmm."

"I've never had anyone flood me before."

"Hmm."

"That was so hot."

"Hmm."

She raised her head and looked at me, her hand resting on my chest. "Lost your voice?" she smirks.

"I don't know what to say."

"Then don't say anything." Sabrina leans down and meets my lips. "Thank you for trusting me." She kisses me again. "I love that I can do that to you."

I reach up and curl my hand around the back of her neck, pulling her in. "Thank you," I whisper, tucking her head beneath my chin. I just about catch her wandering hand. "No, you don't. It's your turn as soon as I can move."

"Not tonight."

I freeze. Doesn't she want me to touch her?

"Lucien, when was the last time a woman did something for you without expecting anything in return?"

I can't believe I'm about to admit this to her. "Never."

She doesn't look surprised.

"That's what I thought. Yes, I'm turned on. It was hot as hell being able to do that to you. But I realized that I want tonight to have been just for you. You never take time for yourself. I was right, so in a minute, we're going to have an early night. I'm going to sleep in your arms, whether you like it or not. Tomorrow, we can visit my mom and your parents. For once in your life, you're going to do as you're told."

The bossy little thing!

Chuckling, I rolled on top of her and groaned when my balls came to rest between her thighs. From the way her breathing has picked up, I think Sabrina likes just where I'm resting. I press down and watch her bite back a moan.

9

Sabrina

I SMILE WHEN I WAKE UP TO FIND A GLASS OF ICE WATER, A dish of melon and cherries, and a cup of coffee on the table beside me. I'm still wrapped up in Lucien's arms, so I'm not sure when he snuck out of bed to leave me these treats. I'm certainly not complaining. I've found that ice-cold water and melon help calm my stomach in the morning, but I still need my caffeine fix. After my first cup of coffee in the morning, I manage to stick with decaf for the rest of the day, so that's good, right?

When I looked up ways to prevent morning sickness online, many people suggested ginger cookies or crackers, but I find that I'm craving something wetter. God, that sounds dirty, especially after what I did to Lucien last night. But it's true. Either that, or the morning sickness has disappeared on its own.

I burrow deeper into Lucien's arms and hear him groan as he clamps down on my wiggling hips. "You need to stop before you find more than you bargained for," he growls.

"I know exactly what I want," I counter, turning in his arms to face him. "It's morning, and I want you to make sweet love to me."

I curve my left leg over his hip and align our bodies. His dick nudges against me, so I push down, and he slides in an inch or two. I'm so wet for him that it won't be a problem. He grips my hips and thrusts all the way inside. He rolls on top of me. I wrap my legs around his hips and cling to his arms with my hands. I run my hands up and down his arms, too frightened to touch him anywhere that I know will stop what we're doing.

Then he starts moving, and all thoughts fly out of my head. I just feel.

Lucien dips his head and captures my lips in a long, slow kiss. I'm sure he's trying to tell me something, but before I can process it, he pulls away and lavishes my breasts with his tongue. When he sucks my nipple into his mouth, my pussy clenches around his cock in pleasure.

He trembles against me.

Because of the pregnancy, my nipples are really

sensitive, and I've just discovered a live wire straight to my core.

Switching to my other throbbing nipple, he sucks it and swirls his tongue around it, causing me to arch up into him. As he grinds against me, I fly apart in his arms. I vaguely hear him grunt while I'm flying.

Lucien brings me slowly back to earth, kissing my chest and collarbone gently. Then, he slips out of me and pulls me into his arms. Holding me tight, he kisses my forehead.

We stay silent, allowing our breathing to return to normal.

I feel as though my heart is about to burst out of my chest. All my nerve endings are alive and buzzing afterward. The only problem is that while I'm wrapped in Lucien's arms, I can't wipe the tears from my eyes without him knowing something is wrong. There isn't anything wrong. It's just that having him make love to me like he did instead of hiding behind me makes me so happy. Lying together like this, I can hope that perhaps there is a future for us. A future where we have a normal relationship and Lucien doesn't worry that I'll walk away.

"You're thinking too hard."

"That was the first time," I say, my voice cracking.

"I know."

He rolls onto his back.

"Things are changing. I don't handle change well." He

kisses my shoulder before rolling out of bed. His long-sleeved T-shirt is still in place as he walks into the bathroom and closes the door.

I'm left floundering.

After what we just did, he could have stayed in bed longer. He could have sat next to me while I ate the treats he left me, as he has the past couple of mornings. Lucien did warn me that he needs time. I just hoped he planned to spend that time with me and not off by himself, beating himself up for reasons only he knows.

Sighing, I sit up and rearrange the pillows behind me so I can eat something before my stomach rebels.

As I finish the fruit, Lucien walks back out of the bathroom. He's fully dressed in jeans and a long-sleeved T-shirt, and his hair is still damp from his shower. He gives me a quick look in passing as he slips his watch onto his wrist. He collects his wallet and keys from the table and gives me another glance before opening the bedroom door. "I'm going to get some breakfast. I won't be long. Then, we'll visit your mom. She'll be around, right?"

I nod.

He pauses, then says, "Okay, see you soon," as he leaves the apartment.

What the hell just happened?

I'm angry now. There was no need for him to leave without saying a proper goodbye. I know we're new, and it's going to take time for us to adjust to being together, but that was damn rude. We're going to have a talk when he returns.

MY MOOD IS RAW, AND THE HEADACHE I'M GETTING IS definitely from my anger toward Lucien. Since arriving home after breakfast, he has done nothing but frown. He was gone for just over an hour, which was long enough for me to get ready. But as soon as he walked in, I knew his mood hadn't lightened since he left. In fact, it had darkened to the point that he could barely say two words to me without snapping at me. So, like any sane person, I kept my mouth shut, even though it pissed me off.

I suppose being pissed off is the best way to be when I'm about to face my mother. It means I won't let her walk all over me like she does too often. She's my mom, yet I spend more time biting my lip to hold back my words than I do actually talking to her. Why? Well, you see, I'm not the perfect daughter. I don't enjoy sitting and chatting about books with her and her friends over tea and sandwiches. Heaven forbid I bring up the kind of books I like to read! I'm sure they'd all choke on their tea if I mentioned Christian Grey from the Fifty Shades trilogy. In fact, when I was annoyed with her for interfering with my life, I purposely bought paperbacks with risqué covers. Minutes before her friends arrived, I laid them out where they would be found. It was a childish thing to do, but it was worth it to see the look on her face.

I've never been good enough for her. Growing up, I preferred the jeans my dad bought me to the lacy, frilly dresses my mother bought me. I'd rather be up a tree than standing beneath it. There was also the time when the son of one of my dad's friends showed up on a bike. I went off with him and ended up covered in mud because it had started raining and there was no mudguard on the bike. I loved it, of course, but, as usual, my mom was disappointed in me. She couldn't understand why I acted like a boy instead of a "delicate young lady." Delicate my ass! Apparently, my marriage prospects were plummeting because of my wild ways.

Well, I guess we're about to find out what she thinks about Lucien. I'm not too sure about him at the moment. He told me that we were going to get married, but I agreed to be engaged for now. The only problem is that he hasn't mentioned it since the hospital. Who knows what's going through his head? I wish I knew, though, so I could help rid him of his dark thoughts.

Realizing that I had been lost in thought for most of the journey, I pulled myself back into the present as Lucien pulled into a parking space directly outside my mother's building. I lived here for a month or two when we first arrived back in Lexington, and it drove me crazy. Needless to say, I moved out as soon as I had the chance.

Climbing out of the car, Lucien gets my door and opens it for me. This time, however, his hand isn't offered, so I climb out myself. He still isn't really looking at me when he takes my elbow, so I yank it free. I catch his startled expression from the corner of my eye before he puts on a mask again.

We walk into the building in silence, greet the doorman, and he shows us to the elevator. Once inside, I press the button for the seventh floor and stand on the opposite side of Lucien. His dark looks have started to get to me. I'm already on edge because of what I'm about to tell my mother, and having Lucien act this way when he promised to support me with her has me worried.

My mom will see the tension between us the moment she sees us together.

As the elevator slowly takes us up to my mother's floor, my anger flares up and I can't hold it in any longer. I turn to Lucien and ask, "What the fuck is going on? And don't you dare say nothing."

"What are you talking about?"

"Are you for real?" I wave my hand between us. "You've been in a snit ever since we made love, and I want to know what changed. What happened?"

He gives me a dark look before running his fingers through his hair. "It isn't you. It's me. You knew that it wouldn't be easy when you started this with me." He looks away. "Let's get this over with so we can go celebrate with my family."

"Not sure I feel like celebrating," I mumble under my breath as I exit the elevator and lead Lucien to my mother's apartment.

After I press the buzzer, announcing our arrival—an arrival she'll be expecting, since the doorman will have informed her that I was on my way up with a strange man—Lucien takes hold of my face. He turns me to face him and seals his lips over mine.

I'm so stunned by this unexpected move that my mouth opens, allowing him entry. His tongue dances with mine as I moan and wrap my arms around his neck, bringing us flush together. He turns me inside out with his touch. I know I have his undivided attention when he holds me tight in his arms, with his mouth devouring mine and his hands on my bottom. I just wish it lasted longer than the kissing and touching.

"Well, really, Sabrina."

When I hear my mother's voice, my instinct is to pull away from Lucien, but he doesn't allow me to as he slows our kiss. Eventually, he leaves my lips, smiles down at me, and kisses me again before letting me turn to face my mom.

With his arm around my waist, he smiles in a way that melts my heart as he greets my mom. "Mrs. Walker. How are you? I'm Lucien McKenzie." He is so smooth! I watch in disbelief as my mom melts before my eyes. Well, that's a first!

"Come in."

Mom opens the door wide for us to enter, but she frowns as I walk past her.

"Please call me Dorothy," she tells Lucien without missing a beat. "Would you like some refreshments? I'm sure Sabrina wouldn't mind finding you something."

Good God! We've only been here a minute, and she's already pissed me off. That's a new record.

"Sabrina isn't going to find me anything." Lucien takes my jacket, ushers me onto the sofa, and sits beside me, draping my jacket over his thighs. "I know you've met some of my family. For whatever reason, I wasn't present, but we're here to let you know that I've asked Sabrina to marry me, and she's accepted."

Words escape me.

I told him I would agree to be engaged to him for now and that marriage might follow once we get to know each other, so his forwardness is surprising. Looking at the shock on my mother's face, I turn and meet his gaze. He winks at me before turning his attention back to my mom. I realize that he told my mom first to give her time to process the news before announcing, "You're also going to become a granny," as he caresses my stomach.

I cringe. "Granny" isn't going to go over well, which he damn well knows. I can't help but snicker.

He's wicked.

"You got her pregnant?"

"Yes, ma'am." He grins. "Strong swimmers in the McKenzie family."

She stutters, and we watch her blush.

He's purposely baiting her.

I know I shouldn't feel the need to come to her rescue, especially since that wouldn't even enter her head if it were me, but I do. "Mom, I'm three months pregnant, and sometime before the baby is born, we might get married. That's not confirmed yet, so we'll see."

Ignoring what Lucien said, my mother stares at me, and I know she isn't happy. Years of disappointment shine in her eyes as her mouth tightens and her voice hardens, "Really, Sabrina? I expected as much from you. Unmarried, pregnant, and now you're only considering marriage? For the baby's sake, I hope you're married before it's born."

I feel Lucien tense beside me at her words. Her tone doesn't surprise me, but her angry words do, which is sad considering she's the only parent I have left.

Lucien gets to his feet and pulls me up. "We're leaving before I say something that will make Sabrina hate me. If you want to be involved in your daughter's and grandchild's lives, then I'm sure you know how to contact us."

Before I can fully comprehend what she just said and

Lucien's reaction, I'm out in the hall, being ushered back to the elevator by a fuming Lucien.

He leans against the wall, drops his head between his hands, and calms himself down. I hate seeing him like this, and I have no idea whether he'll welcome or reject my comfort. There's only one way to find out.

Aware of his aversion to being touched on the back, I move closer to him, place my hand on his shoulder, and rub it.

I feel him shudder at my touch. He turns his head and looks at me from beneath his brows, and I feel my panties incinerate. I love seeing that look on his face. As though I'm the only one he sees. The one he wants to devour.

When he hears the elevator ping, he moves quickly and shoves me up against the back wall. The doors close as his mouth descends to mine.

Lucien

After feeling like I was drowning this morning, I'm feeling pretty smug now. Giving Sabrina an orgasm in the elevator after sucking her breasts through her top, right before the doors opened on the ground floor, is something to feel smug about. She went off like a rocket, causing me to work out complicated mathematical problems to make my raging erection shrink before I embarrassed myself.

That certainly helped lighten the mood from this morning.

I'd been a jerk.

Seeing the hurt on Sabrina's face after making love to her killed me, and I couldn't stop the feelings rising up in me. So, like a coward, I'd gone and hidden in the bathroom. I wanted to grab her and tell her how much she means to me. But those feelings choked me up, and I started to panic. That brought back the last time I saw Alyssa. She had been screaming at me. She told me how hideous I looked. She said that no one in their right mind would ever want to be with me and that if they did, it would only be for my money and who my family is, not for me or how I look now.

For years, every time I closed my eyes, I could only see her face screwed up in disgust. Eventually, I started to believe her and shut myself off from everyone. I suppose the fact that I couldn't get hard for her after the fire might have angered her even more. But if she had loved me, she would have stuck around instead of abandoning me. I thank God every day that my family was there. They always are.

Now I have Sabrina under my skin, and for the most part, I've resigned myself to that fact. What terrifies me is when she looks at me as though I'm the only one she sees. I want that look to always be on her face. I don't want it wiped off because of how I look naked. No matter how many times she tells me to trust her and says that she isn't like that, no one knows how they'll react until they're faced with the fact.

The more time I spend with Sabrina, the more I'm pulled in. Until she moved in with me, I had no idea how lonely I was. I didn't realize how much I was craving company. I wanted someone to call my own, someone to build a life with. Then Sabrina burst into my life, literally knocking the breath out of me.

My brothers already think of her as part of the family. Well, I don't even need to think about my parents. They welcomed her into the family the moment she arrived with Lily. When Sabrina hasn't shown up for a family dinner, Mom has always given me a look that would make me come up with any excuse to get out of her line of sight. Yeah, my mom still has it.

I'm going to give her a minute after we tell her about the baby to reach for the tissues. She loves children and dotes on Charlotte and Jr. so much. It's no wonder she's always hinting for us to get married and give her a house full of grandchildren. No doubt she'll want more children for each of us when she finds out about Ramon, although he could adopt. I need to talk to him and find out what's going on. I hate not knowing exactly what's going on, and he's damn evasive. In fact, Sabrina probably knows more about his life than any of us do, as they seem to have developed a good friendship.

I sigh, wondering what the future holds for Sabrina and me, as I pull up to my parents' house.

I'm lucky to have grown up in this family and this house. This place will always be home to my brothers and me, and no matter where we travel, we always come home.

"You okay?" Sabrina asks, sliding her hand up my thigh.

I catch her fingers and entwine mine with hers. "Yeah, I'm good."

I leave out the part about being nervous. She can probably tell anyway. I'm the oldest at forty-one, so I shouldn't be nervous about bringing a girl home. I wasn't with Alyssa. Probably because she didn't mean as much to me as the woman beside me does. That's why I'm terrified she'll see the light and walk away.

"You're lying to me. You look like you're about to hurl." Sabrina offers me a small smile.

I laugh, which eases my nerves.

"Come on, let's go tell Mom you have a bun in the oven." I smirk, knowing it's going to piss her off.

"You better choose your words more carefully, or you won't see what's beneath this dress," she counters as she gets out of the car.

I get out and meet her beside the passenger side.

She looks so cute that I invade her personal space

and press up against her. I rest my forearms against the car and gaze into her eyes. "You make my libido crazy. But you know that already, don't you?"

She smiles and reaches up, sliding her fingers through my hair. Shards of pleasure run down my spine, waking my dick up as I press right against her covered pussy. Sabrina moans into my mouth, and our tongues dance in a primal way, as old as the stars. I wish we were doing that dance with other parts of our bodies.

Her taste is driving me crazy.

I reach down, grab her bottom, and hoist her up so that she's in a better position for what I want. Her dress needs to disappear. My cock needs to be free.

Fuck! No!

"Shit, babe." I breathe heavily against her neck. "We're in my parents' front yard."

She chuckles. "I know."

"Fucking hell. I hope they're busy elsewhere. The last thing I want is for anyone to see you like this." I mean every word. I don't want anyone to see her in a lust-induced haze. I don't care who sees me, but no one sees my girl.

"Do you need a minute before we go inside?" Sabrina asks, smoothing her dress out.

"No, I'm good."

"You sure?" She looks at my groin, then moves her eyes up to meet mine, grinning.

"I'll be fine by the time we get inside. I just need you

to keep your hands to yourself." I wrap my arm around her waist and pull her along with me.

"What about your hands on me?"

"I figured that if I'm aching to be inside you, then you might as well ache too." I bend down and whisper in her ear, "I want you to imagine my hard, thick cock sliding back and forth, creating delicious friction inside your pussy."

She freezes and gives me an incredulous look.

"How am I supposed to sit with your family with a soaked pussy—without panties, I might add—and imagine you buried deep inside me?" She smirks.

"No panties? Fuck! I had no idea. Now you can suffer like I'm about to. At least your arousal won't be obvious to everyone."

"Hmmm."

"Anyway, when did you take off your panties?"

"In the restroom before we left my mom's apartment building. They were too wet to wear after what you did to me."

"Fuck."

"Lucien...with Sabrina."

I jumped at the sound of my mom's voice and turned toward her.

Unbeknownst to us, she had snuck up and was now standing in the doorway with a mischievous look in her eyes. I just hope to God she didn't hear the sexy banter

Sabrina and I exchanged. It wouldn't surprise me. She doesn't miss anything.

"Come inside. Sebastian and Carla just arrived too."

Oh, great! Just what we need—Sebastian.

"Oh, look what the cat dragged in," Sebastian says, taking my girlfriend into his arms for a bear hug and grinning at me.

"Ignore him," Carla adds, giving me a quick hug before Sabrina gets hers. She hooks her arm through Sabrina's, dragging her toward the sofa. I hear her say, "So you and Lucien, huh? I want all the details later. It seems as though you've neglected to tell your friend all about it."

Sabrina looks back at me, and I start moving.

As I join them on the sofa, I hear the end of her response, "He's amazing."

I grin, and Carla rolls her eyes.

"Next time you tell me about him, make sure he can't hear you. That smug look he's wearing reminds me of Sebastian when we discuss something and he insists he's right."

"Of course I'm right, babe. A McKenzie is never wrong."

"See what I mean?" Carla glares at Sebastian before turning her attention back to us. "It's annoying."

We laugh as Mom and Dad sit down across from us. Mom pours us both a drink from the large coffee pot on the table.

I'm not sure Sabrina should be drinking so much coffee, especially since she's pregnant. The thought of commenting on it makes me slightly queasy. I'm an adult, yet the thought of announcing things like marriage and babies to my parents gives me butterflies as big as golf balls.

Sabrina slips her hand onto my thigh and gently squeezes. I look into her eyes and find myself lost. She's amazing. She offers me comfort and support, or whatever you want to call it. It's something I sure as hell don't deserve, considering how I was with her this morning.

Forgetting that we're in a room with my family, I lose all awareness of my surroundings. I slip my hand around the nape of Sabrina's neck and nudge her toward me. I sigh when our lips meet in a sweet kiss. Sabrina is slightly off balance, so her hand lands on my hip, narrowly missing my rising cock. I groan and hear a throat being cleared.

"Do you two mind? You may want to be alone, but I can assure you, you're not," Sebastian says.

"I know that," I reply, still holding my girl. "We're getting engaged and having a baby."

There's a pin-drop silence after my announcement.

Sabrina smiles against my lips before sitting upright and facing my parents.

They both look stunned.

Mom is the first to pull herself together. Jumping up, she runs around the table, pulls Sabrina into her arms, and holds her so tightly that I'm not sure she can breathe. "Thank you for bringing our son back to us," I hear her whisper into Sabrina's ear. I haven't gone anywhere, but I know what she means. Back to the living. Back to having a normal life.

"Wow, the McKenzie swimmers are good," Sebastian adds, pulling me up from the sofa into a hug. "It's about damn time you got your act together."

I grunt in response and pull Carla into my arms.

She doesn't say anything, but I notice her wiping her eyes.

Sebastian takes his woman back and whispers in her ear, causing her to turn red.

When I turn back to Sabrina and Mom, I notice Dad watching me from the sofa. He doesn't move.

I shove my hands in my pockets and walk over to him, offering him a hand, which he takes. As soon as he's on his feet, he pulls me in close and holds me tight. He doesn't say anything—he doesn't need to.

When we separate, I realize I'm fighting back tears of my own.

"I've always been proud of you," he begins, "but none more so than right now. I know you're still fighting your demons, but you have the love of a good woman and a baby on the way. You're changing the future you said you were resigned to six years ago. I don't think anything will ever be as hard for you as it is right now. So the fact that you're fighting to overcome them has made me damn proud of you all over again. I love you, son."

Fuck!

Sabrina wraps herself around me, offering comfort. I pull her against my chest, burying my face in her neck, while I get my bearings back. My dad's words have floored me. He's always been a man of few words, and even though we know he loves us, he doesn't often tell us.

"Are you okay?"

I raise my head and gaze into Sabrina's eyes, which are swimming. I offer her a small smile and bend to kiss each one. "I think I am."

"Good."

"I'm really happy for you both," Carla says. "And I can't wait until the baby is here. Oh, how far along are you?"

"Three months."

"Oh, wow. You're due around the same time as Lily. How exciting! Have you bought anything yet?" Mom asked, pulling Sabrina out of my arms and down onto the sofa with her and Carla.

"Not yet. I want to wait another month before we start thinking about baby things and the nursery. If that's okay with Lucien," I say.

I sit on the coffee table in front of her, caressing her knees and slipping my hands beneath the hem of her dress. Her eyes glow with my touch.

"I'm good with that."

10

Sabrina

HAVING LUCIEN'S HANDS ON MY LEGS IS DRIVING ME crazy. I'm doing my best not to squirm with need in front of his parents. I'm mortified!

I narrow my eyes as he smirks.

"Mom, Carla, I need to talk to my woman."

Sebastian laughs. "Heard that before."

Carla smacks him on the leg. "Behave yourself, and you might get lucky later."

Lucien stands and wraps his hand around mine, pulling me to my feet. Before anyone can stop us, he drags me out of the family room, shoving me in front of him and telling me to "Just keep walking."

I do as he says, adding a more pronounced sway to my hips, knowing his eyes are on my bottom.

Within seconds, his hands grip my hips as he steps into me. The bulge behind his zipper presses into my bottom, making my pussy clench with arousal.

"Fuck this!" he curses.

Lucien grabs my wrist, and before I know it, he rushes me out of the house and into the barn, having me facing the wall before I can catch a breath. I find my hands resting against it as he pulls my hips out. He spreads my legs with his foot, throws my dress over my bottom, and rubs against me.

"You're ready for me. Christ, Sabrina." I hear his belt and zipper go. "Do you have any idea how fucking hot it makes me knowing how much you want me?"

He spreads me and thrusts inside before I can catch my breath. His hands grip my hips as he pauses, giving me time to adjust to his size.

"Jesus fuck, Sabrina. I've never wanted anyone as much as I want you. I've even had my dick inside you while at my parents' home."

He kisses my spine as I feel him withdraw and then slide back inside.

I bite my lip to keep from moaning. The only thing that could make this experience better is if I were facing him. He used to fuck me like this, but I'm not sure how I feel about it now, even if it does make my toes tingle with pleasure.

My dress rides up my back as Lucien curls one hand

over my pussy, while the other goes up to play with my breasts and nipples.

He bites my ear, and I clamp down on his thick shaft.

We both moan.

"God, that feels good, babe."

"Umm, oh yes."

Lucien straightens up and slowly starts to slide in and out of me. I feel every ridged inch of him as he thrusts deep inside me and pulls out slowly. My knees feel like they're about to buckle.

"Just so you know," he says, grinding into me, "I'm not doing this because I don't want you to touch me." He breathes. "I love watching my dick slide inside you." He slides out and holds still with the tip at my entrance. "And when I withdraw, full of your arousal, it makes me so hard seeing my glistening cock that I can't see straight."

God! Hearing those words makes my head spin.

I push back onto him and groan, "We can't stay in here all day."

He chuckles.

"Don't worry. I won't last much longer being surrounded by you."

He kisses my spine.

My core pulsates around him.

"Oh hell!" he hisses. "Then I'd better hurry and make you scream."

I scream silently.

TODAY HAS BEEN AMAZING! DESPITE OUR DIFFERENCES, everything turned out pretty well.

Since leaving Lucien's parents' place, we've been relaxing at our apartment. Well, I have, at least. Lucien has been working.

He works for the McKenzie business, and from what he's told me, he's very selective about the architectural contracts he takes on for the company. Apparently, the project he's currently working on requires some changes, and he must deliver the final blueprint to Ramon within the next couple of days, as the project has already begun. Ramon is the foreman in charge, and I know from talking to him that there have been a few setbacks, which have worried him. Maybe Lucien has managed to solve the problem.

I don't know much about the construction industry, but I know the McKenzies have a monopoly in Lexington.

At least being on the hospital's fundraising board doesn't put me in competition with anyone. I'm not built for constant battles. However, give me a cause to fight for, and anyone standing in my way had better look out.

Thanks to Lily and Carla, I have that opportunity now. They've gotten me involved with the charity event at the hospital in two months. I'm really excited about it. One of the things I most enjoy is arranging things and ensuring that everything possible has been covered to make an event perfect.

The event is to raise money to help open the new wing of the hospital. Although the building was completed over twelve months ago, it has just been standing empty. All the previously raised money went toward the state-of-the-art building. It's impressive, and we hope that the fact that it will be a dedicated children's ward will attract even more funding.

Being involved has given me something to think about other than Lucien, who pushed me away. However, since moving in with him, I can't stop thinking about him and our growing baby. I'm having a hard time concentrating on anything else.

Glancing back at Lucien, I frown. He's on his phone and looks stressed. I hope he'll tell me if he's receiving bad news. If our relationship is going to work, he needs to start opening up to me, whether it's about us, family, or even problems at work. Talking to me will help him get things off his chest instead of worrying about them, and it will give me a chance to be there for him.

"I'll be expecting Eric," Lucien says, hovering over me. I move my legs so he can join me on the sofa. "Email me his flight details, and either Ramon or I will meet him at the airport." Lucien indicates that he wants my legs across his lap. So I comply. He grins before finishing his call. "We'll talk later, Dante." He hangs up.

After sitting in comfortable silence for a few minutes, I realize just how tired he is. We've been spending time together during the day, and he hasn't complained once about falling behind at work, which makes me wonder just how far behind he is because of me. I really don't like seeing him like this.

Then he turns his head, focuses his dark eyes on me, and everything but Lucien disappears from my mind. I'm determined not to let him distract me like he always does.

"Talk to me, Lucien. What's going on? Why do you look so tired?"

He doesn't deny anything, leaning his head back against the sofa while keeping his eyes on me.

"There's a problem at the site Ramon is on. Materials keep going missing, and accidents that shouldn't happen are happening. It's as if the site is doomed to fail. We've never had so much trouble before, and we take the safety of our employees seriously. If we don't do something about it, someone is going to get seriously injured. That's why we're bringing Eric in." He takes my hand from my lap and intertwines our fingers. He sighs as though I'm giving him strength. "Eric is our cousin and used to work with us when we first started with McKenzie Holdings, so he knows what he's doing. He's also on leave. He's a Marine, so he can handle himself just fine."

"I don't think I've ever heard you mention cousins while I've been around your family."

"They haven't been to Lexington in years. Dante and I are the closest."

"Are they a big family like the McKenzies?" I ask, caressing his thumb with mine.

"Yeah. Francesca was my father's older sister, about five years older, if I remember correctly. She died twenty-seven years ago. Tomorrow is the anniversary of her death, as Dante reminded me. Then, Emiliano married Lucia. His quick remarriage caused a huge rift between him and my father, and my father hasn't spoken to him since. He has five children with his first wife—Dante, Eric, Aiden, Mateo, and Kasey. Then, with Lucia, he had twins, Diego and Emelia. I've only really stayed in touch with Dante, who is a priest. We've helped each other out a few times over the years, and I consider him a good friend."

"Wow. Are they as hot as the McKenzies?" I tease, and I get a frown in return. Maybe I should wait until he's more secure in our relationship to tease him like this. I know what I want, but he isn't quite there yet. "Lucien, stop frowning at me. I'm only teasing you."

"That wasn't funny, especially since you're carrying my child."

I offer him a wry smile. "You do realize that I only have eyes for you, right?"

"Hm."

"Lucien, you're really starting to piss me off. For God's sake, I don't just let anyone rip my panties off and fuck me at his parents' house."

"Hell, Sabrina," he growls.

"Don't you 'hell Sabrina' me."

He starts laughing.

I'm not impressed.

He continues to laugh.

"I didn't think that was funny."

He pulls himself together. "Sorry. It wasn't funny. It was fucking hot."

I roll my eyes at him.

"We're going to have to do something about your language before the baby gets here." I smile to soften the blow of my words.

"I'm not that bad."

"No, but one word is bad enough, and you seem to like the f-word."

He grins so widely that I'm tempted to knock it off his face.

"Who doesn't like fucking?"

I ignore him and concentrate on breathing because I'm wound up now.

He releases my fingers and starts massaging my foot.

I have to admit, it feels damn good and is starting to relax me again.

"Can I ask you something?" he asks, sounding unsure.

"You can ask me anything, Lucien. I thought we'd already discussed this."

He gathers his courage and asks, "When my mom asked about buying things for the baby, you said you wanted to get past the four-month mark." I nod, and he continues, "Please tell me what's worrying you about the pregnancy. Why do you want to wait?"

Has he been worried about me? Is he wondering why I'm hesitant to start planning more for the arrival of our child?

"I'm not worried about the baby. Well, no more than any other pregnant woman. To me, it's still early. I don't want to jinx anything by getting a nursery ready. I guess I shouldn't have researched pregnancy online, but I did, and I don't want to be someone who gets everything ready, only to lose the baby. I don't think I could handle that."

"So, other than the doctor wanting to keep a close eye on you because of the episode in the park, there isn't anything to worry about? I'm referring to you as well."

His words have me choked up. One thing I've been told is that my emotions will be all over the place, and I'll probably cry at the drop of a hat while pregnant. So far, that has been fairly accurate.

Shuffling slightly on the sofa, I spread my legs and watch Lucien's eyes darken. I smirk and say, "Don't get any ideas. I want you to come sit up here with your back resting against me."

He hesitates, then kicks off his shoes and scoots up between my legs. I thought it would be more difficult to get him to do this because of his back issues. But I'm certainly not going to complain because, for now, he's exactly where I want him.

His easy compliance might have had something to do with the fact that I asked him to sit between my open thighs.

Sliding my hands over his shoulders, I pull him back. He moves lower, half lying on me with his head resting on my shoulder.

"Are you sure I'm not too heavy?"

"You're just perfect."

His whole body seems to tense at my words. I hope he realizes they're true.

"Relax," I whisper, wrapping my legs around his waist and resting my feet against his thighs.

"How do you expect me to relax with your feet rubbing my cock?"

I laugh and swat his arm. "Behave. I'm trying to get you to relax without sex being involved."

"Honey, when you touch me, it's hard not to think about having you naked under me or your touch on my cock."

If he keeps this up, he's going to get a hormonal pregnant woman who wants more than a massage.

He chuckles as he wiggles around under me.

"Now, I hope you're ready for my talented hands."

He grunts as I place my hands on his shoulders and slide them to the front of his T-shirt. Slipping my hands inside, I feel him twitch, causing me to smile and nibble his ear.

"That good, huh?"

"Hmm."

I rub over his collarbone and move my hands to caress his arms. "You're a beautiful man, Lucien. When you walk into a room, you're the only one I see," I whisper into his ear, feeling his whole body shudder.

He brings tears to my eyes because he can't or won't see himself the way I do. Instead of massaging him, I just want to wrap my arms around him and never let him go. He'd be angry if I acted on my instincts.

Hopefully, if I continually tell him what he means to me, he'll eventually start to believe me. I need that hope.

I slip my hands over his shoulders and start to apply pressure, hoping I won't hurt him. Although he mentions his scars, we've never talked about his pain. I don't know if he still suffers. I have no experience with burn victims, so I'm going into this blind. But I'm good at research.

As I rub the back of his neck with my thumbs, Lucien freezes.

What's changed? I can't reach his back, so he can't be worried about that.

He moves out of my arms, drops his feet to the floor, and rests his head in his hands with his elbows on his knees.

After a few minutes of silence, he turns his head. As he looks at me, regret fills his face. Shaking his head, he gets to his feet, grabs his cell phone and keys, and walks out of the apartment.

I'm speechless, and I feel my heart break.

Lucien

There isn't enough alcohol in Kenza to make me forget what I just did. I can't explain why I left without saying a word.

I enjoyed her touch more than I'll ever be able to admit to her—not that she'd listen anyway. But that won't happen after what I've just done.

She didn't deserve that.

"Congratulations, brother. About damn time you decided to turn your life around."

I grunted at his words.

"You pissed she's pregnant? Mom said she doesn't remember seeing you this happy."

"I'm happy about the baby."

Ruben leans against the bar next to me, his eyes burning a hole in my bowed head, while he plays with his phone.

"Burying your head in Mr. Daniels isn't going to solve anything, brother."

I choose to ignore him.

"I'm not going anywhere." He drops onto a barstool.

"If you didn't want me to see you, you would've chosen a different bar. So quit with the attitude and tell me what you've done."

I lift my head and meet his gaze. "How do you know I've done something?"

He laughs.

"You're a McKenzie. All McKenzie men mess up and come here to drown their sorrows. So I'll ask again. What have you done?"

"I walked out on Sabrina."

He shakes his head. "When are you going to stop hurting her? And yourself?"

"It's complicated."

"No, it isn't. You want her, and she wants you. What's complicated about that?"

"You're an ass. If I recall correctly, not too long ago, you had a crush on Rosie and acted like a jerk. What makes you the expert?"

"Love," he replies, giving me a smug look while still playing with his phone.

"I'm not going there. Let's just say we were on the couch, and her hands started to wander down my back, and I froze." I empty my glass down my throat. "I'm a bastard. I knew it hurt her when I pulled away, and that made me angry. I left without saying anything."

"So she has no idea where you are? You didn't even tell her that you needed space. If that's the case, then you are a bastard."

Well, at least we agree on something.

"Can we talk about something else?"

I hold his gaze as he studies me.

He nods. "Ramon tells me you're having problems on the site."

Relieved that I'm going to have my mind distracted, if only temporarily, I admit that I've brought in reinforcements. "I asked Dante for help. He agreed to ask his brothers, but said it would most likely be Eric, as he has more experience on a building site than the others. Plus, Eric is on leave and driving everyone crazy. Dante said that Eric would jump at the chance to help, since he'd have something to do. He did mention Diego at first, but Diego has started back at the firehouse. Plus, Dante said Diego has become a bit of a hothead." I shake my head, thinking about my brothers and me being hotheads. I'm not sure how our mother coped with us.

"Isn't Diego's twin out of the country? Studying or something?" Ruben asks with a frown.

"Yes, Emelia. They were inseparable when she was

home and kept him tame. Now that she isn't around, though, he seems to be spreading his wings a bit too far. If you know what I mean."

Ruben laughs. "It's been a long time since both families got together. Perhaps that's something we need to think about. Maybe when the next wedding takes place."

"We've been invited to a wedding." He raises an eyebrow in question. "Mateo is getting married, and he invited us all to Montana for the event." According to Dante, Mateo doesn't sound like a man about to get married. So, I'm more curious than anything."

"Are you thinking of going?"

"Yeah, it would be great if everyone else could go too. Especially Mom and Dad."

Ruben takes a drink and looks thoughtful. "I'll talk to Mom," he smiles. "Then she can talk to Dad."

I grin. Dad's a hard nut to crack.

Ruben pauses. "Let's get back on track. When is Eric arriving?"

"Soon. When he gets here, we need to make sure our relationship doesn't get out. He's going in as one of the workers. See if he hears anything. I'm hesitant about him going in alone. These bastards have been screwing with us for a while now."

"He's a Marine. He'll be fine." Ruben pours himself a drink.

"Since when do you drink hard liquor?"

"Since I looked at you."

I pause, then start laughing at him.

There's no way he would've walked past me. He might not have wanted to get involved, but the McKenzies' brother connection is strong. It always has been, and no matter how much we piss each other off, we're loyal to a fault.

"So, Ruben tells me you've screwed up again." Ramon grins as he walks up to the bar.

"For fuck's sake, Ramon," Ruben curses.

Ramon holds his phone out in front of his face and reads, "L's screwed up. Drinking in club. That sounds like you're telling me he's screwed up," Ramon points out to Ruben.

"Okay, children. Give it a rest. Yes, I've messed up with Sabrina. I'm going to keep drinking this," I say, holding up the half-empty bottle of Jack, "until I can't think straight anymore, and then my life won't seem so bad."

"If you think drinking all this will change the fact that you have a woman at home who cares about you and a baby on the way, you're sadly mistaken. You better also start praying that Sabrina doesn't decide to leave. I wouldn't blame her if she did."

Will she really walk away from me?

Yeah, she will. If you push too far.

I knock back the rest of my drink and no longer feel it burn as it slides down my throat. Since I met Sabrina, I've only had a few drinks on occasion, and even though

I know I'll regret it tomorrow, I can't stop. The look on Sabrina's face when I walked out on her will always haunt me.

When will I stop hurting the only woman I care about?

"Well, hello there. Aren't you three handsome?"

A cute blonde woman who isn't bad to look at pulls me out of my alcoholic daze. I look at my brothers and grin. Ramon looks shocked, as if he wants to leave, and Ruben frowns, then hides his smile behind his drink.

I take the initiative and ask, "And you are?"

"Susan," she tells me, moving in closer and running her finger over my chest. Her finger moves slowly down past my abs, stopping at my belt.

Looking at her closely, I see that she's a cute little thing.

But she's not the woman you want!

I shake my head to clear my mind, but I can't seem to stop myself as I remove her hand from the waistband of my jeans.

"Susan," Ruben says, grabbing her attention. "You might want to go say hello over there before they attract others." He points behind her to where two guys are sitting and watching us.

I agree it's best she moves on. I've hurt Sabrina enough without trying to lose myself in someone else. I laugh. I can't believe that thought even popped into my head! As if I'd move on to someone else! There isn't any way I'd be able to get it up for anyone else—not even myself. I've tried.

Ruben slings his arm around my neck, and Ramon removes the glass from my hand. "You, my brother, are going to come upstairs with us before you get yourself into something you can't dig yourself out of."

Yes, I've had too much to drink, but I'm fully aware of what's happening around me. I'll suffer the consequences tomorrow, but it's nothing less than I deserve.

"Can you walk?"

"I'm not drunk."

"Hm. Well, get your ass up, then," Ruben smirks.

I stand and turn to face him, saying, "I'm up," as I sway into him.

"I'll ask again. Can you walk?"

"Probably not in a straight line."

Ignoring my brothers, who are waiting for me to fall, I make my way through the club. I wait for Ruben, who has come up behind me, to punch in the code to his place.

The stairs feel like more than I can handle, but I'm not about to give my brothers the satisfaction of knowing just how badly I'm struggling.

Once I'm finally in Ruben's apartment, I crash on his sofa. Turning my head, I grin at Rosie, who is trying her best not to laugh at me from the chair she's curled up in.

"What's going on?" she asks Ruben.

"He's messed up again."

"Oh."

My eyes drift closed, but open again soon when I feel a cold cloth against my face.

"What happened, Lucien?" Rosie asks, and all I want to do is fall asleep.

"I keep hurting her. I do it deliberately, testing her. She says she isn't going to walk away, but she will."

"Ruben?"

"Leave him, Rosie. He can sleep it off here," I hear Ruben tell his girlfriend. "Ramon, could you text Sabrina and let her know he's spending the night here? We'll just hope she doesn't decide to walk."

"I'll call—"

I sleep.

11

Sabrina

I GOT UP AND DRESSED, REFUSING TO CHECK MY PHONE for the millionth time in case I had missed a message from Lucien. After Ramon called me last night, I managed to get some sleep. Not much.

I'd been worried about him after he left, even though he hurt me by walking out without saying anything. I mean, who does that? He never said what the problem was. What I'd done or said? I practically told him that I loved him. Well, not in so many words, but anyone reading between the lines could tell how I felt about him.

Then he walked out, leaving me with a broken heart, desperate to go after him. I didn't. He left so quickly that, by the time I'd shaken off the shock, he would have already been in his car and away from the building.

I'm not going to give up on him. I promised I wouldn't, and regardless, he's under my skin. I wouldn't be able to walk away, even if I wanted to.

That doesn't mean I have to wait here for him to come back. I'm not sure he'd even give me an explanation.

That's why I accepted Carla's invitation to meet her for breakfast. She wants to review a few details for the charity event at the hospital, and she wants to give me some baby brochures that Lily picked up for me.

Thinking about Lily hurts. She was my best friend, but now I'm not sure what we are. I know things are strained because of her connection to Lucien, and it's my doing. Lily is in love with Michael and doesn't see anyone else the same way, but her relationship with Lucien is hard to explain. There's a closeness between them that seems much deeper than his connection to me. Sometimes I think he's telling me the truth, that there's nothing between them. But then I see them share a secret look, and I'm not so sure anymore.

I obviously want to believe him. It's just difficult.

I hope that, at some point, my friendship with Lily and our closeness while growing up will return because I miss having her to turn to. She always gave me sound advice, and she is sure to know how I can help Lucien...or at least have some ideas. I'm completely out of my element with Lucien and can't seem to do anything right.

Stepping out of the elevator, I walk through the lobby and smile and wave at Roger at the security desk. He does a great job, and Lucien has said that it's one of the reasons he chose to buy the apartment. As I approach the door, he quickly dashes in front of me to open it.

"Have a nice day, Miss Walker."

What a lovely man.

"Thank you, and please call me Sabrina," I say with a smile.

"Oh, I can't. Mr. McKenzie won't like that."

"Hmm." We'll see. "Thank you, Roger."

Starbucks is only a few blocks away, and since the weather is nice, it's a lovely walk. Just because I'm pregnant doesn't mean I can't do anything. I love walking, and on nice days, I can walk for miles — and often do. It's also a good opportunity to try to get rid of the constant stress I'm under.

Something has to give with Lucien. I'm human. I can only take so much before it becomes too much. The doctor told me in his presence that I need to be stress-free. She has no idea what it's like to live with someone who expects you to leave the first chance you get. Sometimes I feel like screaming at Lucien, but most of the time, I just want to hold him. I can't deny how much I need his arms around me. Lucien has lived a very solitary life until I came along. I can understand him needing time to adjust, but he needs much more than that. I'm starting to think that perhaps I'm not strong enough to hold him together. Tears prick my eyes, and I take a deep breath to stop them. I can't keep feeling so sad. But what else can I feel when I watch my hope for a future with him slowly dwindle away?

"Sabrina!"

Hearing my name, I look up, but I still can't figure out where the shout came from.

"Sabrina!"

Then, I spot Carla waving like a madwoman on the opposite side of the road I'm about to cross.

Carla and I became friends right away, and she's like having a nosy sister. She's worse than Lily ever was, and that's saying something.

"Hey," I greet her. "I see Sebastian has let you out without him."

"Only because he went to Ruben's place." She smirks.

Carla slips her arm through mine, and we continue walking down the sidewalk. "You wouldn't know why he was called to Kenza, would you?"

I catch her eyeing me.

"I'll tell you over coffee."

"Good. Because we're here," Carla says with a sigh.

WE TAKE OUR SEATS WITH OUR LATTES IN HAND. CARLA says, "So, spit it out. I'm guessing Lucien is there," she says, leaning in toward me. Her eyes are alight with mischief.

"Yeah."

I sip my drink, trying to buy some time, but she's on to me. Meeting her unwavering gaze, I laugh.

"Everything was going well. We were sitting on the sofa talking, and I had him sit between my legs so I could hold him. I started to rub his arms and shoulders, and everything was going great. I could feel him relaxing into me. But then, I dipped down the back of his T-shirt, and he froze and left without a word."

I had a feeling it had something to do with his injury.

"I just can't get over the fact that he left without saying anything. Not one word was spoken from the moment I slipped up to when he left. I still haven't heard from him this morning either."

I shrugged, trying to make light of it, before taking another drink.

"He really hurt you, didn't he?"

I nod and whisper, "Yes."

"What are you going to do?"

"I don't know. When he does this, He shuts off. It feels like he doesn't care about me or the baby."

Angrily swiping at a tear, I look out the window, but I can't see anything but our reflection.

Carla moved to the chair next to me and wrapped her

arm around my shoulders. "I know everyone keeps saying to give him time, but that's really what he needs. He wouldn't have drunk so much last night—which caused his brother to intervene—if you didn't mean so much to him. When he gets like this, you need to call him out. Don't ignore what he's done. Make him listen to how he made you feel. Eventually, he'll stop hurting you because he'll finally realize that you're there to stay and that nothing he does or says will make you walk away from him."

I blow out a breath of air.

"I'm not sure I'm built to take hit after hit from the man I love." I look at Carla. "Because I do love him."

"I know you do. It wouldn't feel like your heart was breaking every time he left if it weren't true."

"I just wish he would show me his back to get it over with, you know? His biggest fear is that once I see his back, I'll leave. So I need to get him to show me. When I'm still there, he won't be able to use that as an excuse anymore."

"I'm sorry, Sabrina. I wish there was more I could do to help you."

I pat her hand. "Just being here is enough. Thank you."

Carla goes back to her seat and pulls the folder with the charity event information out of her purse.

"Are you okay looking at this now?"

"Yes, I'm fine, and it'll help take my mind off Lucien."

As I watch her find the page in the folder where she has written notes about what to go over today, I start to feel weird. It's as though there's something wrong between my legs. I'm not in any discomfort, but I feel panic setting in.

I push away from the table. When Carla gives me a quizzical stare, I tell her, "Restroom."

She smiles as I head toward the restroom.

Once inside, I quickly pull everything down and sit on the toilet. When I look down, I see that my panties are covered with blood.

My heart starts to pound.

More blood is coming out of me. It's running out of me. Like water.

"Oh God, no."

I don't know what to do. All I can hear is my heart pounding while I panic.

I realize I have my cell phone in my hand and quickly dial Lucien. No matter what he's dealing with, I need him right now. His phone rings and rings until he answers. No one speaks.

"Lucien?"

"I'm sorry, Sabrina. I can't talk right now."

He hangs up on me.

How could he hang up on me?

I dial Carla instead.

The minute she answers, I tell her that something is

wrong, and she comes running and shoves feminine products at me.

"Here," she says. Use some, and try to get up. We need to get you to a hospital."

I do as she says, not believing anything will work. There's too much blood.

I manage to get out of the stall and meet Carla's eyes, feeling myself go lightheaded.

Lucien

"Why did you refuse to talk to her now?" Sebastian looks angry.

"I need to be with her when we talk," I reply, burying my head in my hands.

Hearing Sabrina's voice alone made my heart beat faster. Maybe I should have said more. At least I could have asked her if she was okay. I could have told her that I would be home soon and that we could talk then. I had a lot of explaining to do. Instead, I was curt and hung up on her.

"Fuck!"

Ruben stood over me, glaring, until Rosie pushed him out of the way.

"You need to call her back right now. Providing she

answers, tell her you missed her and that you'll be home soon."

I did miss her. I missed sleeping with her in my arms. I missed her body heat and the beat of her heart, where I'd rest my hand, making my sleep peaceful and keeping the nightmares away.

Instead of nightmares, it was my pounding head that woke me. After drinking lots of water, taking painkillers, and eating a breakfast roll, I feel almost human. I need to get myself together to talk to Sabrina.

What I'm going to say to her is anyone's guess. I royally fucked up, and it kills me knowing that I really hurt her. I had intended to leave as quickly as possible before she made me turn my back on her. I wasn't ready for her to walk away from me. Instead, I was a bastard and walked away.

"What the fuck?" Sebastian shouts, bringing me abruptly back to the present. "Are you okay?" He listens, but his eyes stay focused on me.

"We need to go," he says. "That was Carla. She's with Sabrina." He pauses, looking around as though he doesn't want to say what he has to say.

My heart thuds in my chest. Something is wrong.

"Sabrina?" I whisper.

He nods.

Ruben wraps Rosie in his arms as we all stare at Sebastian. His face is pale, his lips are a thin line, and he's not wearing his usual smirk. I don't ever remember him being so serious. He's scaring the shit out of me.

I can't find the words to ask what's wrong, but luckily, he tells me, "They were catching up at Starbucks when Sabrina collapsed. Apparently, she was bleeding heavily," he says, wincing. "Carla called the paramedics, and they were just loading her into the ambulance when she called me."

"She's awake now, right?"

He shakes his head. "They couldn't rouse her."

I'm frozen to the sofa, feeling my eyes well with tears. This can't be happening. I might deserve bad things, but not Sabrina.

"Come on, grab your cell phone and wallet. We'll meet the ambulance at the hospital," Ruben tells me. "I'll drive."

WHEN WE ARRIVE AT THE HOSPITAL, SEBASTIAN SPOTS Carla. As if she has a sixth sense, she turns her head in our direction. Before any of us can catch our breath, she's in my brother's arms, crying.

"I'll go find someone to tell us what's going on," Ruben says.

"There's no need." Carla pulls away from Sebastian, but he keeps his hands on her shoulders. "Lucien, the doctor is in with her now. I told him you were on your way, and he said he'll come find us when he knows more."

I drop into the nearest chair and bury my hands in my hair. "She called me," I choke out when I feel Carla sit next to me. "I told her I couldn't talk and hung up on her. I'm guessing she needed help, and I ignored her."

She places her hand on my shoulder and rubs it. Offering comfort.

"I loved hearing her voice, but I didn't want to talk on the phone. I wanted to be with her when I tried to explain my messed up mind. I wanted to hold her hand. I've really screwed up."

"Lucien, the only advice I can offer you is to be honest with her. Don't let what happened in the past dictate your future. She'll always be by your side if you let her. You just have to stop pushing her away."

I turned my head and looked at her. "Thanks, Carla."

Suddenly, she stands and looks toward the doors where Sabrina has been taken. I follow her gaze and see the doctor walking toward us.

"You're Sabrina's fiancé?"

I nod. "Yes."

"The baby seems to be hanging on. You have a strong one in there, but we have to monitor the baby to be sure."

"Sabrina?" I ask. I need to know she's okay before I think about our child.

"Sabrina has come around and is resting."

"Do you know what's wrong? What caused the bleeding?" Carla asks.

"You'd be surprised at how common this is among pregnant women. Sabrina has had a more severe case than most, which is why I'm suggesting bed rest for the next few weeks. She isn't going to be happy about it, but if she wants to reduce the risk of miscarriage, then it's what she has to do. There are no guarantees, but the rest will reduce the likelihood of miscarriage."

"I'll continue to work from home so I can be there for her. I'm sure one of her friends or my mom can be there when I have to go out of town for work. She'll stay in bed and in the apartment, even if I have to remove all her clothes from the place."

Ruben snickers and gets an elbow in the stomach for his trouble from Rosie. "Get your mind out of the gutter."

"I'm just imagining you waking up and finding all your clothes gone," he says, wiggling his eyebrows.

"You're an idiot, but I love you anyway," she replies.

I shake my head at them and their attempt to lighten the mood before turning my head back toward the doctor.

"I need to see her."

"Okay."

I get to my feet and follow him, knowing my brothers and their girls will stay and wait for me. They'll want to know how my girl is doing. "Shit." I pause and turn back to them. "Can someone get ahold of Sabrina's mother?"

Ruben nods. "We will."

I continue on, and the doctor stops outside what I assume is Sabrina's room. Before I go in, I ask, "Are you sure they're both all right?"

He puts his hand on my arm. "Sabrina will be fine with rest. Hopefully, so will your child."

"Thank you." I shake his hand.

"I'll give you ten minutes." He walks away.

I'm nervous and apprehensive about seeing Sabrina. I also have a lot to make up for.

With a heavy sigh, I push through the door, and my heart drops to my feet. Sabrina is curled up on her side, looking broken. Her whole body is shaking. I quickly start walking toward her.

I reach out and place my hand on her arm, but she jumps away from my touch.

"Sabrina, please. Let me hold you."

She shakes her head. "You don't want me."

What have I done?

"Sabrina, I'm sorry. I'm more sorry than I'll ever be able to tell you. I loved hearing your voice this morning, and I really wanted to talk to you, but I wanted to see you in person. I needed to talk to you face-to-face, not over the phone." I drop my hands to my sides. "God, I had no idea you needed me, and I hung up on you."

"I've lost our baby, so you don't need to bother with me anymore," she cries, holding her stomach.

"What the fuck!"

I don't give her a chance to speak or refuse me this time. Kicking off my shoes, I climb onto the bed with her, pull her into my arms, and say, "You have Not. Lost. The. Baby. Are you listening to me, Sabrina? Sabrina?"

Her body slowly stops shaking as she pulls her head away from my chest. I continue, "You're still pregnant. You're going to need to rest a lot, but our child is still growing inside you."

"I thought—"

"I know, babe. I can't believe they didn't tell you."

"They haven't told me anything."

I kissed her forehead. "For the record, in the interest of full disclosure, when I arrived here, the only people I wanted to know about were you and the baby. Don't think for a minute that I don't want you because I do. No matter how much of a jerk I've been, you're always on my mind." I pull her back to me and sigh with relief when she snuggles against my chest.

"You hurt me," she mumbles against me. "You walked away from me after promising you wouldn't. I know I shouldn't accept your apology so easily, but I can't bring myself to not accept it. I need you, Lucien."

Her words terrify me. The truth I don't want to admit is that I need her, too.

12

Sabrina

IT'S BEEN FOUR WEEKS SINCE THE FRIGHT OF MY LIFE. Spending all this time in bed or on the sofa has been driving me crazy. I'm not one to sit back and do nothing, so being inactive is hell. I know it's for the good of the baby, but no matter how hard I try to stay positive, I feel myself sinking deeper into depression.

Lucien has been amazing. Apart from three days a week, he spends all his time here. He either works at the dining table or makes sure I'm comfortable and have everything I need. He must be exhausted. He never lets it show, though.

The trip to the hospital scared us both. I don't think either of us has gotten over it yet. I've tried mentioning it to Lucien a few times since I was released, but he

175

doesn't want to talk about it. He only wants to look forward to the end of the pregnancy, when the baby and I are healthy. It's fine to look forward, but it isn't if the past hasn't been dealt with. It's not a good idea because it doesn't bode well for the future. Despite everything, Lucien doesn't want to see it that way. He prefers to just move forward through the pregnancy day by day. But I'm sure he's only existing, not living. He won't admit that.

Knowing that I'm getting fed up with all this resting, Lucien has arranged for my mother to come over today. Although our visit with her didn't go well, she came around a bit after Ruben called and told her I was in the hospital. It will be a nice break, even though I'm always at odds with my mother. The only other activity I've been allowed is frequent checkups with my doctor to ensure the baby and I are healthy.

I smile as I caress my more pronounced baby bump and think about my baby. I'm not nervous about being pregnant. Although I'm excited, I just can't work up any enthusiasm for preparing for the baby. The doctor has assured me that the baby is fine, but it isn't just about the baby or the nursery. I feel sorry for Lucien because he's hinted a few times that he'd like to look at nursery furniture with me. I'm not interested yet and can't seem to get there. I think I have a mental block about it ever since Lily mentioned that we needed to start looking last week when she was here.

Our relationship is still strained, and yes, I know it's all my fault. I can't get past the thought that Lucien is in love with Lily. He smiles at her and touches her in an affectionate way that he never has with me. I can't watch them anymore because it hurts. Whenever she visits, she doesn't stay long, and I think she senses the tension. After she leaves, Lucien usually returns to the bedroom, stares at me, and then closes the door.

Now, with his presence in the doorway, I'm not sure how I'm supposed to act. It feels like I'm living with a total stranger. I don't feel wanted here.

"Sabrina, I know you're awake."

Sighing, I mumble, "I am."

His sigh is filled with frustration, as though he's had enough of me—which he probably has.

"Your mother will be here soon. Are you going to shower and get dressed?"

It's been a few days since I last showered. I know I'm letting myself go. I just can't bring myself to do anything about it.

Ugh! I'll never hear the end of it if she sees me looking like a mess.

I'm not sure I'm up for a lecture.

"I guess."

I'm startled when I feel the bed dip behind me. I thought he was still in the doorway. Slowly, he moves closer and pulls me into his arms, settling me into the curve of his body.

He always makes me feel secure, and right now, he's making me want to cry. This is the closest we've been in weeks. We haven't made love or had sex since before he left after the impromptu massage. I really miss his closeness, and I think part of my listlessness has to do with that. Now that I'm in his arms, I wish he would never let me go. I wish all the hard stuff between us didn't exist. I wish we could move forward together toward a bright future. The sad thing is that I know that won't be our reality. At least not until Lucien deals with his past.

"I want to take you out to dinner," he whispers, surprising me. "The doctor said you're good to go back to how things were before the scare. Just add more rest to your daily routine."

I understand what he's saying, and he's invited me out to dinner in his own way. Even though I don't feel like putting any effort into doing anything, I agree. "Okay, I'll probably feel better once I've showered and changed. So dinner it is."

Before I can move, Lucien has me in his arms, off the bed, and in the bathroom. He turns on the shower and turns back to me, his expression unreadable. "Will you be all right in here?" he asks, reaching up to caress my face.

I burrow into his hand, wishing his touch would last but knowing it's only temporary.

Cupping my face in his hands, he stands so close to

me that he kisses each of my eyelids, my cheekbones, and the tip of my nose. "I miss you."

His three little words start my tears. I can't stop. They fall quicker than he can wipe them away with his thumbs.

"I miss you, too," I cry as he pulls me into his arms, burying his face in my neck and holding me tightly.

My tears are a buildup of weeks of bed rest—weeks without being close to the man holding me now—and worry that he would walk away from me if I lost our child.

At the hospital, he told me that he was worried about me first and then the baby, but I have a hard time accepting that. He's an amazing guy, and I don't think he'd ever lie to me. Knowing how difficult it is for him to have me as a daily fixture in his life makes it easy for me to imagine him walking away from me if something should happen to our child.

"C'mon."

Lucien releases me slightly, starts to remove my clothes, and then his own, leaving his long-sleeved T-shirt on. Taking my hand, he pulls me into the shower with him.

I long for the day when there will be no clothing between us.

As soon as the water hits me, I sigh with pleasure. It feels good on my face, so I tip my head back and let it run down my body. Lucien stands in front of me, placing his hands on my hips. He kisses my shoulder, sending goosebumps down my spine.

I feel better already.

He removes his hands, but they're soon back, covered in shower gel. He starts washing my body. His hands tremble as they slide from my neck along my collarbone. He misses my breasts and moves on to my stomach, buttocks, and legs.

Kneeling down, he thoroughly cleans my calves before caressing my thighs. The closer he gets to my pussy, the more my legs quiver.

His eyes stay focused on mine as he watches and enjoys my response to his touch. My eyes start to drift down his body toward his erect penis when he slips a finger inside me.

I rest my hands against the shower wall to keep my balance as I throw my head back and moan. He has magic hands.

"You're so wet, baby," he whispers seconds before I feel his mouth.

My legs are about to buckle when he grips my hips and pushes me gently against the shower wall. He places one of my legs over his shoulder and dives in.

Now, he has two fingers pumping in and out of me while his tongue teases my clit, then sucks it into his mouth.

My orgasm is fast approaching, and there's nothing I

can do to slow it down. Instead of fighting it, I go with the flow.

Reaching up, I cup my breasts and start to rub my nipples.

Lucien pauses.

I watch him from beneath my hooded eyes.

"Fuck, Sabrina," he growls.

I don't stop. "Please," I beg.

"You're killing me."

His fingers thrust in and out of me as his mouth sucks my clit into its warm embrace. With his other hand, he starts stroking himself. I'm mesmerized. I can't look away. Then, I...

"Ahhh... Oh God, Lucien."

My stomach tightens as my orgasm rushes over me, draining the last of my strength from my weak limbs. Lucien slowly brings me back down to earth with his fingers, placing kisses all over my pussy. The largest kiss lands on my stomach.

He helps me slide down the wall. Spreading my legs, he kneels between them and kisses my lips so tenderly that I feel tears threatening. Resting his forehead against mine, he tells me, "You taste amazing," still breathing heavily. His hands slowly move along my thighs.

Pulling back, he grabs the shower gel and washes between my legs, grinning.

My eyes caress him, creating a desperation in me to taste him. I see his well-defined muscles, his nipples protruding through his wet T-shirt, and his strong thighs rippling under my gaze. But what's twitching between his legs has my full attention now. He's hard as a rock and standing proud.

Unable to move my eyes from his cock, I see his hands clench into fists against his thighs out of the corner of my eye.

I smile and shuffle onto my knees. I push his legs open wider and trail a finger down his jerking shaft, watching pre-cum leak from the head.

Meeting his gaze quickly and holding it, I lower my head until I'm hovering above his shaft. It jerks in antic-ipation, and my tongue darts out to trace his slit, collecting the sweet taste of his arousal.

He hisses between his teeth.

"You don't have to do this," he grinds out.

I don't reply with words. Instead, I wrap my fingers around the base of his shaft and gently caress the puck-ered skin there. I have no idea if he has any sensation where the scarring is, and now isn't the time to ask.

He's growing thicker, so maybe he does have feeling there. I'm going to try to find out.

Licking down his shaft, I lick his balls and feel his shaft lengthen and thicken, dripping with more pre-cum. I make eye contact with Lucien again. I trace over some of his scars with my tongue and carefully gauge his reaction. At first, he looks unsure, but then I hit what must be a particularly sensitive spot. I smile as his eyes practically roll back in his head.

I continue licking back and forth and start stroking him. I feel his hands slide into my hair, tightening the more he throbs in my hand.

My hands caress his balls as I work my way back to his leaking tip with my tongue, then suck him into my mouth.

He gasps and comes in my mouth over and over again.

"Fuck... Sabrina... Stop," he groans.

I suck him one last time and hear him curse.

He slumps back onto his butt and leans against the wall opposite me. He grabs my hands and pulls me onto his lap. His arms wrap around me, filling my heart with hope.

"How are you feeling?" he eventually asks, his breathing still not back to normal.

"Much better." I smile against his chest.

"Really?" He sounds unsure.

I lift my head and try to read him through his eyes. For once, I can. He really is unsure about me. Nervous, maybe?

"Lucien, I've missed you. I've missed being close to you and having your arms around me. I felt like we were drifting further apart, and I didn't know how to bring us back together. Right now, I feel close to you. I don't think I could cope if that was taken away from me again."

He gulps before leaning forward and kissing me on the lips.

"I know it's all my fault."

I try to interrupt, but he covers my mouth with his fingertips.

"It is my fault for giving you mixed signals and walking out on you after promising to talk through my uncertainty. This," he says, pointing between us, "is terrifying."

"I need you, Lucien. At first, I thought that I could do this alone, but I can't. I don't want to."

"I'm here now."

I can't help but wonder how long that will last.

"Can I ask you something without you shutting down?"

He kisses the top of my head.

"Ask me, babe."

"When I had my tongue on you, around the base of your cock, could you feel me?"

Well, I'm certainly feeling him now as he starts to grow between us.

"I felt you." He sits me further away from him on his thighs, slightly spreading his legs.

He smirks, takes my hand, and places my fingers against the puckered skin. "I can't feel anything here," he says, moving my hand. "But I can here."

This is the spot that made his eyes roll back. I gently press down, watching his eyes narrow and his shaft jerk between us, tapping against my wrist.

I smile and meet his gaze.

Lucien removes my hand and brings my fingers to his mouth, kissing them. "As much as I'd love to have you riding me," he smirks, "your mother will be here any minute."

"I'd forgotten," I groan.

His smirk is filled with mischief. "We'll carry on tonight after dinner."

We scramble to our feet, quickly wash, and exit the shower.

Lucien

After my shower with Sabrina, I felt like my heart was lighter than it had been in weeks. She mentioned that she felt like we were drifting further apart, and she was right. We have been. I've struggled with how to act around her. I'm always watching what I say or do so I don't upset her, yet somehow I still manage to.

I was angry when she didn't give Lily the time of day. Not only because Lily is my closest friend, but also because Sabrina really needs a friend and keeps pushing away her oldest friend, Lily. Since then, I've had a hard time getting through to her, and she seems to be sinking into depression.

But now, I'm hopeful that she's coming out of it. The doctor gave her the all-clear, although she still has to rest for long periods of the day. I'm also hopeful that we're back on track after showering together.

Maybe she just needed attention from me. Maybe she just needed proof that she isn't alone and that I care.

My lips slip into a smile as I remember her wet, naked body writhing on my mouth while she caressed her breasts. Watching her pleasure herself made me hard as fuck, just like I am now as she walks into the closet behind me.

"You look nice. Are you going into the office?"

"Hmmm," I mumble, keeping my back to her.

"Lucien?" She comes up behind me, stands to my side, and looks up into my face. "What's wrong?"

I sigh and take her hand, placing it on my erection. I have the pleasure of hearing her gasp as I flex against her hand.

"That's what the image of you in the shower has done to me."

"Wow."

She smirks and slowly licks her lips.

My eyes narrow.

Her hand presses against my cock and rubs back and forth, sending my arousal up a notch. But it's her thumb pressing down on the head of my dick that makes me take her face in my hands and kiss her passionately.

I press her up against the closet mirror and feel her legs wrap around my hips as I continue to devour her. Our tongues swirl together, sucking and teasing, sliding and mating. I slow the kiss down, using my hips to keep her in place, creating a small amount of space between us so I can caress the small bump of her stomach.

I rest my hand on her growing belly and place my forehead against hers, looking into her eyes. "Thank you," I say, giving her a light kiss on her waiting lips. I hope she realizes that I'm giving her my heart without having to find the words to tell her, and that admitting how much it terrifies me to say the words out loud is enough.

She smiles and wraps her arms around my neck, and I wrap mine fully around her waist. I move back slightly and let her legs fall to the floor, even though I don't want to let her go.

"I'm yours," she whispers.

Realizing that time is running out, I slide my hand down over her bottom through her stretchy yoga pants, wanting to keep her with me. "I don't want to leave," I admit.

Keeping her hands around my neck, she meets my gaze, goes up on tiptoes, and kisses me. "You have to. You've given up so much time to be with me, and we need to get back to normal." She straightens my tie over my chest and stomach.

"I've never regretted a moment of my time at home with you. I know you've found it difficult to be on bed rest, but you're on the other side of it now. Providing you follow the doctor's orders, you won't go back to that." I kiss her on the forehead, pull away, and slip my arms into my suit jacket.

"I know." But she doesn't sound sure.

"Are you sure you'll be okay today? Your mom is running late, but—"

"I'll be fine. I feel ten times better after being in your arms. You've given me the strength I need to get through the rest of the day. I promise I'll rest."

"Good." I can't hide my grin as it spreads across my face at her words.

She rolls her eyes and steps in front of me.

My hands go to her shoulders.

"You always look handsome," she says, flattening the lapels of my jacket. "But there's something about you being in a suit that has me wet and aching for you to take me."

My whole body tightens with desire. Does she have any idea what she does to me? Then I see the slight smile at the corner of her mouth. She knows!

I inhale, trying to loosen up, but that only draws her scent deeper into my lungs. I close my eyes instead and picture her naked in the shower. There's no escaping her.

When I open my eyes, she's grinning up at me, and then she rubs against my erection. Slacks aren't the best at hiding a man's arousal.

"You'd like that? For me to take you?" I need to know that she isn't just teasing me. "Would you let me tie you up and lick every inch of your body? Would you let me get my fill of your sweet pussy before sliding my thick cock inside you?"

Kissing my jaw, she whispers, "Yes."

My breath catches in my throat.

"Knowing you'd be tying me up for pleasure, not to keep me from touching you, will heighten the pleasure for both of us. I trust you, Lucien. So tell me, do you own a gray tie?"

After gauging whether she's serious for a moment, I throw open a top cupboard, revealing my ties.

Her eyes widen when she sees them. Most of them are different shades of gray.

"Jeez, that's a lot of gray ties."

She eyes me while smoothing them with her fingers. "Are you sure you're not a closet Christian Grey?"

I frown. "Christian who?"

"Never mind."

"Um, I don't think so."

I slip my arms around her waist and snuggle into

her. I bite down on the curve of her neck, and she shudders in my arms. "Who is Christian Grey?"

"Seriously?"

I growl. "Sabrina?"

"Lucien?"

Then, the bell chimes, announcing a visitor, and her grin widens.

"My mother's here."

She wiggles out of my arms and is out of the closet before I can collect myself. Saved by the bell!

"This conversation isn't over," I shout, laughing as I hear her open the door to let her mother in.

I glance at the ties again and exchange the dark blue one I'm wearing for a dark gray one.

See if she notices.

After straightening my tie and jacket, I close the cupboard, exit the walk-in closet, and adjust my slacks. Now that I'm more presentable, I walk out of the bedroom to greet the future mother-in-law. Well, only if Sabrina ever agrees to the whole wife thing. It's the right thing to do. Which reminds me—after all this time, she needs a ring on that finger. Neither of us has mentioned that she agreed to be engaged to me. It's something that needs to be rectified, and hopefully it will make her more secure in our relationship. It just makes me nervous. The thought of her wearing my ring gives her the power to hurt me.

She already has that power.

I put on a smile and walk over to her mother. "Dorothy, It's nice to see you visiting Sabrina."

As soon as I finish speaking, Sabrina pinches my butt as she walks past. "Lucien, don't you have a meeting or something, dear?" She looks at me pointedly as she turns and sits beside her mom.

After taking a sip of her decaf coffee, she notices my tie. Her eyes widen in surprise, and she hides her smile behind her cup.

Hmm. I need to do some research.

Looking at her now, I'm tempted to tell her that I canceled and will be staying home.

Grinning, I counter, "Now, where would the pleasure be in that, babe?"

After a lingering kiss, I leave her in peace, feeling her eyes on me.

She knows how to reach me if she needs me. Hopefully, her mom will keep her entertained for a while without causing stress.

13

Sabrina

I FOLLOW LUCIEN WITH MY EYES AS HE LEAVES, AND I'LL admit they stray south a few times. He looks mighty fine in that suit, the slacks clinging to his perfect rear end and muscular thighs. He knows he makes my mouth water.

Sighing, I remember that my mom is in the room with me. When I turn back to her, I see her ogling my guy, and a grin spreads across my face.

"He's, um, nice," she says, flustered.

I chuckle. "He's more than nice."

I'm tempted to say more to embarrass her but think better of it. Since I was released from the hospital, we've talked more than we have in years. It's sad but also a relief because I really want my baby to know her. We've always had our differences, but now that my father is gone, I need her in my life more than ever. She's the only family I have. No matter how she acts, I just can't bring myself to walk away from her.

I'm happy that she's trying, or at least appears to be. No doubt we won't see eye-to-eye about something at some point, but for now, I hope we can develop a closer relationship.

"So, how are you really doing, Sabrina? I don't want the same response you give me over the phone."

She gives me a stern look.

I've been telling her I'm fine, but I haven't actually been. No matter how many times she asked, I always replied the same way, trying to convince her that I was really okay. She obviously has the motherly intuition to know when I'm lying.

Wrapping my hands around my mug and curling my feet under me, I decide to really talk to her for the first time in my life. "The baby is fine and has been doing well. Lucien had the doctor come, and the doctor brought a nurse and a portable ultrasound device. As long as I rest during the day, she doesn't see any reason why I won't carry to term."

"Well, that's good news. I'm really looking forward to having a granddaughter to spoil." She smiles, and I can tell she means it, which, if I'm honest, makes my heart feel lighter.

However, she has to accept that it could be a boy. "It

could be a boy," I mention out loud. I know she has always loved dresses, lace, and frills, but that's just not me. Never has been, never will be.

"Well, what do you want?"

I roll my eyes. "I'm not bothered by what I have, as long as he or she is perfectly healthy." But if you ask Lucien, he'll agree with you. If I were given the choice, I'd choose a boy who looks like his dad."

I met her gaze over my mug and paused. "What? Why that look?"

"You're in love with him."

It was a statement, so it didn't need an answer.

"Well?"

Maybe I should say something. "Yes, I love him. He's been hurt badly in the past, so he doesn't trust easily." I cringe at my poor choice of words.

"Anyone who has seen the way he looks at you knows how he feels about you."

What is she talking about?

Frowning, I ask, "Why? How does he look at me?"

"Sabrina, open your eyes. That man loves you, and I won't accept any denials."

"Um."

She smiles. "Well, it looks like I've left you speechless for a change."

"I'd say," I mumble.

"Whatever is going on between the two of you seems

to be working. I'm in my sixties, but I recognize the blush running along your cheekbones."

I throw my head back and laugh. For once, my tears are tears of laughter.

Some mothers might say things like that all the time, but mine—well, let's just say she's prim and proper. So that was a surprise.

"Were you about to tell me how you're really doing?"

She doesn't let up.

"Truthfully, I've been feeling useless and in the way." She arches a brow at me. "Lucien hasn't made me feel that way. It's just difficult to explain. One minute, I'm happy that our baby is growing inside me. The next, I feel like I'm trapping Lucien. Like I'm forcing him to be with me when he'd rather be alone. He's told me that he wants me to live with him, and that he'll always be there for me and our child. It's just difficult, you know? I love him. I love him so much. If he had asked me to be with him without the pregnancy being a factor, things would be so different, and I'd know exactly where I stand. Most of the time, I feel as though I'm walking on eggshells.

After my confession, we fall into a comfortable silence, which is surprising. I think about what I've just admitted.

I think every girl in my situation wants to know that the guy she's with wants her for herself and not just because of the child she's carrying. Lucien is different.

There's always been an electric connection between us since the moment we met.

Part of my problem is my insecurity about Lily and Lucien's feelings for her. I hear what everyone has said. It's just hard to accept whenever I see them together. It always hurts. The only way to stop the pain and get used to the idea of another woman in his life is to talk to him about it. I need to make him see that it bothers me. I'm sure he's figured it out by now, given how reserved I've been around Lily. I've avoided her for months, making any excuse I could think of. Putting off addressing my concerns isn't going to change anything or give me the answers I need.

Lucien is always defensive of Lily, and I guess it pisses me off.

Hell! Having these thoughts isn't making for a light and cheerful day.

I started the day in bed, not wanting to do anything or talk to anyone. But I ended up with Lucien's arms wrapped around me for the first time in weeks. He surprised me even more by showering with me—and what a shower that turned out to be!

"You know," Mom says, bursting through my thoughts. "You need to go out more. You haven't over the past four weeks because you were on bed rest, but now there isn't any excuse. Go to the museum, the mountains, or out to dinner. Just spend more time together doing what people who are dating do."

I shake my head.

"Well, then, what are you waiting for?"

"Lucien asked me out to dinner tonight. I guess that's a start. I'll ask him about going out over the weekend. He's been working constantly here, except for the days he goes into the office for meetings and to catch up. I really feel bad that he's spent so much time working from home."

"I'm sure he was more concerned about your health and that of his child than he was about work. He has four brothers who help run the family business, so I'm sure they've managed fine with him being here.

"They all have different responsibilities, but that's actually what he said."

She grins at that. "I can see I'm going to enjoy being his mother-in-law."

Shit. How do I tell her that I haven't agreed to marry him yet?

Not only that, but we haven't even discussed being engaged.

"Um, Mom. We still haven't made any plans to get married." I cringe, knowing this isn't going to go well. The last time the topic came up was a disaster.

"What?"

"I've been sick, and we haven't discussed it," I say, trying to buy us some time.

She narrows her eyes. "Why do I get the feeling you aren't telling me everything?"

"Mom, you need to trust us to do the right thing. Please."

"For now. But don't keep me waiting long. I've dreamed about you walking down the aisle looking like a princess." She has a dreamy look on her face. "On the days when you weren't being awkward, you'd dress up in one of your Disney princess dresses and pretend to marry one of your dolls or have a tea party with the Mad Hatter. It was cute. Too bad it didn't last."

"Mom," I say warningly.

"I know, I know. You were cute like that."

"If you say so."

All of a sudden, a serious look comes over her face as she looks at me.

"I'm sorry," she begins, "for not being a better mother. I should have listened to your father more about what you wanted and needed to be happy. I shouldn't have tried to push my upbringing on you." She swipes at a loose tear. "I'm just happy that you're giving me another chance. When you came to visit me and Lucien said what he said, it woke me up to the fact that I was about to lose you. I never want that."

I feel tears on my face as I get up from my chair. I go over to her, lean against the chair arm, and wrap my arm around her.

"I'm glad we have this second chance together. We're going to make it, and you're going to be a wonderful grandmother. So let's move forward, okay?"

She nods her head.

"You know, we need to watch a chick flick," I say, trying to lighten the mood. As soon as the words leave my mouth, I realize it's exactly what we need. It's also something we've never done before.

"A chick flick?"

"Mom, you need to get with the times. A chick flick is a girly movie. Hot guys, usually no violence." I grin. "We'll watch Pretty Woman."

"All right. I'm game."

Today has certainly turned out differently than I expected.

I wonder how tonight's dinner will turn out.

Lucien

It was frustrating to be in a meeting all morning because all I wanted to do was look up this Christian Grey that Sabrina seems to know a lot about. She's been reading a lot, especially over the past four weeks, so I assume he's a character from one of her books. And holy fuck, was I right! Needless to say, I spent most of the afternoon flipping through Fifty Shades of Grey and discovered that Mr. Grey has a fetish for gray ties.

I've been so hard ever since that, at one point, I was tempted to jerk off in the restroom.

I just hope my girl is serious about being taken and tied up because my body is humming with sexual tension.

It was so bad that, when I parked in my spot in the underground parking lot, I nearly bit the security guard's head off when he stopped me. He stammered and forgot what he wanted to say, so at least I got on my way.

Looking in the elevator mirror, I grinned as I straightened the gray tie. Maybe I won't tell Sabrina that I know who Christian Grey is. I'll see how long I can keep it up before admitting that I didn't get any work done because I was too intrigued by the stories to pass them up.

Finally, the doors open onto my floor. I quickly made my way to the door, punched in the ten-digit security code, and pushed the door open.

The blinds are closed throughout, but the lamps are on, giving the place a warm glow.

I put my satchel of documents on the table at the end of the hall and hope Sabrina is home. I can't imagine her doing all this and then leaving. With how much I want her, I hope she wouldn't do that.

"Nice day at the office, dear?" she drawls.

Her words startle me.

But I am speechless when I turn and see her sitting at

the dining table with her legs crossed at the ankles and resting on top of it. She's wearing nothing but stilettos, a tie, and a smile.

I chuckle and slowly walk toward her.

She's killing me.

I come to a stop at the side of the table and stroke her ankle, really looking at her. Starting at her red, lethal shoes, my gaze travels up her long legs and narrow hips until it hovers around her pussy. I lick my lips.

"Are you hungry?" she asks huskily.

My eyes shoot up to her desire-filled ones.

"You have no idea."

I travel back to her pussy and drink in the sight before moving up to the swell of her stomach, where our baby is nestled.

The gray tie is loose around her neck but drops between her breasts and curves under one of her swollen breasts, which I caress with my eyes. They've grown during her pregnancy, usually overflowing her underwear, which is why she's been wearing sports bras. I really need to take her shopping for more clothes.

The plumpness of her breasts makes me want to dip my head and nuzzle between them, tasting her rosy-colored nipples with my tongue.

She's a fucking wet dream in the flesh.

She untangles her feet and plants them on the floor,

spreading her legs and giving me a view that makes me throb behind my zipper.

"You look good in a gray tie."

I try not to grin, but I feel my lips twitch at her comment.

"Is that a fact?"

I move between her spread thighs, gazing into her eyes as she raises her head.

"I'm thinking I prefer you in a gray tie. You're so damn sexy."

"Hmm."

She grips my thighs and slides her hands up to my hips.

My cock pulses.

As she nuzzles against me, I inhale and clamp down on my jaw, trying to hold off my orgasm.

"I've missed you today. This pregnancy has made me twice as horny as I was before."

Her fingers trail up my shaft. Then, I feel the zipper go down before she wraps her hand around me. I grind my teeth, desperate for release.

"I'm so turned on that my pussy is already wet for you to sink inside."

Fuck!

She hums against the head of my cock.

Before she can take me fully into her mouth, I slide my hands into her hair, gently tugging her head back and allowing my cock to slip away from her lips.

"You are gorgeous."

Releasing her, our eyes stay connected.

My breathing increases. I stay in place and remove my jacket, letting it drop to the floor. But who cares? I kick off my shoes, followed by my socks.

I unfasten my tie and watch her eyes narrow as I drop it on the table. I pull off my shirt and let it follow my jacket, but I keep the long-sleeved T-shirt on.

I pick up the tie and let it slide through my fingers. "What should I use this for, I wonder?" I tease her, watching as her eyes turn hot with desire.

"Do you trust me, Sabrina?"

After a few minutes, she replies, "I trust you to never physically hurt me."

Her choice of words bothers me and gives me pause.

I'm only planning to tie her wrists together. Being tied up and at someone else's mercy requires a lot of trust in the other person. Her answer makes me wonder how she expects me to hurt her. Does she think I'm going to hurt her mentally? I suppose we don't have a good track record with that—or rather, I don't.

Feeling her hands on my cock again, I pull her out of the chair, grab her face, and seal our lips together.

I show her with my tongue what I'm going to do with my dick sooner rather than later. She's not the only one who's horny.

"Hold on to me."

I grab her hips and lift her up as she wraps her arms around my neck. I hiss when my cock meets her pussy.

Her shoes clunk to the floor.

I set her on the table and help her lie back. I nearly come when she puts her feet on the table to make sure I see everything.

Unable to ignore what she's showing me, I slide my finger through her wet pussy and circle her opening. Her hips arch, trying to take my finger inside her.

"No."

I pull her to the edge of the table, making sure my balls are wedged against her. I lean over and fasten her wrists with the tie above her head.

"Keep them there."

"Yes, sir," she replies cheekily, wrapping her legs around my hips and pushing me inside her with her feet.

My control is about to snap as my cock lengthens.

"Mmm, I felt that," she whispers.

I bury my face in her neck and start trailing kisses along her collarbone. Then, I cup her breasts in my hands and lick each of her nipples in turn.

Moving further down, I dip my tongue into her navel before reaching between us and taking hold of my cock. Throbbing in my hand, I guide myself into her. As I meet her eyes, I thrust all the way inside.

I hold still and grab her hips, really looking at her. The woman attached to me is everything to me, in the most basic way. I just need to find the words to tell her, but I can show her... just not like this.

Leaning over her, I kiss her lightly on the lips as I untie her wrists. "I want your hands free."

I caress down from her wrists, under her arms, and to her waist, feeling her clench down on my dick, nearly sending me into oblivion.

I glare at her as I caress my way back up to her hands, entwining my fingers with hers. I give a few shallow thrusts. Her whole body vibrates beneath me as she gets closer and closer to her release.

Whoever said it was hot as hell to fuck your girl on a table is insane because it's fucking uncomfortable, and I can't get into a proper rhythm.

Standing tall, I grip her hips, slowly withdraw, and then slowly slide back inside. My balls are so heavy that I'm afraid I'll come before she does, which won't do. With each withdrawal and each thrust, she lets out a little whimper, driving me insane.

"Lucien," she pants. "Fuck me hard and fast."

I pause, wondering if I heard her right.

"Please..."

Okay, I needed to be told twice, but I don't lose another minute. I tighten my grip on her hips and start pistoning in and out of her. My movements become uncontrollable as I feel my orgasm rising to meet hers. She clamps and releases around my dick as though she's preparing to detonate. Her breasts jiggle, but not for long. Sabrina arches up from the table and starts to rub her nipples.

I slip one hand between us and pinch her clit. She gasps and groans as her orgasm rips through her. It clenches around me like a tightening fist, pulling and releasing as our climaxes overtake us.

Slowing down finally, I drop face first against her stomach. Within seconds, I feel her stomach quiver.

No way—was that the baby? Was it?

I don't think it's appropriate to be buried deep inside my child's mother while she's wiggling around in there. I pull my spent dick out of her and lay my hands on her stomach, feeling a light movement.

"Wow, how does it feel when she moves inside you?"

She smiles and covers my hand on her stomach. "She might be a he, and it feels amazing."

"Let me help you up."

I take her hands and pull her into a sitting position, realizing she's a mess down there because of me.

"We need a shower," I say, wiggling my eyebrows.

Rolling her eyes, she asks, "Again? I've had a few showers today."

"Yes, again."

I pick her up and carry her toward the bathroom. When we get there, I say, "Thank you for that welcome-home scene. I'd only been gone a few hours, but it was hot as hell walking in and finding you like that. Especially since I've been hard all day thinking about you while reading Fifty Shades of Grey."

I start laughing at the startled look on her face.

"You knew?"

"Only since this afternoon."

"Bummer. Thought I'd be able to keep you wondering a bit longer."

"No chance, babe. But tell me, was that idea from the book?"

"Pretty Woman. I watched it with my mom this afternoon." Seeing my quizzical look, she continued, "You must have seen Pretty Woman. I mean, you're a guy. Weren't all guys crushing on Julia Roberts when the movie came out?"

"I know who starred in Pretty Woman. I'm just surprised that you watched it with your mom."

"Don't worry about that. Right now, I need you to wash my back."

14

Sabrina

Lucien has been amazing, and the more time I spend with him, the more I fall in love with him.

I took my mom's advice, and we've been on dates over the past two weeks. We've gone to the museum, out to dinner, and on walks in the mountains. We've basically just spent our time together getting to know each other. However, there is still a wall between Lucien and the fire. He told me outright that he doesn't talk about it and isn't sure if he'll ever be ready for me to see the full extent of his scarring.

I've told him that I'll be here when he's ready because I'm convinced that one day he'll be ready to talk to me about it and show me his scars. I just wish he had done it already, so we could move forward with me by his side.

I touch and feel his groin and penis nearly every day, unless he has other ideas. They're scarred, but I don't run away because of that. I can't get enough of him.

The fact that he doesn't trust me is starting to hurt. I keep telling myself that he's obviously been made to feel like he'll lose anyone who sees him. He won't lose me. The only way he'd lose me is if he chose to walk away.

So, I'm avoiding any mention of his past, which is stressful for me. I always have to think carefully before speaking when we're intimate because I don't want to ruin our time together. It's a huge elephant in the room, and I'm sure he's as aware of it as I am.

When I'm with him away from the apartment, I always feel close to him, as though the relationship we're trying to build because of our child will really work. I feel as though he's really going to stick with us and that he doesn't regret anything or blame me for trapping him.

It's only when we're in the apartment that I'm not sure about him or myself. Even though he's been attentive and made sure I haven't wanted for anything, I know that I'm pulling away from him. Self-preservation is a powerful force, and I guess that's what Lucien has been doing for years. I can't help it. No matter how hard I try to pull myself back, I can't. I think it's because I know in my heart that he'll never trust me enough to stay with me. I'm basically in a relationship where the man I love is waiting for me to walk away. How is that supposed to make me feel?

The rustle of a magazine pulls me out of my dark thoughts. I glance around the crowded OB's office at the happy couples quietly talking or reading to each other. I look at the clock. Another scan...another missing Lucien. He's never late for anything, unless circumstances are beyond his control. Yet again, I find myself offering my turn to another lady waiting to see the doctor, hoping he's going to be here. What the hell is it with these appointments? Nothing ever comes up at any other time, and now my cell starts to ring.

I glance at the caller ID before answering and my heart sinks when I see Lucien's name flashing on the screen.

"Hello," I answer.

"Sabrina, thank God. I just realized the time. I'm not going to make it. I'm so sorry, but Lily fell."

"How did she fall? Is she all right? The baby?" I quickly asked, my voice full of concern.

"She said she felt dizzy and lost her footing on the stairs. Luckily, she was only two steps from the bottom, so she didn't have far to fall. The doctor thinks that, other than shock, she and the baby are going to be fine, but Michael is freaking out, so I'm here at the hospital with them."

My heart sinks.

"Sabrina, are you there?"

"Yes," I whisper, unable to hide my disappointment.

"I'm really sorry. I can't leave. They need me here. You'll be fine, right? You know how much I was looking forward to being there. I'm disappointed, but at least you'll get a DVD, and we can watch it together later."

He sounds disappointed that he isn't going to be here. But I keep telling myself that if he wanted to be with me, he would be. Lily is going to be all right, so there isn't any reason for him to stay there.

He chose Lily over his child, over me.

A lump forms in my throat, and I find it difficult to breathe. I struggle to find the words, but I can't. All I want to do is rail against him and cry out about the pain lancing through me. I shake my head to clear it and hang up. There isn't anything else I can do.

"Sabrina, you're the only one left," Crystal says. The word hangs between us again. I glance around the room, startled that I lost track of time.

Just by looking at her, I can see the pity on Crystal's face. I'm pregnant, and the father isn't as committed as I thought he was.

Why am I surprised that he's blown me off because of Lily? I know I shouldn't be, but I am, and it hurts so much.

Yes, Lily was hurt and taken to the hospital, but she has a devoted husband with her. Mom and baby are okay. Why can't he leave to be with me? As I follow the nurse into the small room, I feel a strange mixture of sadness and numbness taking over.

Lying back on the table while the doctor works, I stare at the ceiling, trying to keep the tears at bay. When I'm handed a tissue, I realize my tears are falling and my face is wet. I can't focus because tears are clouding my vision.

I vaguely hear India, my doctor, ask Crystal to give us a few minutes before the door clicks shut.

"Why are you in tears in my office? It's been a while since I've made someone cry."

At least she gets a small smile out of me. "I'm sorry." I sniffle into a tissue. "It's not you. I can't talk about it. Otherwise, I'll be an even bigger wreck than I am now."

She nods. "I'm not going to push you, Sabrina, but it helps to get things off your chest. I'm here for you if you ever change your mind."

"Thank you."

I mop up my tears and try to breathe through my heartache.

"Do you want to know the sex of your child?" India asks with a smile in her voice.

Do I?

Before he stood me up, we agreed to find out the sex of our baby, but now I'm not sure I want to know.

I shake my head. "No."

Her hand pauses on my stomach before she continues taking measurements.

I still can't bring myself to look at the monitor.

Twenty minutes later, I find myself back on the sidewalk in a daze. I took a cab today so that we would only have one car here and could go straight from here to buy my engagement ring. We finally discussed it over a romantic dinner together. Now, I'm exhausted and just want to lie down and forget about my disastrous life. But first, I have to get home.

I take my cell phone out of my purse and dial Ramon, hoping he's free to give me a ride.

He answers on the first ring.

"Sabrina, how are you doing?"

"Are you free to pick me up?" I ask, getting straight to the point.

"I'm in the car and pulling out of the lot. Where are you?"

"I'm outside the doctor's office on East Maxwell Street."

He pauses.

"Isn't Lucien supposed to be with you?"

I sag against the wall.

"He decided he had something more important to do," I tell him, feeling my heart crack again.

"Fuck. Don't move. We're about five minutes away."

"I won't."

He hangs up as I grip my phone.

Lucien hasn't tried to call me since. No missed calls or texts. Nothing.

How are we supposed to have a relationship when he runs to Lily at the slightest problem? Not that I think falling is a small problem. I'm not a selfish person, and I'm truly concerned for my friend. But knowing she was okay and that Michael was with her should have freed him up to come to me. Instead, he stayed there. I don't think he realizes how much his actions hurt me.

When I lift my head and hear a car horn, I sigh in relief when I see Ramon pull up to the sidewalk. But not only does Ramon emerge from the car, a strange, handsome man emerges too. I can't help but stare at him. He's tall, muscular, and he rocks his jeans and T-shirt. His dark hair is messy, but it's his green eyes that sparkle with mirth when I finally meet them that make him handsome. I blush, realizing I've been staring.

I start moving and meet Ramon as he comes around the truck. He grins, but I can see worry for me in his eyes. After giving me a quick kiss, he smirks and introduces me to the man standing behind him.

"Sabrina, this is my cousin, Eric."

I hold my hand out to him. "It's a pleasure to meet you, Eric."

"The pleasure is all mine," he says, bringing my hand up to his lips and kissing my knuckles.

"Eric, knock it off."

He rolls his eyes. "Ramon, chill. Let's get this young lady seated. She can sit in the back with me."

"She can sit in the front with me. You can keep your-self company in the back."

Ramon lifts me into his truck.

After buckling in, I stare out the window during our short ride to the apartment building I share with Lucien. I can't even bring myself to call it home anymore. I know it's probably killing Ramon to know that some-thing is wrong with me but not know what it is or how to help. I'm not sure there's anything anyone can do to make me feel better right now. Even Eric has stayed quiet in the back of the truck, which surprises me since he isn't shy. I must look like a thundercloud.

Ramon walks me up to the apartment, and then he pulls me into his arms.

"Please talk to me," he begs. "I can't leave you like this. I know there's something wrong, and you're upset."

I pull away from him, take his hand, and pull him toward the sofa. He sits down and pulls me close with his arm around me.

Talking to him about today helps me figure out if I'm being unreasonable for being upset.

After he's listened to everything, I turn to face him and ask, "Do you think I'm being unreasonable? Am I upset and angry for nothing?"

Ramon shakes his head and cups my face in his hands. We're practically nose-to-nose. "You have every right to be pissed. Lily is my sister-in-law, and I love her like a sister. But if they'd been told she was okay and that Michael was there, then there was no reason for him to stay. He should have been with you."

Great, racking sobs take over my body as I feel Ramon pull me against him and wrap his arms tightly around me. He makes me feel safe.

HOURS HAVE PASSED SINCE RAMON LEFT, AND LUCIEN still hasn't returned. I'm not sure what I'll say to him when he arrives.

I've been unable to sleep with everything on my mind, but part of me is listening for the door to open. That's why I find myself heating milk in the microwave when I see my purse on the breakfast bar. I'd forgotten that I'd left it there when Ramon brought me home.

Opening it, I pull out the baby brochures I'd picked up from the doctor's office. At the time, I still thought Lucien would be there, so I sat looking through them. Now, though, I don't care about them, so I let them drop into the trash beside the sofa as I sit down.

Lucien

Exhaustion set in a few hours ago, but barging into my apartment at one in the morning wasn't part of the plan. Neither had missing the ultrasound yesterday afternoon.

Lily had given us a scare with her fall, and the fear on Michael's face made me call Sabrina to cancel. I knew it was wrong, and that I should have been there for her. However, she wasn't in as much pain as Lily was.

Hopefully, the bouquet I bought her from the hospital florist will be accepted as a peace offering. I'm not sure what I'll do if she doesn't accept them. I'm so out of practice with this kind of thing. For years, I've only had myself to think about. Now that I have more, I keep messing up.

My apartment is dark, with only a soft glow from the bedroom lighting the sofa. I find Sabrina curled up asleep there with a throw blanket keeping her warm.

Why is she asleep out here? Was she waiting for me to come home?

I wince. That's probably the last thing she'd do after my call.

Not wanting to disturb her, I sit down opposite and don't move until a bit of white catches my eye. I walk back to her side and find torn pieces of paper with pictures on them in the trash. I retrieve them and realize they're baby brochures. Why did she tear them up? Have I hurt her that badly?

Knowing I won't be getting any sleep soon, I slump back into the chair, heart heavy, and watch her sleep.

THE BEST I CAN DO BEFORE HEADING BACK INTO THE lounge is showering and putting on clean clothes.

I slept in the chair across from her all night because I couldn't leave her alone. I thought about carrying her to bed, but since she looked comfortable, I decided against it and let her sleep.

She's beautiful, and she causes an ache in my chest.

Lost in thoughts of her, I had no idea her eyes were open and fixed on me.

Now that I'm faced with an alert Sabrina, I'm not sure what to say.

As we stare at each other, I notice her swollen eyes and pale skin. She looks like she's been crying all night.

"Are you all right?" I ask, dropping into the chair.

She looks at me before averting her eyes. "What time did you get in?" she asks, ignoring my question.

"One. I took Michael and Lily home around eight." Michael put Lily to bed and then insisted that I stay and talk to him. He wanted me to keep him company. He was pretty shaken up by the whole thing."

"Oh, I need to shower," she tells me. Before I can respond, she jumps off the sofa, locks herself in the bathroom, and turns on the shower.

What the hell is going on?

I knew she was going to be upset that I missed the appointment. I just didn't think she'd be this upset. After all, Lily is her friend—or at least she was.

I was about to go wait in the bedroom for her when my cell started ringing.

"Is this Lucien McKenzie?"

"Yes, it is."

"This is Crystal from the OB's office."

I looked toward the bathroom, wondering why they would be calling me.

"Go on."

"Well, Sabrina was a bit of a mess yesterday. She forgot to take the pictures of the baby and the DVD with her, so I was wondering if you could stop by and pick them up."

I frown. "She was upset?"

"She was upset. Well, more than upset, actually, since she never once looked at the monitor during the ultrasound."

"Does she know the sex of the baby?"

Sabrina was beside herself yesterday morning about the ultrasound. She couldn't wait to find out if we're having a girl or a boy.

"I'm sorry, but she refused to be told when she was given the option."

"Thank you. I have to go."

I hung up and stared toward the bathroom.

Have I messed this up more than I thought?

Sabrina completely ignores me as she walks out of the bathroom in clean yoga pants and a T-shirt. After slipping her feet into her boots, she heads toward the kitchen.

Needing answers—knowing I'm probably not going to like them—I follow her.

She pours two cups of coffee while I sit at the breakfast bar and wait for her to finish.

I notice her glance at the flowers I put in a vase last night, but they don't elicit a reaction.

She finally meets my eyes after placing my coffee in front of me, and I'm worried because I don't see anything reflected in them. They're dead.

"I can't do this anymore, Lucien," she whispers, as though her voice has deserted her.

"Why?" I ask, my hands tightening around the mug.

"I can't and won't spend my life always being a second thought. I deserve so much more than that."

"I don't treat you like that." My immediate response sounds hollow, even to my own ears.

"You have no idea how much I wanted you with me yesterday. You told me that Lily was fine, but in shock. There wasn't any reason for you to stay. You could have made it to the ultrasound if you'd really wanted to be there."

She stumbles into the living room and sits in an armchair, looking sick.

This upset can't be good for the baby. A baby I'm not sure she wants anymore.

I'm losing her and our baby.

My heart freezes at the realization. I wish I knew how to make things right, even though I'm not sure if anything can be done.

In my defense, I say, "I'm sorry, Sabrina. I don't know what else to say. I told you that Michael was a mess and that I was worried about Lily. Someone needed to stay with him while the doctors examined Lily and ran tests. He's my brother, damn it, Sabrina!" I drag my fingers through my hair, wanting her to understand. "My family has always been there for me, and I'm not about to let them down when they need me."

Her heavy eyelids flew up in shock.

I closed my eyes. I just told her that she isn't family, but she is. She's my family. My future. I hadn't meant it the way it came out. I've always put them first in the past, but now I should be putting Sabrina first. I didn't, though. I love her and our unborn child. What the hell have I done?

The hurt on her face nearly kills me.

She just looks at me, silent tears falling down her face. "I guess I finally know how you really look at me."

She slowly gets to her feet while my words of apology get stuck in my throat. "Please don't come after me. If you can't show me any respect, please respect my wishes. My mother will let you know when the baby arrives."

Unable to move, I watch her leave, purse in hand.

I can't breathe. There's a pain in my chest that won't subside. My whole life passes before my eyes, spinning out of control like a tornado, all without Sabrina.

I throw my mug across the room, not caring what else shatters with it. I cry like a man who's just lost everything because I have.

15

Sabrina

TWO DAYS AGO, I WALKED AWAY FROM LUCIEN. INSTEAD of going to my mother's house, I ran to Ramon. I know I shouldn't have, given that he's Lucien's brother, but he's the only one I wanted. He's the only one who would understand.

Lucien's words cut me up inside. Hearing him say that he was there for Michael because he was family was the final blow to our so-called relationship. I was living in an illusion. I'm not sure what he thought we had, but it wasn't what I thought it was. A relationship.

Lily, Carla, and Rosie have tried calling me, but I can't speak to any of them. I just want to forget and try to move on with my life, which is laughable. It's already past lunchtime, and I'm still wearing my pajamas.

Ramon and Eric are at work, so I guess it doesn't really matter. Eric, whom I didn't know was staying with Ramon while he's here, has also turned out to be a good friend. He even threatened to carry me into the shower and wash his back if I didn't get out of bed today. I didn't want to find out if he was serious.

Instead of lying around, I need to find a way to move on without Lucien. I relied heavily on him for my happiness before he destroyed all my ideas about us. I can't get the look on his face when I turned away from him out of my head. He looked as though I were the one doing the destroying.

I hear a lock turn and stare at the door as Eric walks through, kicking off his work boots. No Ramon?

He smiles as he drops onto the chair opposite me. "See, you made it from the bed to the sofa. You showered as well? Too bad." He smirks. "I wouldn't have minded carrying out my threat."

"No one wants to see this body in the shower."

"If I thought for one minute that I stood a chance with you, we would have showered together by now, and done other things," he smirks.

"You're a big flirt."

"Been accused of that a time or two."

I change the subject. "Why are you home now? I thought you were working all day."

He shakes his head. "I needed to get out of there for a

while before I pushed an asshole off the tenth-floor scaffolding."

"That doesn't sound too good."

He stretches out in the chair and crosses his feet on the coffee table, letting his head drop back.

"Are you all right?"

"Exhausted. I'm getting too old for this shit."

He does look worn out.

"Let's forget about why I'm mad at someone at work, and I'll tell you about my brother, Dante." He looks at me, his eyes sparkling with mirth. "And all the women at his church who won't leave him alone."

My eyes widen.

He chuckles. "He's a priest and has been for a while now. Anyway, he called me this morning because he needed to let off steam. Apparently, working out at the gym didn't help this time. I see I have your attention."

"Please get on with it. This sounds like a story I might enjoy."

"Okay, well, women love a guy who takes care of his body, and the same goes for a man of the cloth. My brother works out to burn through the demons he's been running from for years. The women at his church drool over him. Anyway, one of these women has started to stalk him." He grinned.

"Um, why are you grinning?"

"You'll understand when I finish." Pause. "At some point

during the day, he would find a single red rose somewhere around the church. He was starting to get worried and tried to be more vigilant. I told him it was probably one of the stiletto-wearing women. He emailed me this morning to tell me that he caught the culprit red-handed. Her name is Betty, and she's an eighty-two-year-old widow. Apparently, Dante reminds her of her late husband, and the roses are reminiscent of their courtship. He was lost for words and didn't know what to say to her. On the one hand, it's funny because he was terrified it was one of the younger women who always stare at him. On the other hand, it's sweet and sad. I mean, what a life she must have had to live to be eighty-two years old! I can't help but wonder how long she and her husband were together when he died.

"That is so sweet," I blubber.

"Oh, hell, Sabrina. I didn't tell you that to make you cry. I thought it would make you smile."

"I've been crying on and off all day, and these pregnancy hormones make it ten times worse. Thank you for telling me that story. I hope to meet Dante one day. He sounds nice."

He rolls his eyes.

"I'll keep that to myself. I don't want him to think you're stalking him."

I laugh as my tears dry up.

I've enjoyed Eric's company over the past few days, but I think he's lonely. He's a Marine, but he hasn't been active for months. I'm not sure why. They said it was convalescent leave, but since no one has explained it to me, I haven't asked. If he wants me to know, he'll tell me. I mean, he tells me everything else.

"So tell me," Eric pauses and waits until I meet his gaze before continuing. "Did that distract you from my cousin?"

"Yeah, temporarily," I admit.

"I've seen how unhappy you are, Sabrina. Are you sure there isn't anything anyone can do to help you two get back together?"

I shake my head. "I don't think so. I love him, Eric," I say, swallowing down the sob trying to burst forth. "The problem is that he doesn't love me or consider me part of his family. I lived with him like a normal couple. I'm carrying his child, so I thought I was at least part of his family. But when he practically told me that I wasn't, I realized that I couldn't stay anymore." I shrug. "We might have been able to work through what happened with the ultrasound, but it hurt to hear him say that he passed me over for family. A lot."

"So, what are you going to do?"

"I don't have any choice but to carry on. I have a growing baby to think about. I'm just not sure where I'm going to go. To be honest, I'm worried about Lucien. He looked as broken as I felt when I left. I can't get his look out of my head."

"He has his brothers. Don't worry about him. Just worry about yourself and your baby for now."

"I know I need to. It's difficult. The love I have for him isn't going to disappear just because of his callous words. I'm not sure it ever will."

Eric's cell buzzes, and he scrambles to find it. Glancing at the screen, he frowns—obviously, the text message isn't good.

"Hell. I need to head back. I'm sorry, Sabrina. Will you be all right on your own?"

I smile. "I was fine all morning."

"Okay."

He stands up, hesitates, then kisses me on the head.

Without another word, he puts on his work boots and slips through the door, leaving me with my thoughts.

Lucien

As usual, my brothers think they know best. They're now in my kitchen warming up food that the girls sent. If I stop hiding in my bedroom like a coward, this will be the first meal I've eaten since Sabrina left. I don't blame her for leaving because I was a complete bastard.

What the hell possessed me to say she wasn't family? The minute the words left my mouth, I knew what I'd done. Seeing her face as she processed what I said killed me. To be honest with myself, I said them because I felt backed into a corner, so I snapped. I knew she was right about the accusations she was throwing at me. I knew I was wrong, but I couldn't admit it, and I ended up hurting her badly.

After three days of misery, my brothers arrived and let themselves in because I refused to answer the door. I'm just thankful the girls stayed away, because I'm not sure how I would have handled seeing them together, given the love they have for my brothers. I had all that, and I threw her away with my callous words.

Now, I have to go out there and talk to them. I have to tell them what a bastard I was to her. They probably already know, as I'm sure Ramon has told them everything. I'm not just jealous. I'm fucking jealous as hell that my brother has a closer relationship with my girl than I do.

I know they haven't slept together and never will, but she talks to him. Part of me is glad she has someone to turn to, but yeah, I can't help but be jealous of my own brother.

I shove my arms into a clean T-shirt, making sure I'm covered, and inhale deeply before slowly exhaling in an effort to calm myself down.

I'm the oldest and should dish out the grief, but today, I'm about to receive it. Something's wrong here.

It's usually me telling them what bastards they've been.

Walking into the living room, I'm met with four pairs of eyes staring at me as though they haven't seen me before.

I sigh and, ignoring them, grab a bowl of chili, a fork, and a beer from the breakfast bar. I take them with me as I drop onto my chair in the living room. I could have shaved, but why would I? I have no enthusiasm for anything.

As I start to eat, my brothers join me, spreading out on the sofas and in the other chair with their dinner.

Eating in silence is unusual, but looking at Sebastian, I know it won't last long.

He grins and asks, "So, what did you do to mess up?"

Michael and Ruben curse. I glance at Ramon, whose frown probably matches mine, but he remains silent, which is probably a good thing.

Being prepared for the question helps keep my anger in check as I place my bowl on the coffee table. I take a long drink from my beer as I gather my thoughts, then sigh.

"Have you not told them?" I ask Ramon.

He replies, shaking his head, "No. It wasn't my story to tell."

I'm glad at least one of my brothers doesn't gossip, but it would be easier if he did.

Feeling heavyhearted, I admit, "I missed Sabrina's scan at the OB's office."

"How the fuck did you forget that?" Ruben demands.

"If it was Rosie, you can bet your ass I'd be there, no matter what else I had going on."

I should have been there for Sabrina like that. I let her down by not being there. The truth is, I wanted to be there so badly, but when I called her, I tried to make light of it. In fact, I'd been hiding my disappointment from her. I hadn't even mentioned Sabrina's appointment to Michael when he asked me to stay because he'd worked himself up over Lily.

I glance at Michael and admit the truth, "It was the day Lily had her fall." I have Michael's attention and notice my brothers glance at him as I continue, "I called Sabrina from the hospital and told her about Lily. I basically blew her off."

"Because I was a selfish jerk and asked you to stay with me while Lily was having tests," Michael says, then curses.

"You had no idea what I had planned that day because I'd only just arrived at your place when Lily slipped. If you must know, I blamed myself for Lily's fall. She was rushing to let me in because the door was locked."

"Fuck. It's not your fault she fell. She was rushing, had a dizzy spell, and slipped because she had socks on instead of shoes."

"Tell them the rest," Ramon said unhelpfully.

I tug at my hair and add, "I snapped when I realized

she was right, and I basically told her she wasn't family and that family comes first."

"Fuckin' hell," Ruben curses.

Sebastian adds, "Even I don't mess up that badly."

"You do realize that the fact it was Lily, which indirectly prevented you from being with Sabrina, probably made the situation ten times worse?" Ramon adds.

"What?"

What the hell is he talking about?

"You seriously don't know? Why do you think she doesn't respond to Lily anymore?" Ramon questions me.

"Fuck. I didn't even think about that," Michael adds.

"Why would she be jealous of Lily?"

Now, they all glare at me.

"You have a special relationship with my wife, which seemed strange to me and the others at first. Sabrina is jealous because you always put Lily before her." Michael shakes his head, telling me to stay quiet. "Basically, she's an outsider looking in, and she thinks you're in love with my wife. I know you don't love her like that, and everyone else does too. It hasn't been a problem before because you didn't have someone with you. But you did, and she was finding it hard to get past your relationship with Lily. Have you ever sat down and told her why you are so close to Lily? Or were you as clueless as I think you were?"

There isn't any reason to answer him—he'll see the shock on my face. I'd assumed, wrongly, after my earlier conversation with Sabrina, that she had dropped the whole thing about Lily. The signs were there if I'd only taken more notice.

"I need to talk to Sabrina."

Ramon winces.

"What?"

He doesn't answer.

"Ramon, if you know something, then please tell me."

He looks at anyone but me, avoiding my gaze. "I'm not sure she'll be willing to talk to you… *Yet*," he stresses. "This morning, she was up before Eric and me. She had breakfast ready for us, and then she said she was fine and was going to run some errands. She just looked— well, not heartbroken, like she has been these past few days."

"That's good, right?" I ask. At least, I think it is. I'm not too sure. It would be easier if she missed me. Then, she would accept my apology and return here, where she belongs. But if she isn't, well, I don't want to think about that.

"I'm not sure. Eric followed her to make sure she was okay because she was acting oddly. We couldn't work it out. Anyway, she met some guy in Starbucks."

"She what?" I roar.

"Ramon, you idiot! I told you not to tell him that!"

Ruben gets in Ramon's face, but Ramon shoves him back.

"Don't start on me." Ramon pokes Ruben in the chest.

"He's the one who screwed up, not me. Lucien needs to know so he doesn't sit around and let someone else walk away with his woman."

He turns to me.

"I hope you're listening, because that's what's going to happen if you keep being a jerk. That woman loves you and has taken nothing but shit from you. You don't deserve her, given the way you've treated her. If you were anyone else, I would beat the crap out of you. But you're my brother, and I want you to be happy for once. I'm telling you this because I love you both, but don't go after her unless you're willing to commit to her and talk to her. You need to tell her about your past so you can move forward. Until you do, you're only going to keep hurting her. Once that's out of the way, perhaps you'll be able to tell her how much you love her. That's what she needs to know, Lucien."

"Well, fuck me. I didn't know my baby brother had all those words inside him," Ruben comments, staring at Ramon in shock.

"Fuck you," Ramon responds.

Every word Ramon just said is true, and I know what I have to do.

16

Sabrina

TO SAY THE LEAST, MY BREAKFAST WITH GAVIN WAS uncomfortable. We managed to finalize the arrangements for the upcoming fundraiser. He's a nice guy, but he tends to flirt with me rather often. This is despite my stomach protruding more with each passing day. I should be happy that another man finds me attractive. But at the end of the day, I miss Lucien. He's the only man I want to be in a relationship with.

Last night, after I woke myself up crying, I decided that the tears and heartache had to stop because they couldn't be good for our baby. Deep down, I know Lucien regrets his choice of words. I just wish they hadn't hurt me so much.

I know myself and know that I won't be able to stay

away from him for long. Thanks to Ramon, I have my clothes, but he only brought me enough for a few days, so I have an excuse to go see Lucien. It gives me a reason to be at his apartment, so I won't look like a desperate fool or a lovesick girl.

As I pass a store window, I look in to see if I have a desperate, heartbroken look on my face. I stop and stare inside when I realize it's a baby store. This is something I'd planned on doing with Lucien, but I'm not sure I can go inside alone without having a meltdown. How stupid is that?

"Sabrina?"

I nearly jump out of my skin and lose my balance, but Eric catches me.

"Sorry," he says, looking sheepish.

What is he doing here?

Instead of thinking, I should ask!

"Why aren't you at work?"

"Errand." He grins.

My eyes narrow as I realize he has probably been following me since I left Ramon's apartment this morning.

"You can stop following me and come shopping with me."

He groans and looks panicked.

"Oh, stop it. I need clothes that actually fit me. I'm sick of living in yoga pants."

"Well, mama," he grins, offering me his arm. "Let's go

get you some new clothes." I slip my arm into the crook of his elbow. He continues, "But I hope you know I'm only doing this if I get a fashion show."

I roll my eyes.

"We'll see. It depends on how nice you are to me."

"I can be really nice."

I laugh. "Come on, Romeo."

DESPITE ALL OF ERIC'S COMPLAINTS ABOUT SHOPPING, HE had a great time. He dragged me all over the place until I announced that he would have to carry me back if we didn't call it a day. We finally made it back to Ramon's apartment, where I crashed on the sofa, exhausted. I grinned down at Eric at the other end of the couch and sighed at how wonderful his massage felt on my aching feet.

He has talented hands. But, I'm afraid to say, the only hands I really want on me are Lucien's. Eric knows this. I can't fault him. Between him and Ramon, they've stopped me from wallowing in despair too much, or at least they have after letting me stay in bed and cry for three days.

Ramon left early this morning, mumbling something about a brothers' meeting. I've managed to put the meaning behind his words out of my head all day, but now that I'm relaxing, I can't help but wonder if the meeting was at Lucien's place. I'm desperate for news about Lucien, but neither Ramon nor Eric will tell me anything. I'm not sure if Eric knows anything, but I know Ramon does, and I plan to pin him down when I see him. He can only avoid me for so long, especially since I'm living in his apartment.

I groan inwardly at that thought. Although Ramon said I could stay as long as I like, I can't stay forever. It's just too awkward, especially since he's Lucien's brother. It's also getting harder to stay now that my mom knows about my split from Lucien. Ever since, she's been trying to persuade me to move in with her. She argues that it isn't appropriate to live with two single men and that others will think I'm in a relationship with both of them. I'm glad she was on the phone, otherwise she would have seen my eyes bug out when she mentioned that. It made me wonder what kind of books she reads behind the book club ladies' backs. That's something I intend to find out. She isn't going to get away with it, especially after making such a fuss about those kinds of books. Is she a secret erotic reader?

I smiled at the thought.

"Ouch."

I pull my foot away, but Eric grabs it and rubs the spot where he just nipped me.

"What was that for?"

"I want to know what you're thinking about that has your face alight with mischief."

I smirk. "I was imagining the kind of books my mother has been reading to suggest that people will think I'm really with both you and Ramon living here. I mean, Jane Eyre doesn't talk about threesomes."

He pauses, glaring at me. I can see the wheels turning in his head, wondering what I'm getting at.

"Your mom is under the impression that, as long as you live here, everyone will think you're sleeping with both of us."

"Yes," I grin, and then I start laughing when Eric wiggles his eyebrows.

"I'm game if that was a hint," he laughs.

I push him with my foot as I scoot back into a sitting position.

"You're incorrigible, and you remind me a bit of Sebastian. Yes, my mom suggested that, but if you knew her, your mind would work overtime. She has always done the proper thing, as if she were raised to do so. For years, I felt like I was living in a castle, but from the outside looking in, you know? She could never understand why I preferred jeans to frilly dresses. We've only really started talking and spending time together since I was in the hospital last. It's nice."

"I'm glad you're finally spending time with her. Make the most of it. My mom was amazing. After losing her all those years ago, I still remember her singing me to sleep when I was a child. It may sound crazy, but as I got older, she was always there, guiding my brothers and me out of trouble. There wasn't anything she wouldn't do for any of us. I was nine when she died, and her passing left a hole in our family that still hasn't healed."

"I'm sorry you lost your mom, Eric. She sounds like she was amazing."

"Thanks." He shakes his head. "It's been a long time. All we need to do now is make you irresistible to my idiot cousin. I have an idea."

I groan. "Do I want to know? Your grin is frightening me."

"Ramon told me a while back that Gavin asked if he could take you to the fundraiser."

"Huh."

"Sabrina, think. There's nothing that'll piss Lucien off more than seeing the woman he loves on a date with another man. I'd offer to be that man, but I have a feeling he wouldn't go for it."

"Lucien doesn't love me."

I wish he did.

"Think about what I said. If it makes you feel better, tell Gavin the truth and see if he'd help you."

"I don't know." I bite my lip. "What if we do all this, and Lucien doesn't show up? Or what if he does show up, but he doesn't react? Or even worse, what if he brings his own date? Oh God, I can't do this." I place my hands protectively over my stomach.

"Don't worry about it. We'll get Ramon involved, and he can make sure Lucien attends—and that he comes alone. Now that everything is arranged, I should have left ten minutes ago." Eric gets up from the sofa, kisses my head, shoves his feet into his boots, and leaves, locking the door behind him.

My mind is buzzing with thoughts about the fundraiser. I just wish I were as confident as Eric seems to be about Lucien's reaction to it.

Before contemplating making him jealous, I need to try talking to him. My heart and body crave the sight of him. Even if we only talk about the baby, I need to see him. Speaking of which, the DVD and photographs of our baby are still at the doctor's office. I left them there after my last ultrasound because I was too upset to wait for them. I could call and pick them up and use that as an excuse to see him. Hopefully, things will progress from there.

As I enter Lucien's apartment building, I bump into Ruben, who is leaving.

He looks surprised to see me.

"Sabrina, what are you doing here?" he asks. "Sorry. I didn't mean for it to sound so harsh. I'm distracted by something. How are you?"

"I'm okay, I guess. I'm on my way up to see Lucien. Ramon won't tell me how he is. I need to... I mean..."

"Sabrina, I understand. But I'm afraid he isn't here. He left town."

I can't hide my shock.

Ruben puts his arm around me and directs me outside to his truck. He opens the door and helps me climb aboard the massive vehicle before turning the ignition and activating the heaters. I wasn't cold before, but I am now.

"Look, Sabrina, I know he messed up with you. He didn't mean to. He just needs some time on his own. Michael dropped him off at the airport a couple of hours ago."

He left. He didn't want to see me.

"Where...where did he go?"

"He went to his place in Colorado."

I averted my gaze and looked out the window. I really didn't think he'd leave Lexington. I thought he'd want to make sure the baby was okay. I even hoped he would come for me.

"Sabrina, please don't do this to yourself. He'll be back. He's gone to lick his wounds. Trust me." He took my hands in his. "He'll be back for you and his child. Just give him time."

"How much time? I can't do this without him, Ruben.."

He pulls away from the sidewalk. "I don't think you'll have to wait long."

I turn my head and watch his lips turn up in a smile and his eyes light up with mischief.

"He can't do anything without you, either. But that's all I'm saying. He can beg for your forgiveness himself."

The rest of the drive is spent in silence, and I wonder if I will see Lucien again.

Lucien

Until Ramon's speech, escaping to Colorado hadn't crossed my mind. I need to tell her everything, man up, and show her my damaged skin. But before I can do that, I decided to return to my home in Denver.

It's a large, luxurious cabin surrounded by nature, and I want to reveal everything to Sabrina here. We need to be away from my family and all outside influences. I just want to be alone with the woman I love— the woman who will be the mother of my child and, hopefully, more children in the future. My cabin is perfect for that, but it needs to be aired out, as I haven't been here in months. I also need to buy new furniture to make it a home that I want to share with her instead of the home of a single guy. This is the home I want to live in with Sabrina. Not in our apartment in the city, but here.

As our child gets older, he or she will be able to play outside and hopefully benefit from the fresh air of the great outdoors instead of the city. I'd even buy another one in Lexington if Sabrina wants to stay there.

I have a lot to do while I'm here, and hopefully the time here will help me build up the courage I need to show her my body. I need to overcome the nausea I feel when I catch a glimpse of myself in the mirror. If it makes me feel that way, how can I expect Sabrina to react any differently? I really need to get my head around this quickly, before someone else steps in and gives her what she needs.

She needs you.

I wish I could trust my conscience.

As I drive along the mountain road to my place with my window down, letting the cold air blow through my truck, I try to clear the cobwebs clouding my head.

Knowing what I have to do is so much easier than doing it.

It's no wonder Dante escaped and became a priest. Six years ago, he had just been officially accepted into the church. To this day, I have no idea what caused the sudden change in him. Either way, he's doing a damn good job of turning the church around. He's certainly brought the younger generation back inside its walls. I smile, though, because I'm sure that has more to do with his looks and physique than with religion itself. I don't think it bothers him as much as it used to.

Dante helped me carry on with day-to-day living after I ran here to lick my wounds following the fire. In a way, I guess it's Dante I've come back to.

He lives in a small cabin about twenty minutes from his church and refuses to live in the adjoining house. Over the next couple of weeks, I know we'll be hiking and fishing just like old times.

Hopefully, he'll already be at my cabin by the time I arrive, assuming he picked up his voicemail. I called him at the last minute as I boarded the plane.

Out of all my cousins, he's the one I'm closest to. He's the same age as me, and when we were younger, before his mom passed away, we used to hang out. Those were great times until his mom died and his dad remarried right away. That upset him and his brothers badly, and we drifted apart for a while, until the fire.

As I pull up to my place, I swear I can smell snow in the air. It's almost the first snow of the season, which I hope happens while I'm here. I'd love to bring Sabrina here when it snows because the place looks magical. That reminds me to add the house lights to my list of things to do.

Hopefully, with Dante's help, everything will be perfect.

I smile as I come to a stop beside his SUV and climb out. There's nothing like being here in the mountains.

"Hey, about damn time," Dante shouts, bringing my gaze up to him. He shuts my front door on his way to greet me with a hug.

"It's been a while," I tell him.

"That it has," Dante replies. "I've had the electricity switched back on, and I've put the supplies in the kitchen."

"Thanks."

We walk inside, and I notice that it's already heating up.

"How long are you staying?" Dante asks as I follow him to the kitchen.

He already has a pot of coffee on. It looks fresh, too, still steaming.

"Two weeks." I pour us both a cup of coffee, then rest my hip against the countertop. "I'm here to make some changes to the place. If you're free, I could use your help."

"What kind of changes?"

"The whole place needs furniture, but it needs to be suitable for a family."

He pauses mid-drink.

"I know it's been a while since we've really spoken, but family? What have I missed?"

"I've screwed up badly." I wince. "Sabrina. I told you about her a few months ago. We...uh...we've been dating."

Dante's eyebrows shoot up in shock.

"I want to bring her here, tell her about the accident, show her where I was burned, and hopefully, if she doesn't run screaming, ask her to live here with me."

I sit opposite Dante at the kitchen table.

"So you want to furnish the whole place to try to do what?" He throws his arms out. "Won't she stay with you, even in the sparsely furnished rooms?" He frowns.

"Sabrina would stay with me in a shack in the mountains if I asked her. Or at least she would have before I hurt her. I need to make this right. She's the one, Dante. I knew it from the first time I laid eyes on her. She scared the shit out of me, and I fought it, but she's in here," I say, pressing my hand against my heart. "And she's not going anywhere. She's also carrying my child."

I shoot up and pass him a napkin when he starts to choke.

I'm not surprised he's shocked, considering he knew about my sexual problem. It's not exactly something you call a friend about and say, "Hey, I'm back. My dick's working again."

"She's pregnant? Are you sure it's…?" He sees my pissed expression and backpedals. "Good," he finishes with a wince.

I stare at him for a few minutes.

"Yes, it's mine. No matter what I do, I've been messing up with Sabrina, and it needs to stop. I want to make this place look like a home. I want it to look like a place where she would want to live with me. I need your help to do it."

He placed his mug back on the table and sat back, grinning. "Of course I'll help you. But first, I want to meet this woman you're going to all this trouble for."

"She isn't anything like Alyssa."

"Oh, I know that. You didn't love Alyssa."

"What?"

"Alyssa once asked you to change the sofas in your apartment's main room because she thought the color was hideous. Do you remember? You told her that they were comfortable and that she knew where the door was if she wanted to leave.

"She was surprised, and I had to turn away so she wouldn't see the grin I was trying to hide. She had a wicked temper. Truth be told, I'm glad she left, just not the way she did. She wasn't right for you. Anyone could see it."

"But me," I finish for him.

"Yeah, but you."

"Sabrina is different, and as soon as you meet her, you'll realize that."

"Good. So, when do we start this project of yours?"

"Tomorrow."

"Okay, then tonight, we'll heat up the casserole in the fridge, and I'll sleep here. At least tomorrow night, I might get a bed."

I grin at him. "So, how long are you planning on staying?"

"Until you're sorted." He grabs a notepad and a pen from the table in the hall and disappears into the family room.

I lean against the wall and watch him walk around the room, making notes. I ask him, "So, why are you so keen to come and hide here?" I grin, knowing him well.

Dante's head snaps up, looking shocked.

I'm right. It's not just our friendship that has him here helping me out.

I fold my arms across my body and wait him out.

"You're a pain in the ass, you know that?"

"Not the first time I've been called that, and it won't be the last."

"Family. My sister, to be precise. She's also a pain in the ass." He shakes his head. "I don't want to talk about her. Let's start with the downstairs rooms before we eat."

I stay silent and watch him, wondering what Emelia has done now. She's always been a handful, but now that she's living in a different city from her twin, Diego, I suppose she's spreading her wings more. If I remember correctly, she was angry and upset when Dante joined the priesthood.

Maybe Dante's problems will distract me from worrying about Sabrina and how she'll react when she finds out I left Lexington.

17

Sabrina

EVERY EVENING, I STARE AT THE ENVELOPE CONTAINING our baby's picture and DVD. I do the same thing before getting out of bed each morning. So far, I have been unable to look at them. I desperately need Lucien to be with me when I finally open them. He doesn't deserve my consideration in this matter. Not after he chose not to be here for me...for our baby. No matter how many times I tell myself this, I still can't open the envelope.

I picked them up six days ago. It was the day Ruben told me that Lucien had headed to Colorado to get his head on straight. Each day that passes makes it harder for me to believe that he will come back for me and our unborn baby. Ruben spoke as though he'd be back for us soon. I hope with all my heart that he will, but the doubts are growing stronger each day. Being away from him was difficult when he was in the same city. Now that he's gone, it's unbearable. I miss him more than words can express.

With the fundraising event around the corner, I've been spending more time helping finalize the arrangements. This means Gavin has been around constantly, flirting with me. He's a nice guy and a great doctor, just not for me. If he asks me one more time to go to the event with him, I might just give in and say yes. He knows all about Lucien, so I wouldn't be leading him on. The thought of attending alone makes me nervous. I've never been good at walking into crowded rooms, so it would be nice to have someone with me.

The night of the fundraiser will also be the first time I've seen Lily and the rest of the McKenzies since leaving Lucien. Part of me is nervous, but part of me is also longing to see them and have all the support I can get. I may not be family, but I know they will support me. Of course, that assurance doesn't calm my nerves. What if they blame me for Lucien leaving? I'm sure it's just my mind making all sorts of assumptions, but I can't help it.

Overall, I am looking forward to the event, and I hope it will be a huge success. If it is, it will mean that all of our hard work has paid off.

I think it's safe to say that the only thing I need to do now is buy an evening dress that accommodates my growing belly. When I went shopping with Eric, I didn't think about buying an evening dress, so I need to do that soon.

Thinking about it makes me realize that I should figure it out sooner rather than later, and now is a good time. There's a boutique a block away that sells amazing dresses. I hope they have something suitable for a pregnant woman. I'm not too fussy as long as it covers the essentials. If it happens to show some of my plump breasts, though, I'm not about to complain. After all, Lucien is supposed to make an appearance if Ramon has anything to say about it.

As I collect my jacket and shove my arms inside, Gavin appears. He looks disappointed when he sees that I'm about to leave.

"I'm too late," he says, walking toward me. "I thought you'd still be here for a while, so I figured I'd come see how you were doing and maybe take you out to lunch."

I pull my hair from the collar of my jacket and grab my purse and cell phone. Then, I look back at him. He's a good-looking guy, and if I hadn't met Lucien, perhaps something might have developed between us. Still, there's only one Lucien. Still, I can't help but compare them. Gavin is blond, smooth, and quick to laugh. Lucien, on the other hand, is dark, rough around the edges, and more prone to smoldering glances that leave me hot and out of breath.

"I'm sorry, Gavin."

"But you're still in love with the other guy. I don't like it, but I get it."

He shouldn't care either way, since we've never dated or spent time alone together. It's just weird.

"I'm going to grab a sandwich on the way home after I find something to wear for the event."

"You don't have anything to wear yet?" he asked as he walked out with me.

"No, I don't." I place my hand on my stomach and watch the bell drop.

"Ah, you mean with the pregnancy?"

I smile in reply.

"Okay, well, if you're sure about lunch?"

"I am."

"I'll see you at the final meeting next week."

He waves as I leave the hotel, and I sigh in relief. I hate disappointing him, but I'm not going to use him as a date for the fundraiser like Eric suggested. Lucien will have to accept me as I am. Besides, I don't think I have it in me to do something that might make him jealous. In fact, who am I kidding? It would hurt him. That much I know.

The walk to the store is short, and the cool breeze is so welcome to my overheated body. Pregnancy hormones.

When I open the store's door, I pause when I spot Lily inside. She looks up and sees me, making it difficult to quickly leave and pretend I wasn't shopping there. I'm acting like a jealous lover, which I suppose I am. Lucien chose to stay with Michael and Lily over seeing his child, so I have every right to be hurt by all of them.

"Sabrina," Lily says, finding her voice first. "Please don't go." She comes over to me. "Let me get dressed again, and then we can go somewhere and talk. Please."

I'm standing in front of her, being stupid, so I finally respond. "I need a dress too. There's no need to rush off if you haven't finished. Let's just get this done so it's over with, and then we can go talk."

"Still hate dress shopping?" she asks, a smile hovering on her lips.

I snort. I know it's very unladylike, but I seriously hate shopping for evening dresses—or any dress, for that matter. More often than not, it's because of the high prices stores charge for them.

"Come on, I'll show you the maternity section." She takes my hand, gives it a slight tug, and gets me moving with her.

I've missed having Lily to talk things through with. If only I could figure out Lily and Lucien's relationship, things might not look so bad. Michael is possessive as hell toward Lily, but he accepts their relationship, so perhaps I should too. But first, Lucien needs to explain it to me properly. First, I need to truly believe him.

"Do you know what you're having yet?" Lily asks. But she continues before I can answer, "I'm only having one this time. Thank goodness. I would have coped if it had been twins again, but it was such a relief when the OB said it was one baby girl." She grins. "Michael keeps saying he's going to go gray soon."

I chuckle and respond, "He's going to have his hands full, that's for sure. And no, I don't know what I'm having. I didn't want to know." I avoid her eyes as I start looking through the rack of maternity evening gowns.

After a minute of uncomfortable silence, I take a red silk gown from the rack. "I think I'll try this one on."

"Okay, I'll get out of the way while you try that one on."

We disappear into our respective dressing rooms. I hang the dress up and dump my things onto the chair in the corner. The dressing room is large, with two full-length mirrors and wooden pegs on the wall for my clothes.

I slip out of my clothes and find the zipper on the side of the dress. I slide it down and remove it from the hanger. The dress caresses my skin like a feather as it falls to my feet. The red silk feels wonderful against my skin. The halter style with black beads around the neck adds to the dress's beauty.

After some maneuvering due to my belly, I manage to zip it up and take a look at myself in the mirror.

I take in my curves, which are more defined by my pregnancy, as well as my large breasts. They must be twice their original size. Looking at myself now, I realize the dress would look better without underwear, which makes me moan. There isn't any way I can go without a bra—or is there?

With a huff, I unclip my bra and pull it down my arms and off. Oh, wow! My breasts have always been firm, and now that they're being caressed by the silk, I think one look from Lucien will give away how aroused I am. He'll see my erect nipples perfectly, just as they are now, with thoughts of his reaction running through my head. Standing to the side, I caress my bump, wishing Lucien were here with me. I wish he were here to witness the changes to my body because I'm carrying his child.

"Sabrina, are you okay in there?"

I take a breath and reply, "I'm fine. Give me a minute," as I wipe the silent tears from my face.

I have to believe Ramon when he said Lucien would be at the fundraiser because it's the only thing keeping me going and getting me out of bed every day.

I'm excited knowing he will be there. However, there is a hint of apprehension because even though Ruben told me Lucien was coming back for me, I still have a nagging feeling that it's all a dream.

I NERVOUSLY PICKED AT THE SANDWICH LILY ORDERED FOR me while watching her do the same across from me.

After the dress store, she directed me here. It's a small bistro that serves delicious Italian sandwiches and coffee. Neither of us are drinking coffee. We have a glass of iced water with lemon. It's refreshing.

"Okay, I'm going to go first," Lily says. "I know you're upset with Lucien because he missed the scan because of me. I'm so sorry, Sabrina. I'm sorry not only for you but for Lucien as well. He's happy that he's going to be a father, and he should have been there for you. If Michael had known, he never would have asked Lucien to stay with him at the hospital. I was fine with having more tests done. Michael was a wreck, but he would have been fine. He's kicking himself for being selfish and not realizing that he messed Lucien up.

I shake my head, reach out, and put my hand over Lily's. "I understand that, and it's something we could've probably gotten over. It's just...he's in love with you," I blurt out.

Nice going!

Lily pauses, then starts to laugh. She soon stops, though, when she realizes I'm serious. "Oh, Sabrina. I wondered about that, but I seriously didn't think there was anything to it. Is that why you've stopped calling, or why you refuse to answer when I call?"

"Perhaps."

"Sabrina, I'm not going to lie to you. I love him, and I know he loves me, but not in the way you think. I love him like a brother, and he loves me like a sister. I was the first woman to show him that not all women are bad, so I guess that has created a bond between us. But that's all it has ever been or ever will be. Michael and our children are my life, just as you are Lucien's."

I stay silent while taking in everything she's telling me. I've always wondered about their relationship. I can't help but sift through memories of them together—the looks, the secret whispers. I realize she's telling the truth. They weren't the actions of lovers, but of siblings. I believe her. I really do. However, I still need Lucien to tell me the same thing and take my concerns seriously instead of dismissing them.

"Does Lucien know you feel this way?"

"I don't know," I whisper. "I think he may now. We argued before I walked out. But it was when he said that family will always come first that I realized he doesn't see me as part of the family. It hurt Lily. So much."

Tears again!

I take a swallow of water to regain control before continuing. "Why can't Lucien tell me all this? He'd probably still be here with me if he'd talk to me instead of getting defensive when he knows he's wrong."

"He's a man who hasn't had anyone but his parents and brothers to think about in a long time. And yes, he includes Carla, Rosie, and me with his brothers. You know about his ex, right?"

I nod.

"I really hate her for what she put in his head. She's a

wicked woman, and if I ever see her, she's going to hear from me."

Lily grabs my hand.

"Please come back to me. You're my only friend, and I miss you." I could see the longing in her eyes and hear the hurt in her voice. I swallowed the guilt I hadn't realized I had been feeling.

"I'm sorry, Lily. It was hard to be around you when Lucien was there too because he'd look at you and make me wish he was looking at me."

She laughs, startling me. "Sabrina, if you can't see the way that man looks at you, then you really don't have eyes in your head. He's changed so much since you've been with him. I know it's hard without him around, but once he gets back, he'll sort everything out. Give him this time, and when he talks to you, don't make it easy. He needs to learn that you're not a pushover." She grins.

"Do you want him to suffer?"

"Not really, because I think he's suffered enough. Five minutes will be fine."

"I'm not promising anything because I'm going to be too excited to see him again. I miss him, Lily."

"I know."

Lucien

It's amazing what you can accomplish when you have drive and money.

Over the past week, Dante and I have furnished my home with every modern comfort we could think of. I know Dante thinks I'm a fool for doing all this for a woman, but I don't. My only problem now is that I'm getting impatient waiting for Saturday evening. Had I not had the house to occupy me, I would have been on the next plane back to Lexington to claim my girl. I'm prepared to beg if necessary, as Ruben said I would have to do after seeing her at my apartment the afternoon I left for Denver. He's an ass, and I hope he exaggerated when he said she was pissed and upset.

I've planned my "get my girl" strategy down to the last detail. Michael has the McKenzie Holdings jet ready in the hangar at the Lexington airport, ready to whisk her back here. She's coming back with me, one way or another. Leaving without her isn't an option. If that doctor is anywhere near her, she'll find out just how much I believe she belongs with me. I just hope he has health insurance. I grin, liking that idea.

"What are you grinning at?" Dante asks while trying to put together the coffee table.

"The thought of harming someone," I reply, getting down on the floor to read the instructions he's trying to follow but keeps messing up.

"As long as it's not me, I'm fine with it. Although, I shouldn't be," he frowns. "Being a priest and all. But, considering it's you, I guess you have a good reason." He raises an eyebrow in question.

"He's after my girl, so I guess that's a good reason." I take one of the table legs from him, turn it the right way up, and pass it back. "It won't come to that. At least, I hope it won't. I don't think Sabrina would be impressed if I punched him over her."

"From what you've told me about her, I don't think she would be."

"It would feel good."

He shakes his head, a look of confusion crossing his face. Dante is brilliant at many things, but assembling something from instructions isn't one of them.

"You screw the pieces together as I hand them to you."

He scowls.

"I want this done today, and it's just a coffee table."

"Stop moaning. You moan like a girl," Dante says as he tries to follow the instructions.

"Says he who has done nothing but complain about his sister wanting to visit him," I counter.

The last time I saw Emelia, she was shorter than me with pigtails. Apparently, she's grown into a beautiful woman, and Dante wants to keep her away from his church. More specifically, he wants to keep her away from the single men at the church because he doesn't think any of them are good enough for her. He's damn picky, if you ask me.

"I have a better idea. Why don't you put the kitchen stuff away, and I'll finish this?" I grin, knowing there isn't any way he's going to refuse that offer. He loves being in the kitchen. That's probably why I didn't lose so much weight while I was recovering—he's a good cook and really took care of me. I owe him more than I'll ever be able to repay.

"I'm out of here." He gets to his feet. "I'll rustle something up once everything is sorted," he says, running out of the living room.

I smile and drop to the floor to finish putting together the coffee table—the last piece of furniture in the room.

I'm proud of how everything is coming together. I hope that when I bring Sabrina here in two days, she'll think so too and want to stay with me.

"So, Casanova, how exactly do you plan on getting your lady on the plane?" Dante points the sauce spoon at me, then goes back to stirring.

The thought of his mother's amazing sauce makes my mouth water. Francesca's best friend was Italian, and she taught her to cook real Italian food. After she died, she did the same with each of Francesca's sons, so Dante cooks like a purebred Italian.

He glances back at me, reminding me that he's waiting for answers I haven't even thought about yet. I'd planned on walking up to her and asking if we could talk. Then, I was going to take her to the airport. It hadn't occurred to me that she would refuse.

"You don't have a plan, huh?"

"She won't refuse," I say with more confidence than I feel.

"I'm not saying she's going to refuse. I'm just suggesting you have a backup plan."

I wish I'd never told him about my plans.

"You're damn lucky you don't have woman troubles," I mumble.

He laughs. "I may be a priest, but I can tell you that my problems with women are far from over."

"You're not celibate?" I blurt out in confusion. He's a priest. What the hell is he admitting?

"I can still have women problems even though I'm a man of the cloth." He rolls his eyes. "Mass tends to be more like bumper cars at a carnival. As soon as Mass is over, I'm dodging all the young women. They're like a flock of birds."

I grin at his blush. "So, do young Catholic girls have crushes on you?"

"Crushing? What, are we ten?"

"They're crushing on you. This is the most fun I've

had in a while. I need more details. How young are we talking?"

"How the heck would I know?"

Hmmm, I bet he has an idea.

"You might be a priest, but you're not dead yet."

"The youngest is probably in their early twenties, and the oldest is around ninety. Happy now?" he asks, tipping pasta into bowls.

"Not really. Are you sure you're a priest?"

He growls.

"Okay, you really are. I was there." I smile. "You know, until I met Sabrina, I'd been celibate almost as long as you have."

"Yours wasn't exactly by choice."

"Maybe not, but nonetheless, it's a fact. I can't imagine giving up sex willingly."

"Can we talk about something else?" he asks, shoving a bowl under my nose as he joins me at the kitchen table.

"Like what?"

He doesn't answer, but instead starts eating. I suggest, "Tell me why you don't want Emelia to visit you. She's your sister, so no one will say anything about a priest and a young girl."

"Now you're giving me heartburn." He pushes his bowl away. "Emelia is going to want to get out and visit the surrounding areas. She's also suggested that we go camping. People will talk regardless of whether she's my sister. I don't want them to hurt her. Plus, the women who are driving me crazy might not be too friendly toward her. I think she's lonely and could use some friends. Visiting me isn't the best option for her. I suggested she go to Lexington and stay with Eric for a while." He wipes his hand down his face. "She won't listen. She wants to come and stay with me."

There's more to this than he's telling me.

"I thought you were hungry." He glances at my bowl, which is still filled with food.

"I'll figure you out. I like puzzles."

"You don't want to work it out. Please leave it."

I watch him get up and start cleaning the stove, then wash the dishes.

There's a story there, but I have enough in my own life to sort out without interfering with Dante's for now.

18

Sabrina

EVEN THOUGH TONIGHT'S FUNDRAISER IS GOING smoothly, I still have butterflies in my stomach. My mom thinks I'm silly for looking forward to seeing Lucien again. But I'm nervous about seeing him, too. What if he comes back just to tell me that we're through but that he'll always be there for our child? I don't know much about Lucien, but I know he would never abandon our child. I just wish I knew if he'd walk away from me because of his fears.

Because he's been absent, I've been unable to watch the DVD of our baby, but I'm hoping that will change tonight. The envelope containing the DVD and photographs is securely tucked away in my evening purse. Now, all I need is Lucien.

As I look around the ballroom, I can't help but admire all the work we've done to make tonight a memorable evening for the city. The room is decorated with black and silver tablecloths, balloons, and flowers. Even the plates and dishes match. Many influential people with fat wallets are in attendance, and some have already donated large sums of money toward opening the hospital wing.

The men look handsome in their tuxedos, and the women look beautiful in their evening gowns—some long and elegant and others short and tacky. But there's a rare gem in the crowd—Sylvia. She's stunning in her plain black gown. Her blonde hair is tangled in a twist. The only sparkle is the silver necklace around her neck. She smiles as she dances with Ramon, and from his expression, I can tell he's noticed how amazing she looks.

"Sabrina." Michael says my name, distracting me from the dancing and his brother. "You look lovely." He kisses me on the cheek.

"Thank you."

"It looks like you ladies did an amazing job with tonight's event."

"That we did," Lily adds, hugging me before being wrapped in her husband's arms. "I think Michael should escort us both so the vultures don't descend on you. We don't want to piss Lucien off when he finally gets here."

Michael frowns down at Lily, who grins and shakes

her head at him. "Sabrina already knows Lucien is going to be here. Ruben told her."

"He has a big mouth."

"I agree. He also has a big heart," Rosie adds as she joins us. "He should be back soon. He picked Lucien up from the airport about thirty minutes ago."

My heart thumps in my chest.

"Will you two ladies let me talk to Sabrina for a minute?"

"We'll go flirt with the bartender. He's hot," Lily teases Michael.

"Rosie, please keep my wife out of mischief."

Rosie laughs as she drags Lily off, leaving me alone with Michael.

"Let's sit down." He directs me to the chairs beside us. "How do you feel about Lucien coming back specifically to talk to you?"

"Nervous." I shrug. "I'm not sure what you want me to say."

"Please don't hurt him, Sabrina."

"I—"

"Let me finish," he interrupts.

I nod.

"I know he hurt you with his words, but he's been hurting for a long time, and we all believe you're the only one who can help him. He needs you, Sabrina. All I ask is that you listen to him and not rule him out just because he let you go."

I place my hands over my stomach. "I love him, Michael. I've missed him so much over the past two weeks. I'm not going to play hard to get because I'm his. I have been since the minute we met. Yes, he hurt me badly. When I think about what he said, it hurts all over again. But at the end of the day, I don't want to live without him."

"You have a good heart," he says, smiling at Lily as she dances with Rosie on the dance floor. "I also need to thank you for listening to Lily. She missed having you around."

"I missed her as well."

"Would you like to dance?" Michael stands and offers me his hand. "Or do you need to rest?"

"Michael, I'm pregnant, not an invalid. Besides, I may be wearing an evening dress, but I have my well-worn red Chucks on my feet." I grin and lift the front of my dress to show him.

He leans close to my ear and whispers, "Don't tell anyone, but Lily has flip-flops on."

"My lips are sealed. Come on, take me for a spin around the dance floor before Gavin catches me alone."

He frowns as he takes me into his arms. "Gavin? I thought you liked him."

"I do. I just wish he'd stop asking me out. I don't want to give him false hope."

"You have a loving heart, Sabrina, and I'm glad you tied my brother in knots." He grinned and bent to my ear again, saying louder than necessary, "He's needed a good kick in the ass for years."

Then, I feel hands on my hips and freeze.

Lucien.

"I can take it from here, brother."

Michael laughs before grabbing Lily and pulling her into his arms, and Ruben does the same with Rosie.

I still haven't moved.

He brushes up against my back. "Look at me, Sabrina," he whispers, sending shivers down my spine.

I shake my head.

"Please, baby." He nibbles my earlobe.

As I start to turn toward him, he moves around until we're facing each other, his hands still on my hips. His eyes caress my face. When they travel down over my chest, I feel my nipples pucker into tight buds of arousal. His hands tighten slightly on me as my pulse quickens with desire.

"You're beautiful, Sabrina." One of his hands slides from my hip to caress my expanding belly. I feel as though I've jumped two sizes since I last saw him two weeks ago.

His hands are doing things to my body that I hope no one else can see.

"Please say something," he says. "At least give me something that tells me you don't hate me. I don't deserve anything, but I need…"

I cover his mouth with mine.

His hand slides into my loose hair and cradles the back of my head.

"Sabrina," he says, his voice full of hope. "I need you."

He kisses me.

Our tongues tangle. I pull him closer with my hands in his hair, and he pulls me flush against him. But it's frustrating having a larger stomach because I want to feel him against my throbbing core, but I can't.

I break the kiss in frustration.

"I want to feel you," I whisper desperately.

"God, Sabrina." He closes his eyes. "Let's dance before we give everyone a show."

He starts swaying me to the music, and I sigh with relief when I finally feel his erect penis against my stomach. I suppose I should be grateful that he's taller than me, otherwise this wouldn't be possible.

The throb between my legs is growing, but it's Lucien growling when I rub against him that makes my knees weak.

God, I've missed this man.

He still hasn't apologized.

"When can you leave?"

I raise my head from his chest and meet his gaze.

"I want to take you somewhere." He looks nervous. "I'll understand if you don't want to go anywhere with me, but please give me a chance to apologize properly. You deserve more than just an apology. You deserve so much more. I want to apologize in a way that leaves no doubt that I'm truly sorry. I want to explain what happened six years ago. Finally, if you still want me to, I'll open up to you."

He brings tears to my eyes. It wasn't easy for him to say that to me.

I rise up on my tiptoes, and before kissing him, I say, "I'll go anywhere with you, Lucien. You hurt me badly, but I missed you, and I never want to go through those two weeks again."

"So you'll come with me? No questions asked?"

I frowned, wondering what he meant and where he intended to take me. I assumed it would be his apartment, but maybe not.

"Yes. Why are you so nervous?"

"Because you could say no."

A tear slips free and he tracks it with his eyes, catching it with his thumb before it reaches my jaw.

"Take me with you now, Lucien. I can't be here when we need to talk, and I just need to be with you."

He briefly rests his forehead against mine.

"Let's go."

He wraps an arm around me and leads me away from the room, keeping me close to his side.

Lucien

As I lead Sabrina out of the ballroom, I feel over-whelmed. The relief I feel knowing that I haven't lost her is overwhelming. Now that I've accepted that she and our unborn child hold my heart in their hands, all I have to do is get through reliving the fire and the after-math and pray she's still with me at the end.

I open the door and help Sabrina outside. She shiv-ers, and this time, I'm sure it's from the fresh night air and not from my closeness. I quickly remove my dinner jacket and drape it over her shoulders, noticing her hard nipples pressing against the bodice of her dress. She's the sexiest woman alive and is playing hell with my intentions.

"Are you all right?" I ask, wrapping my arm around her shoulders to keep her close.

"I am now." She snuggles closer to me as we wait for the car I'd hired for tonight to be brought around.

I need her, but I won't make love to her until I've apologized. The only way I'll be able to give her the apology she deserves is when we get back to our home in Denver. I plan to tell her everything, so there won't be anything between us except our future together.

Over the past few weeks, I've given a lot of thought to my life before Sabrina, and I've come to the conclu-sion that I want to fight for the life hinted at while I was with her. I loved waking up with her in my arms every morning and falling asleep with her there.

I don't think I'll ever be able to tell her how sorry I am for the words that caused her to walk out my door. I never want to experience that pain again. That's why I decided to get her away from Lexington, so there would be no interruptions.

The car pulls up in front of us. Before the chauffeur can help Sabrina into the car, I open the door and help her in myself. Given how I'm feeling, I don't trust anyone else to touch her, no matter how innocent their touch may be.

I settle beside her, take her hand, and entwine our fingers, needing to maintain our physical contact.

I was surprised by the size of her stomach when I first walked into the room and saw her dancing with Michael. Our child has obviously grown while I was in Denver. When I took the chance to touch her, I was tempted to slide my hands around her to protectively rest over our child.

Once we're on the plane and up in the air, I intend to make her comfortable and keep my hands on her body. I'm not going to make love to her, even if it kills me. But I've missed her and her changing shape.

"What are you thinking about?" she asks with slight hesitation in her voice.

I bring her hand up, place a gentle kiss on it, and say, "I was thinking about you and our child. How much she's grown in the past two weeks. I was thinking about how much I want to put my hands on your stomach and feel our child. Most of all, I'm thinking that I'm the luckiest man in the world right now. I just hope…"

"You hope what? You can tell me anything, Lucien."

I take a deep breath and admit, "I just hope you'll still be with me after I've told you everything."

Sabrina turns in her seat and, cupping my face in her hands, brings me closer to her. "I intend to sleep in your arms tonight. When I wake up in the morning, I hope you'll still be there, feeling the hockey game going on in my stomach. No matter what you tell me or show me, I'll still be by your side." She gives me a quick kiss on the lips before sitting back and looking out the window.

For the first time in a long time, I feel positive, and I'm going to hold on to that feeling so it doesn't get clouded by my conscience.

"The airport." She turns to look at me. "What do you have planned, Mr. McKenzie?"

"I'm taking you home."

"Home," she whispers as I climb out of the car and run around to help her out.

At least she seems willing to come with me. In fact, she's walking faster than I am.

"What's the hurry?" I ask, tugging on her hand.

"I want your hands on me." She pulls me behind her until I pull myself together and follow her up the stairs of the company jet.

Sabrina stops at the entrance, covering her mouth with her hand.

I had given instructions that the main part of the cabin had to be clear when we first arrived. The last thing I want is an audience while I romance my woman.

Red rose petals cover the aisle down the middle of the plane. There are two glasses of fresh milk in champagne flutes. Ruben told me that Sabrina was drinking gallons of milk because of heartburn and refused to take anything from the doctor.

"Go ahead and take a seat." I follow close behind her as she sits in one of the plush leather seats on our plane. "We'll be taking off soon."

"I don't know what to say. You've done all this for me?"

I nod and take my jacket off her shoulders, replacing it with a soft, cream-colored knit blanket. "The heating will warm you up soon."

"I can't believe you'd go to all this trouble for me."

"I want you to feel special. I want you to know how special you are to me. I've let you down more than once. That has to end."

I offer her a wry smile. "I'm sorry for everything, Sabrina. I'm not sorry for getting you pregnant. Don't think for one minute that I only want you because you're carrying my child. I would have shown up at your doorstep later, but I would have been there begging for your forgiveness. You scared the hell out of me, but you're special to me. The baby is an added bonus, and from tonight on, this is going to be a new start for us." I brush the hair from her forehead. "That's all you're getting for now. It will probably be too late to talk when we get where I'm taking you, but you're sleeping with me, and we'll talk tomorrow."

"I don't know..."

"Don't say anything about what I just said. Sit back and enjoy the flight."

I quickly check that her seatbelt is fastened securely, as well as my own, as the engine comes to life. Within minutes, we're pulling away from the hangar.

She looks completely bewildered by everything. I've probably bulldozed my way back into her life without giving her time to think, but she's not leaving again. I'm tired of not accepting that what I want is right in front of me. I'm sick of being too scared to seize the moment, but that stops tonight. I'm not letting go. Within minutes, we're up in the air, at a safe height to unfasten our seatbelts. I unclip Sabrina's seat belt, take her hand, and help her up from the chair. With my hands on her face, I kiss her...and kiss her some more.

She's addictive. My passion for her is beyond anything I've ever experienced, and instead of frightening me, I relish it.

The swirl of her tongue around mine makes my cock so hard and ready that it isn't funny. I'm not changing my mind about no sex until we've spoken. But God, I've missed her taste, her touch, her mind, and most of all, I've just fucking missed her.

I break away from the kiss and sweep her up into my arms. Cradling her against me, I carry her into the bedroom at the back of the plane, whispering, "I need to lie down with you in my arms. Is that okay?"

She nods. "More than all right. But Lucien, I've always wanted to join the mile-high club."

What the fuck?

I stumble while placing her on the bed and fall next to her.

"You're testing my resolve not to love you until we've spoken."

"Lucien, I want to be naughty," she says, grinning sexily as she wanders her hand down to my aching cock and rubs it with her seeking fingers.

I exhale, remove my hand, and try to control the rising temperature in my blood as she writhes next to me—her arousal obvious.

Staying clothed will probably kill me, but I've been told that I have a will of steel. Well, I guess I'm about to put that to the test.

I roll off the bed and smirk at her when she pouts. "You're leaving me like this?"

"Hell no!"

I kneel at the foot of the bed and laugh when I see the red Chucks sticking out from beneath her dress.

"Michael had the same reaction."

"I was expecting stilettos, but I'm glad you're wearing something comfortable."

"I can't walk in heels anymore. They wreck my back."

"I'm here to kiss any aches and pains away."

"Well, I have a major ache between my thighs right now."

I pulled each shoe off and let them drop to the floor. "Hmm, is that right?"

I caress up from her feet, past her calves and knees. She parts her legs as I feel them quiver beneath my touch. I plan on touching her everywhere, but right now, I'm headed for her belly. I need to see her stomach, unobstructed.

Kneeling between her legs, I watch her unclasp the halter from her neck and push it down past her breasts. Trying not to stare at her hard, standing-at-attention nipples, I climb onto the bed, pulling her dress off the rest of the way as I go. I turn back to the bed and catch my breath. She's lying on her back, spread open for me, completely naked.

The longer I stare, the more her smile slips away.

I yank off my tie and loosen the top buttons of my shirt. I drop back onto the bed, bringing her legs closer to me as I straddle them.

"Can I touch your stomach?"

She nods, tears shimmering in her eyes.

I slowly caress her belly with both hands, back and forth. I can't get enough of touching her. Our baby is snuggling inside her, right where my hands are. I'm in awe. After a few minutes, I tease her nipples before moving back over our baby. Then, using my thumb and finger, I pinch one of her plump globes.

She tries to arch her back, but she can't because I'm sitting across her legs and holding her still.

"You like that?"

"God, yes," she exclaims.

Keeping in mind that I can't drop my full weight on top of her, I lean forward and lick and suck one nipple into my mouth while my hands continue to play with her other nipple.

"Ahhh, don't stop," she begs. "Lucien."

Her fingers slide through my hair, then tighten to hold me against her. I massage one nipple against the roof of my mouth with my tongue, then switch to the other while her hips push up from the bed.

"Why am I the only one naked and having fun?" she whines.

"I'd smack you on the ass after that question if I could reach it."

"Humph."

I start to laugh. "I didn't mean...never mind."

I place a kiss on her stomach, rear up, and grasp her hand, guiding it to my throbbing cock. "I'm having fun. But my dick is staying behind the zipper tonight."

She squeezes.

My eyes practically rolled back in my head before I knocked her hand away. "Enough of that."

I crawl down her body with licks and kisses, spreading her thighs again. Lying down between them, I kiss the top of her pussy.

"Oh God."

I chuckle.

Sabrina raises her head and rests on her elbows. "Did you just laugh at me?"

"I wouldn't dare. Now, lie back and let me taste you."

She smirks as she drops onto the bed. "You have a sexy bum."

Pausing, I repeat, "Bum?"

"You know, ass, or arse as the British say."

I'd forgotten that she had spent a long time working in England.

"Bum, though? Really?"

"You do. You are aware that there's a mirror behind you, right? I can see your butt rather nicely through it. If you were to strip, I'd be able to see straight between your legs to your balls, just as you can see my pussy. Your ass is nice and firm. One of these days, I wouldn't mind sinking my teeth into it."

"Fuck, woman."

"Yes, please."

Without further ado, I open her up with my fingers and shove my tongue straight inside her.

She drops onto the bed, finally silent—well, unless you count the moans and groans coming from her.

As I pull up to my home in the early hours of the morning, I watch a look of delight appear on Sabrina's face.

Dante had gone back to his place a few hours earlier and turned on the outside lights so that Sabrina would see the house looking like a Christmas card. A light sprinkling of snow earlier made it all the more perfect.

Sabrina turns to me and whispers, "I don't know what to say." She covers her mouth with her hand. "You have the most amazing house."

We have the most amazing house.

I don't correct her.

"There must be one heck of a view from those large windows." She points to the floor-to-ceiling windows to the right of the house.

"There is. You'll see it in the morning." Smiling at her enthusiasm, I add, "Our bedroom is above those windows, and we have a balcony directly outside." I refrain from mentioning that it will be nice to sit out there with a glass of wine during the summer.

We're going to freeze if we stay in the car any longer, so I climb out and run around to open the door for

Sabrina. I take her hand and help her out of the car, thanking God that she's wearing Chucks instead of heels in the snow.

"I can't wait to see the inside," she says. Her head moves around, trying to take it all in at once. "Oh, wow! You have a huge Christmas tree in your driveway."

I laugh.

The driveway is long from the road, but once you arrive at the house, it's circular, with the tree in the middle.

"Come on. Let's get inside before we freeze to death."

"Okay."

I wrap my arm around her, telling myself it's so she doesn't slip. It does have something to do with it, but I just want to keep her close.

19

Sabrina

I WOKE UP TO SUNLIGHT BLAZING THROUGH THE BLINDS. I stretched my lethargic body and ended up kicking Lucien with the heel of my foot.

I hear him grunt and try to turn over, but he stops me by putting his hands on my hips. "Go back to sleep, babe."

I wiggle back against him, smiling when I come up against his hardened length twitching against my bottom.

"I'm wide awake, just like something else is."

"That's always wide awake when I'm with you." He chuckles. "In fact, it's awake when I'm not, with you on my mind."

"Mmm." I wiggle again, and with a hiss, his arm wraps around my hips, holding me against him.

"Sabrina," he whispers in my ear, warning me. But after the two orgasms he gave me on the plane last night, I'm desperate to feel his cock slide inside me.

"Lucien, I'm throbbing for you," I moan.

His arm tightens slightly.

"I want you to know everything before I make love to you."

"Then tell me."

"Not while we're in bed. This evening, after dinner. Please, just be patient with me a little while longer."

He's frustrating the hell out of me, but I understand where he's coming from.

That doesn't mean I can't play. After all, he must be extremely frustrated with a permanent erection. He was rock hard last night after having his hands and mouth all over me, so it's only fair that I return the favor. If he'll let me, that is.

Reaching behind me, I slide my hand over his hip and squeeze his firm ass.

He hisses between his teeth, his cock rubbing between the crease of my bottom.

"Please don't stop me from touching you," I beg, knowing he's probably two seconds away from grabbing my hand.

I slide my hand to the front of him, slowly wrapping my fingers around his erection. He groans in pleasure.

My thumb rubs the crown, coming away coated with his excitement.

Feeling wicked, I turn my head to meet his gaze over my shoulder. I bring my hand up to my face, suck my thumb into my mouth, and watch his eyes darken with lust.

Returning to his pulsing cock, I wiggle my bottom away slightly, push him down, and then wiggle back against him. His cock is now nestled between my thighs from behind.

I move my hand to the front and take his hand, which is still holding my hips in place, and bring it up to my breasts. Then, I reach down to massage the part of him that's against my pussy.

With him in this position, he stimulates me, covering me from my ass to my front with his length. I bite back a moan as his throbbing sends tremors through my body.

I rub him with my fingers and he starts a slow back-and-forth motion, causing us both to moan.

"You feel good," I whisper.

"You've just stolen my line."

"Mmm, God, do that again," I moan.

He'd just pinched my nipple and does as I ask, sending desire straight to my core, which starts to clench.

"Lucien...please."

He kisses my shoulder as his hand slips over my hip and covers mine on his cock.

"Move your hand, babe."

I do, placing my hand on top of his, and my eyes roll back in my head.

He's pushing his dick against me, but it's the finger he's slipped inside me that's making my eyes roll back.

His breathing has become as choppy as mine as he thrusts behind me. The head of his penis rubs against my clitoris with each thrust.

"Oh God," I moan. "I wanted you to come this time."

"I will. I'm right there with you. Let go and come all over me."

His fingers and cock aren't the only things stimulating me. His hand is also rubbing himself off, which is arousing as hell. With my hand still on his, I can feel him touching himself, which causes my stomach to start contracting and my pussy to quiver. Then, he slips his other arm between us and starts pulling and twisting my nipple.

"Ahhh..."

I'm coming. Oh God, it feels good! Lucien doesn't let up as my climax takes over my body. Intense pleasure befuddles my brain as our baby somersaults in my stomach. But I want him to come with me.

I move my hand from covering his and wrap my fingers around the head of his penis, squeezing with my thumb and rubbing the slit on the tip.

"Fuck," he curses as bursts of white heat coat my fingers, hand, and thighs. "Jesus." He sags behind me.

"You came with me."

He kisses my shoulder.

"I did. Let me go get a cloth to clean you up."

After kissing my shoulder one last time, he slips from between my thighs and heads toward the bathroom.

I watch him go, admiring his strong thighs and solid butt, mostly covered by the bottom of his T-shirt.

Hopefully, after we talk tonight, he will stop wearing his T-shirts to bed.

"Sabrina, please stop fidgeting."

"I'm not fidgeting." He smirks.

"Okay, I'm fidgeting a little bit. I've never had lunch with a priest before."

He rolls his eyes. "Dante is a priest, but he's also my cousin, and he's a great guy. The only reason the house is in this condition is because Dante has been helping me furnish the place these past couple of weeks."

Is the house the way it is because of me?

I open my mouth to ask, but he beats me to it. "Yes," he says, answering the question I was about to ask. "I've owned this place for years, and although it's always had the basics—a bed, a sofa, and a television—it's lacked everything else. I wanted you to fall in love with this house, so maybe you could see yourself living here with me."

He shrugs as though it's no big deal, but it is, and he's trying to hide behind nonchalance.

Ignoring the fact that we're in a public restaurant waiting for Dante to join us, I take his face in my hands and make him look at me. "You did all that for me? Yes or no?"

His eyes burn into mine. "Yes."

My eyes fill with tears. "Don't you realize that I'd sleep on the floor if it meant spending my life with you?" I kiss him and rest my forehead against his. "Thank you," I say, smiling. "Thank you for everything. Your house is beautiful inside and out, just like you."

I silence his protests with my lips. It was corny, but I couldn't resist, and I mean every word. He is a beautiful man, and I'm finally starting to realize that he is truly mine.

He wants to live here with me. Moving nearly all the way across the country is frightening, but with him by my side, everything will be perfect.

We hear a throat being cleared and look to our left. I watch as a smile breaks out on the priest's face.

I hold out my hand and introduce myself, "Dante, I assume? I'm Sabrina."

Taking my hand, Dante engulfs it in his and grins. "Pleasure to meet you, Sabrina. Pity I didn't meet you seven years ago."

"Yes, well, you didn't, so stop flirting with my woman before you give that getup a bad name," Lucien grumbles.

Dante's grin widens as he looks as if he's about to respond, but he's interrupted.

"What can I get you, Father?" the server asks, silencing him.

"Water is fine." He looks at us. "Have you two ordered?"

"No, but we can now if you know what you're having," Lucien tells him.

"Surprise me. Something with chicken," he says, passing the menu back to the server.

"Are you okay with chicken?" Lucien asks me.

"I'm fine, but I'd like a chicken salad, please."

After Lucien orders, the server leaves us alone.

Dante is a handsome man, though I'm not paying much attention. His dark hair is windblown, and his five-o'clock shadow gives him a bad-boy look. It's a pity he's a priest because he wouldn't have a problem getting any woman he wants to drop her panties. Even dressed as he is in a black shirt and white collar, women are passing sly glances his way. Some are even directed toward Lucien.

My hand tightens in his as I glare at one woman in particular.

"Hey, what's gotten your panties in a twist?" Lucien asks, following my gaze with Dante.

"My panties aren't in a twist."

Dante laughs.

"So, I have to ask, what do you think of the house?"

"It's beautiful." I smile at Lucien, then turn back to Dante. "I believe you had something to do with it."

"Hey, it was all Lucien. All I did was get under his feet and cook."

"Dante loves to cook, and I'm afraid he's stocked the kitchen with every pot, utensil, and dish he could find."

"There's nothing wrong with having a well-stocked kitchen. It's better to have full cupboards. When I come to visit, I'll have everything I need to cook for you both." He grinned as our food was placed in front of us.

"Oh, this looks good," I say, my stomach rumbling. "I think, by the sound of that, our child is hungry as well." I waggle my brows at Lucien.

"She's a McKenzie and needs feeding regularly," Lucien says with a smug smile on his beautiful lips.

Chuckling, I counter, "*He's* a McKenzie and needs feeding regularly."

I collect a large portion of salad on my fork and shovel it into my mouth. I sigh when the flavor bursts on my tongue.

Dante chuckles. "Well, whatever the sex of your child is, he or she is going to be healthy with all that salad you're eating."

"I love food, but I can't eat a big lunch or I'll sleep all afternoon. I want to make lasagna for dinner."

"That sounds good."

"You're not eating with us tonight," Lucien points out to Dante. "I plan on talking to Sabrina this evening, and we could do without an audience."

"I was only teasing. I'm picking Eric up at the airport later. He's coming out for a few days. We'll hike, fish, and maybe camp out."

"I met Eric in Lexington. I lived with him and Ramon for a couple of weeks. He's a great guy, but he gets grouchy when you drag him from shop to shop trying to find maternity clothes." I smile, remembering his face when I told him I needed bras. "He threatened to leave me when I wanted to go into a lingerie store, so I went back the next day alone."

Lucien chokes on his chicken and scowls at me.

I nudge him with my shoulder. "Notice I said I went back alone." I kiss his cheek.

"I never thought I'd see the day, and I'm glad I have." Dante gets up from the table, takes my hand, and places a kiss on it before meeting my gaze. "Take care of him."

"I will. He's not getting rid of me this time."

"Good." He releases my hand and looks at Lucien, who has gotten to his feet. They embrace in a manly hug. "You've got this," he whispers to Lucien.

Lucien replies, "I have," and I can hear the emotion in his voice.

As we watch Dante leave, I realize that we aren't the only ones watching. The eyes of every woman—and a few married ones—follow him as well. Lucien shakes his head. "He always attracts attention. Wherever we go. It's as though they can't believe he's actually a priest."

"How long has he been a priest?"

"Fully? About six years. Something happened—I don't know what—but one minute he was happy and planning to open a restaurant, and the next, he was selling the restaurant and joining the priesthood. I've never been able to get him to tell me what happened. Every once in a while, I get the feeling he regrets his decision, but I don't really know because it's the one subject that is off-limits between us."

"Is he a good priest?"

"He is. The church was a disaster when he was appointed there, but he turned it around and now gets a full house every Sunday. There are a few ladies who like to follow him with their eyes, which scares him."

"I'm not surprised. He's cute," I say, putting the last bit of salad in my mouth while feeling Lucien's eyes on me. "Okay, he's not that cute. Happy now?"

"Hmm."

"I'm tired." I lean back and rub my stomach. "I didn't want to sleep this afternoon, but I'm struggling to keep my eyes open."

"Okay. Let me get the bill, and then we can go home." Lucien waves to the server and pulls out his wallet, but I'm barely aware of it. All I can think about is home.

"Home." I whisper, watching his eyes darken with desire. "I really like the sound of that."

"So do I." He leans toward me and kisses my waiting lips. Pulling away, he whispers, "You are so beautiful, Sabrina."

He prevents me from answering by placing his fingers over my lips.

"Don't say anything. Let's go so you can get some sleep."

He wraps an arm around my waist and practically hauls me out of my seat, much to the amusement of our server.

"Have a good afternoon," she says, turning her back—but not before I see the grin on her face.

Returning to my conversation with Lucien, I say, "Please don't let me sleep too long. I'm craving lasagna for dinner."

"I won't, babe." He smiles and kisses the top of my head.

Lucien

Tonight, I impressed both Sabrina and myself with my cooking skills.

When Dante had remodeled the kitchen, he had also

stocked it with easy-to-follow cookbooks. Not wanting to wake Sabrina, I looked up lasagna and followed the instructions in one of the books to a T, and the end result was delicious. Considering Sabrina is on her second piece, I'd say she's enjoying it as well.

"I can't believe you made this for me. You always said you could only cook toast." She grinned.

"Dante has wanted to give me cooking lessons for as long as I can remember. So, when I gave him free rein to organize the kitchen, he made sure I had a shelf full of cooking tutorials."

"I think I need to thank him the next time I see him."

No way!

"Let's keep him in suspense."

She stops eating and laughs.

"He's more like a brother than a cousin to you, isn't he?"

She always manages to figure me out.

"I stayed with him after the fire." I pause, not wanting to say her name out loud. But it's going to be unavoidable tonight. "After Alyssa walked away."

Sabrina pauses and, letting her cutlery drop to her now-empty plate, says, "You can mention her name, Lucien, but don't expect me to not have evil thoughts about what I'd love to say to her if I ever see her."

Her outburst surprises me. I know she's as possessive of me as I am of her, but hearing her speak like a mama bear protecting her cubs silences me.

Soon, I'm going to tell her everything about the fire and show her my back. She's seen my groin, hip, and buttock, as well as the slight scarring on my thigh, but I've never given her the opportunity to really look. It's going to be different tonight because my arm and back took the brunt of the fire. The sight of it still makes me want to hurl.

"Hey, where'd you go?" Sabrina asks, bringing me back to her.

"Sorry." I shrug, deciding to start by telling her how I intend to move forward. "I was thinking about our talk later and showing you the damage to my body. It makes me sick whenever I catch a glimpse of it in the mirror, so—"

"Are you afraid that I'm going to react the same way, or worse?"

I nod.

She stands up from her place at the table, and I push my chair away so she can straddle me.

I smile at her. Because of our growing child, she can't get as close as I'd like, but as my hands settle on her bottom to keep her from falling off, I groan when she rubs my hardening cock.

"Will you stay still, please?"

"I love feeling you nestled against my pussy." She grins.

I throw my head back and close my eyes at the sight of her.

She's wearing a red wrap dress that barely contains her breasts. With her straddling me, the dress has fallen open, showing her smooth thighs. Knowing that only my pants and her panties are between me and what I want is driving me crazy, causing my dick to throb with need as she wiggles around on top of me.

"After you've told me everything. I want you to sit naked as the day you were born on this chair. I want to feel your chest against mine as you bury your cock deep inside me. I need to be able to touch you everywhere and not just where you say."

Her words and the rotating of her hips make it difficult for me to breathe.

I pull her dress up at the back and work my way beneath, freezing when I feel her naked ass.

"Surprise."

"Oh God."

I grip her bottom tightly and pull her toward me. Rising up from the chair, I walk to the opposite end of the dining room and lay her out on top of the table.

Her nipples are ready to burst through her dress, so I lean over and free them before descending upon them with my mouth, sucking and licking them into tight peaks.

"I'm going to love watching you nurse our child."

"I like that idea."

I straighten up and open her dress, finding that I can't look anywhere but at my woman. Her breasts are now twice their original size, with dark, dusty nipples that are hard pinpoints of arousal. Moving down, my gaze caresses her stomach, which is also swollen because of her pregnancy, before moving to her trimmed pussy.

I lick my lips, nearly coming on the spot, as I watch her place her feet on the table and open her legs wide.

I drop to the floor, pull her legs over my shoulders, and slowly lick her. Back and forth, back and forth, all the while keeping her hips in place as she tries to wiggle away from my mouth.

She's panting and squirming, trying to close her legs, but I won't let up. I shove my tongue inside her, and she shatters.

Nothing tastes better than her release on my tongue.

Fuck!

I grab the base of my cock through my pants and squeeze, trying to ward off my own release. But I'm too late, and I come in my pants like a fucking teenager.

Still panting from my own pleasure, I bring Sabrina back to earth with my tongue.

Her legs are like jelly now, loose around my neck. I move her legs back down, stand, and gaze into her swimming eyes. I frown.

"I'm okay." I take her hand and pull her into a sitting position. "It's just that I want to feel you inside me."

Have I made her doubt my intentions by refusing to make love to her until we've talked?

That's the last thing I want.

I take hold of her dress and wrap it back around her. I kiss her on the nose. "Let's get cleaned up and talk."

"Okay... And Lucien? Don't worry. I'm here with you, no matter what you say or show me."

I nod, trying to accept her words, as I lift her into my arms and head for the stairs.

She snuggles into me. The closer I get to baring it all, the worse the pressure in my chest gets.

Maybe I'll feel nothing but relief once I've told her and she's still here with me, as Dante suggested.

I've never felt more vulnerable.

20

Sabrina

I WISH I KNEW WHAT TO DO FOR LUCIEN. HE SETTLED ME on a large, thick rug in front of the fire and now he's pacing back and forth.

He is my everything, and I wish he could believe that I won't leave him because of his past, which includes a scarred back.

He turns to pace again, and I can't watch him anymore.

"Lucien, please." He stops and looks at me startled, as though he thought he was alone. "If you don't want me to come over there, you need to come sit with me and tell me everything. Now."

I hope that was firm enough.

After a slight hesitation, he moves toward me and sits opposite.

"Thank you," I say, reaching out to touch his knee. "I know this is difficult for you, but I promise you'll feel better once you've told me. It'll be off your chest, and it won't be between us anymore."

I settle back against the large throw cushions he propped me up with and watch him stare into the fire. "Does the fire bother you?"

"No," he says with a wry smile. "It used to. For a while, I couldn't see fire of any kind without having flashbacks. I can't say I'm over it. Otherwise, I wouldn't have such a hard time talking to you about it. But I've learned to live with it."

"Okay. Tell me your story, Lucien."

He continues to gaze into the fire while I watch him. I want to hold him and wrap my arms around his shoulders, but I stay where I am and wait.

I don't have to wait long.

"I was driving from my parents' place when the truck in front of me ran a stop sign and hit a car that had the right of way. The truck pushed the car toward the embankment, and it went over. I pulled off the road and called emergency services while the driver of the truck climbed out of his cab. Seeing that he was okay, I made my way to the embankment. I smelled alcohol as I ran past him. I froze, turned to look at him, and saw the moment he realized I knew. I didn't stop. I made my way down to the car that had gone over the embankment.

"There was smoke, but no fire, when I reached the car. I discovered that a woman and a child were trapped inside. The woman's window was already down, so I managed to unclip her and drag her to safety, even though she was unconscious."

He glanced at me before continuing, "I had to crawl back into the car to get Samantha because her foot had gotten stuck between the seat and the side of the car during the rolling of the car. It didn't take me long to free her. As I was trying to get her out of the car, I saw the front of the vehicle ignite." He rakes his hands through his hair, and silent tears track down my face at the anguish I hear in his voice.

"I knew we had to get out of there fast. I pushed her through the open window, and as I was pulling myself out, my T-shirt caught fire. I managed to free myself from the car. I picked Samantha up and threw her as far as I could. I threw her away, Christ. For years, every time I closed my eyes, I could hear her cries as she landed hard on the ground."

I can't stay put any longer. I crawl between his legs, wrap my arms around his neck, and hold on tight to him. "You saved her life by doing that. You have to know that?"

He eventually nods. "Let me get this out."

I sit where I was and wait for him to get his emotions under control so he can continue.

"Before," he hesitates. "I could take off my shirt, but the whole thing was on fire. The pain, the smell... Unfortunately, I remember everything until I was shoved to the ground. Thankfully, I lost consciousness after that. I was in and out of it for days." He sighs and finally meets my gaze. "I'm not going to bore you with my treatments. You know what Alyssa said to me. When I was finally given the all clear to travel, with Michael's help, I made it to Colorado and Dante. I spent two years out here. First, I stayed at his cabin because he'd just started his appointment at the church where he still works. Later, I moved here. I fell in love with the mountains. It was like home, but I had my own privacy. I owe Dante everything, Sabrina. He saved me."

My tears are falling uncontrollably now, and I lean into Lucien as he moves to my side and wipes them away with his thumb.

"Samantha and her mom, were they okay?"

"Samantha suffered a broken ankle, and her mom suffered a concussion."

"Sabrina, please don't cry. I don't want you to feel sorry for me."

"I can't help how I feel. I wish we had been together back then. You would have had me to help you. Things would have been so different these past six years."

He kisses me, lingering over my lips. "You have no idea how much I want you."

I rake my fingers through his hair, gently tugging him back to me. "You have one more thing to do. Then, you can put your past behind you. You'll be able to look forward to the future with me and our baby. I'm not going anywhere. If you suggest otherwise, I'll cause you serious bodily harm."

A slight smile appears on his handsome face as he holds my gaze. He nods in acceptance.

Settling back on his haunches, he closes his eyes and quickly removes his T-shirt, tossing it away.

As much as I want to look at his chest and touch him, I keep my eyes on his face and wait for him to look back at me. When he finally does, he takes a deep breath, but his mouth remains tight with stress.

I need to look at him so he can relax because I hate seeing him like this.

Very slowly, I move toward him, spreading his legs as I crawl between them. Bending over, I kiss his belly button while caressing his abs with my fingers. I leave a wet trail upward, meeting his eyes as I swirl my tongue around each of his nipples in turn.

A shudder runs through him at my touch. Without moving my mouth from his chest, I reach toward my hips where his hands rest and intertwine my fingers with his. I'm ready to explore him, but first, I want to make sure he's ready.

Pulling away, I hover over his lips. "It's only me, Lucien. Please trust me."

After a few heartbeats, he whispers, "I do trust you."

I realize he's telling me the truth, and it gives me the courage I'm looking for.

I know in my heart that I will never walk away from him because of his scars, but I'm still nervous that I'll burst into tears when I see them and he'll misunderstand and think that I find him repulsive. He could never repulse me. I love him.

Settling back, I look at our joined hands and slowly start moving up the scarred skin of his arm. I'm guessing this isn't as bad as his back, but it's still pretty bad.

Most of the skin on his arm is scarred. Starting at the puckered skin on his wrist, I trace my way up to the ugly ones on his bicep that reach up his arm and over his shoulder. I'm positive they probably go down his back as well. I glance at Lucien, who is staring at my hands on him but won't meet my eyes.

He's ashamed that I'm seeing him like this.

I lean forward, tracing some of the scars with my lips. I feel his other hand tighten on me the further up his arm I travel with my tongue.

"You don't need to do that," he growls, trying to pull his arm free. I'm not letting go.

"Kissing you like this is the only way I can think of to prove to you that I accept you the way you are."

His eyes stay on me, but he doesn't say anything else as I continue kissing him. The closer I get to his shoulder, the more nervous I become. I wonder how badly his back was injured and hope the sight won't cause me to give in to the tears I feel behind my eyes.

Lucien is in control of everything in his life except for what happened to him. Now, for me, he's made himself vulnerable. I can't fall to pieces on him now.

Climbing over his outstretched leg, I move around behind him, feeling him tense under my hands and hearing his breathing turn shallow.

Without removing my hands from his skin, I settle behind him before looking.

I thought I was prepared. I wasn't.

My hand trembles on his shoulder when I feel his hand enclose mine.

"Let me grab my shirt."

What?

I quickly slide my legs onto either side of his and tell him, "Don't you dare." Then, more softly, I add, "Please don't hide from me now, Lucien."

His entire back is covered, and I'm not sure where to touch first.

"Will I cause you pain if I touch you?"

"No, I can't feel most of my side, but I can feel the rest in degrees, depending on where you touch. But you don't need to do this."

"I know I don't need to," I whisper, tears sliding

down my face for the brave, vulnerable man sitting in front of me. "But I want to. You're just going to have to accept that I'm not going anywhere."

My hands shake as I reach out and gently trace the uneven skin and scars on his back. Some spots still look raw, even six years after the fire. Wanting to show him the same way I did with his arm, I lean forward and kiss the skin I can reach despite my stomach being in the way.

When I hear a whoosh of air escape his mouth, I know I've found a sensitive spot. I lick the area and feel him shudder.

Hmm.

I get up on my knees and kiss more of his back, even the really bad areas. Suddenly, I get the urge to hold him. I slip my arm beneath his and splay my fingers on his stomach, continuing to kiss him.

He can probably feel my silent tears on his back, but I don't care if he does anymore. At least I'm showing him how much I love him. This is the only way I can think of to show him how much I care about him.

He takes my hand from his stomach and holds it tightly without saying a word.

I slowly make my way back around to his side. When I look at him, Lucien avoids my gaze, but I see the sheen of tears on his lashes.

"I love you," I blurt out, throwing myself into his arms.

He has no choice but to hold me close. I climb into his lap and wrap my legs around his waist. It's a bit awkward, with my stomach in the way, but I manage to wrap my arms around his neck and hold on tight.

My tears are still flowing as I kiss his neck, his shoulders, and finally—after he wipes my face with his discarded T-shirt—his lips.

"I love you, Lucien. So much that I need more than a lifetime to tell you how much."

"But—"

I silence him with my lips.

"No buts. I know it's going to take time for you to feel completely comfortable taking off your shirt in front of me. But please, don't ever think you have to cover up for me. You don't. From now on, when we make love—unless it's a quickie in your office—I want you naked so I can feel you against me. I want to be able to touch your skin when you make me come."

Purposely pressing down where I felt his cock twitch, I start to rock on him.

His eyes darken with lust as he grabs my hips to keep me still. "Let me get this out before you distract me completely."

"Okay."

He cups my face in his hands and tells me the words I've wanted to hear, "I love you, Sabrina. From the minute I laid eyes on you, I knew you were going to be trouble."

I laugh.

"You've made me whole again, and I never want to live without you. No one has ever filled my heart the way you do, so I'm not going to let you go."

He pulls me close and kisses me sweetly on the lips.

"I suppose you're not going to let me get a fresh T-shirt?"

"You suppose correctly...at least for now."

I sit back on his legs and untie my black wrap dress. I discovered that they're the most comfortable to wear while pregnant, so I purchased the same dress in multiple colors. I had discarded the red one in the laundry after dinner. I let the dress fall around me, knowing I need to distract Lucien from what he revealed and lighten the mood so he won't feel uncomfortable again. However, I'm not sure he'll be able to relax until he has his T-shirt back on. Perhaps showing him that I find him attractive while he's naked will make him feel more comfortable around me.

Lucien caresses me with his eyes and says, "I don't think I've ever seen a more beautiful woman."

I melt.

He caresses both my breasts with his large hands, giving me pleasure. His naked torso begs for my attention because I've been deprived of it until now.

Wiggling out of his grasp, I grin and demand, "I want you naked."

He raises an eyebrow questioningly, but quickly shucks the rest of his clothes. I scoot back against the pillows and pat the space between my legs. "Sit right here with your back to me."

I've surprised him. Good!

"I'm waiting."

"I don't think—"

"Don't think. Just do as I ask."

"Such a demanding little thing, aren't you?"

I stay silent while I watch him debate with himself.

A minute later, he slowly sits back down between my thighs, scooting back until my belly touches his back.

"This is going to be very frustrating for me. I wanted to feel you against my breasts. Never mind. I'll improvise."

I kiss his back and press as close to him as I can. Reaching around to the front, I stroke the length of his impressive erection and his balls, which I can barely reach.

"Sabrina," he growls. "You don't have to do this from there."

"Are you asking me to take my hands off your dick? Which, by the way, is hard and throbbing in my hands." I ask, squeezing his balls.

A hiss escapes his lips.

"I didn't think so."

I caress him a few more times, playing with his balls

at the same time, but I start to get uncomfortable in this position.

I rub the tip with my thumb, release him, and manage to maneuver myself around until I'm between his thighs.

"God, you're huge."

He starts laughing.

He grows before my eyes.

I wrap my fist around him, lean forward with my ass in the air, and suck him into my mouth. His hands tangle in my hair and tighten as his legs start to quiver. This big man beneath me is so ready to explode, all because of me. That makes me feel on top of the world.

"Ahhh, God, babe. No."

I freeze. "What?"

"The chair."

"The chair?"

He carries me into the dining room and sits down on one of the chairs. He pulls me in and has me straddle his lap.

Ah, the chair!

My eyes darken as he takes hold of his penis and pumps a few times.

"That's so hot."

"I know you like to watch me."

"I'd like it even better if you put that thing inside me. I want to feel its length caressing my insides. They're so wet from wanting you."

He groaned. "Stand up a bit."

I stand up, and my pussy clenches as his hands grip my hips and pull me over him. Then, he's there—big and hard at my entrance.

"Go slow. I don't want to hurt you."

I slowly slide down his length. Before I'm fully seated on him, I feel my climax begin. "Oh God, I'm coming."

Lucien pulls me down onto him, then lifts me off in an agonizing withdrawal and pulls me back down to his groin. He holds me as my orgasm continues to wash over me. It starts to ease, and then I feel Lucien lengthen inside me just before his cum starts to spurt against my inner walls, sending me into another state of bliss.

My baby tosses around in my stomach. I need to pee, but my orgasm won't stop. His long, thick shaft strokes me in a way that prolongs the pleasure. I've never felt that before.

He curses as his cock finally stops jerking and he rests his forehead against my shoulder.

My pussy is still quivering around him, but not as intensely as during my orgasm. Christ.

I wrap my arms around him, stroking his shoulders and the part of his back I can reach.

"That was...I don't know."

"Me either," I agree, understanding what he's trying to say.

Lucien

After our shower, I felt as though a weight had lifted as I got dressed. I was tempted to cover up when Sabrina suggested showering together, but I stopped myself.

Having a slippery Sabrina against my chest felt good, and feeling her hands on me while she washed me had given me another erection. I'm starting to understand that just thinking about her slick body bringing me to orgasm again is arousing.

"Hmmm," she said, squeezing me through my sweats. "I don't need to ask what you're thinking about."

"Someone's slick body in the shower," I tease.

"Mmm, you taste good."

I'm fully erect again. Fucking hell. I went six years without an erection, and since I met Sabrina, I can't keep it flaccid.

"Lucien," she says, and I glance at her, noticing the serious look on her face. Her brows are drawn, and she's pulling her lip between her teeth. "I need you to promise me something. No matter how you think I'll react, I want you to promise me that from this moment forward, you will talk to me. About anything and everything."

I need to show her, over time, how much our relationship means to me and how much I don't want to mess it up again. Dante will help me with part of this, but I guess the rest is up to me.

"Apart from my family, I've never thought about anyone that way before. That's why I said what I did after your scan." I take her face in my hands and hold her gaze. "I knew I was in the wrong, and I should have been with you. I wanted to be with you. I'd been looking forward to seeing our child again, but then Michael asked me to stay. He was a wreck, but I could have called someone else to stay with him so that I could get to you. I need you to believe me when I say that I love Lily only as a friend and sister. She was the first woman who didn't flinch when I offered her my hand, but we're only friends."

"I know. Lily told me, but it's nice to hear it from you. I do believe you. I couldn't help being jealous when it felt like you were choosing them over me."

"I'm sorry. You'll never know how much I wish I could take those words back. You and our child are part of my family now. You and this one in here come first," he said, pressing his hands against my belly. "Always."

"Thank you."

I wrap my arms around her, and she slips hers around my waist. She starts to slide her hands over my ass, which I think she has a crush on. She pauses when she finds the tag hanging out of my pocket.

Pulling it free, she moves away from me slightly and reads what I've written.

Sabrina,
With this ring, I'm giving you my heart.
Lucien

Tears swim in her eyes as she looks at me.

I kneel down, take her hand, and ask the most important question of my life, "Will you marry me?" My heart is in my throat.

I hold my breath, waiting for her answer.

Sabrina joins me on the floor. "Yes," she says, tears running down her cheeks. "I love you."

I pull her into my arms and whisper into her ear, "I love you, too."

"That was sneaky. Now put my ring on my finger."

I laugh. "Okay, bossy pants."

She snaps the tag from her ring and takes it from me. "I'm keeping this forever."

I kiss her briefly on the nose.

I slide the ring along her finger and tell her, "You're my one and only, Sabrina."

"And you are mine." She holds her hand out to admire her engagement ring.

The saleslady at the store tried to sell me a ring with a much larger cluster of diamonds, but as soon as I saw this ring, I knew it was for Sabrina. She has small hands, so anything else would look terrible. The ring I chose has a slightly larger diamond in the center of a cluster of smaller diamonds, all set in platinum. It looked stunning in the store, but even more so on her finger.

"It's beautiful. Thank you."

"Can I ask you something?" I hesitate, feeling unsure about taking her back to the scan I missed, but I need to know.

"Anything."

"Did you get the photographs and DVD from the doctor's office?"

"Oh, wow," she whispers, jumping to her feet and running toward the closet. "I was too excited to see you and too tired when we arrived to remember. I have them here."

She retrieves an envelope from her evening purse.

"I couldn't watch them. I needed us to be okay first."

The reminder of what I did to her makes me feel sick. But she won't allow it, and she kisses me. "Stop thinking about that. Let's go watch our baby."

She takes my hand, leading me out of the bedroom and downstairs into the living room.

"Here," she says, passing me the DVD. "You better sort that out."

I insert the disc into the correct slot, switch on the TV, and join Sabrina on the sofa.

"I wonder if we can tell what I'm having by watching this."

"We'll soon find out."

I pull her into my arms and take the photographs out of the envelope. After studying them for a few minutes, I pass them to her with a big grin. "You may want to look at these."

She takes them from me and gasps.

Then, the DVD starts playing.

EPILOGUE

Sabrina

I'M ON CLOUD NINE! I MUST BE, BECAUSE I'M LIVING MY dream. My dream involves a sexy, dark-haired man of Spanish-American descent with a hard, muscular body who only has eyes for me. Over the past three weeks, he has shown me through his actions how much he loves me and how devoted he is to our child and me. Our son.

Lucien was just as delighted as I was when he found out the sex of our child. Needless to say, the very next day, he bundled me up in his SUV and drove me into town to a large department store and the baby section. He bought so many things that he had to arrange to have them delivered. He also ordered twice as much of some items to have them delivered to our apartment in Kentucky.

I'm now twenty-five weeks pregnant. As my last trimester approaches, we both want to be settled in Lexington before the baby arrives. After careful consideration, we've decided that I'll give birth close to my mom and Lucien's family. When our son is a few months old, we'll officially move to our home in Denver. In two days, we'll be back in Lexington, which makes me nervous because, apart from Ramon and Dante, no one in our families knows that I'm now a McKenzie.

Five days ago, I became Mrs. Lucien McKenzie after a beautiful but short marriage ceremony performed by Dante in his church, with Ramon as best man. Lucien couldn't wait to make it official, so he arranged everything with Dante. He promised me that we'd celebrate with our families and that I'd get to wear a beautiful bridal dress and have lots of wedding photos taken with our families.

Honestly, none of that had crossed my mind until Lucien mentioned it. I just wanted to call him my husband.

Coming out of my daydream, I noticed Ramon with his hands on his hips, staring out toward the mountains, looking troubled.

He must be freezing out there in just a shirt.

"What's so interesting outside?" Lucien asked, coming up behind me and wrapping his arms around my waist.

"Ramon? Do you know what's wrong with him?"

"The trouble on the site is still happening. Although Eric has become friends with them, he thinks there is more going on than we realize. So, it's really a waiting game. But Eric has been called back to base for his medical assessment and PT, which puts us back at square one unless the contact Eric has can come in and help."

I turn in his arms and wrap my arms around him.

"I hope so, because Ramon looks like he has the world on his shoulders."

He's meeting the new guy in town tonight before flying back home. Let's hope this guy can go with him and figure out what's going on before someone else gets hurt."

Hurt?

"Has someone been hurt? Recently?"

He sighs. "Yeah. Craig, one of the joiners, had a fall. He's lucky he only broke a leg, considering he fell from a whole floor up."

"Oh, God. Do you think he was pushed?"

"If he was, he isn't saying."

"So, who's this guy Ramon's meeting?"

"I don't know. Eric set it all up. I'm not sure if Ramon knows anything either."

"Well, I hope you get it sorted out soon."

"Me too, babe."

Lucien

Holding Sabrina close and knowing that she really has my back is unlike any feeling I've ever had. For the first time in years, I feel free. I'm free to be myself without hiding.

Telling Sabrina about the fire wasn't as hard as I thought it would be, but taking off my T-shirt was.

I'm not sure if I'll ever be completely comfortable without it to hide behind. With Sabrina, though, I'm managing. Since that night, I've been tempted to reach for my shirt on more than one occasion, but Sabrina wouldn't allow it. On those nights, she'd hold me so tight that I never wanted her to let me go.

She really is the love of my life, and I can't describe what it's like knowing she's my wife. I was unsure whether she'd agree to marry me with only Ramon present, but she jumped at the chance. Nothing has given me as much pleasure as hearing her repeat, "Mrs. Lucien McKenzie." She only stopped when I sealed her lips with mine.

I smile, remembering what followed, as I bend and kiss the top of her head while we watch Ramon make his way toward the house.

Sabrina nudges me in the side.

I grin.

"Sabrina has something to ask you," I tell my brother as soon as he appears through the kitchen door.

She wanted me to ask him because she was shy about it. But I'm not letting her off that easily. Plus, I think my brother will love hearing it from Sabrina.

"You'll suffer," she mumbles to me.

"Well, this must be good." Ramon grins at our banter.

Sabrina releases her grip on me and walks over to Ramon, taking his hands in hers.

"You've become a good friend to me, Ramon. You're the only person I can think of to trust with our child if something happens to Lucien and me. Would you do us the honor of becoming our baby's godfather?"

Watching my brother struggle with his emotions at Sabrina's question makes my own heart flutter.

Ramon nods and pulls her into his arms. "I'd love to," he says loudly enough for us both to hear. Sabrina returns his hug and lets it last longer than I normally would. But what the hell. He looks as though he needs it.

Finally pulling away, Sabrina reaches up and kisses him on the cheek. "We're both here if you ever need us, Ramon." I hope you know that. You don't have to do anything alone."

"You're one in a million, Sabrina." He kisses her on the cheek before walking over to me.

"Take care of her and yourself." He held out his hand, which I took before pulling him into a proper hug.

"Take care of yourself. If you need anything, get in touch." We break apart. "I mean it, Ramon. Anything. You only have to ask."

He nods and says, "I'll see you both back in Lexington. Have a good night," and walks out of the room.

Sabrina is now back in my arms where she belongs.

I pick her up, place her on the kitchen island, and step between her spread legs. My hands automatically go to her stomach to cradle our child.

I bend my head and place a kiss right where our son kicks. "I love you, Buster," I whisper to him.

I raise my head to look at Sabrina and see the unshed tears in her eyes.

She threads her fingers through my hair.

"You're amazing, Lucien. Our baby is lucky to have you as his father."

I cradle her face in my hands and tell her with my heart in my eyes, "You've given me everything I've ever wanted, and I love you so damn much."

"I love you too. Always, Lucien."

I catch her tears with my thumbs and gently kiss her. But gentle isn't how Sabrina wants it. Her fingers grip my hair as she takes over the kiss. Her tongue slides against mine, and her legs wrap around my waist. Her feet dig into my ass, pulling her closer to my aching dick.

The talking is over for now, but the lovin' has just begun.

THE END

DEAR READER

Thank you for reading *Playing with Trouble,* and thank you for
your reviews! It's really appreciated.

Subscribe with your email to be alerted about new releases,
sales, and events.

www.lexibuchanan.com

LOVE STRYKER
MMA ROMANCE

When my childhood friend, Cora, dared me to write a sexy novel about a martial arts fighter, I agreed, albeit under the influence of alcohol. It was something for me—something different and exciting.

It was supposed to be research, pure and simple. But then I met him——a six-foot-six mountain of a man with no name. The way his muscles flexed and rippled when he trained made my belly quiver. The way his dark hair flopped over his forehead made me want to brush it back from his strong face. His nose had been broken, but it made no difference, he was still a handsome man. He had eyes dark as the night that would land on me the minute I entered his gym…Every…Time. He was their star fighter, the one that brought in the big money. At first I feared him because of his size and the way he would look at me. But then I discovered that I was his biggest distraction, and no matter what my head told me, my heart told me to fight for the man who didn't know how to live outside of the cage.

NYT & USA Today bestselling author Lexi Buchanan brings you her new sexy standalone novel about fighting for freedom when the odds are against you.

INDECENT VILLAIN

A DARK MAFIA ROMANCE

My parents descended into the ground while I stood
motionless and unresponsive to the penetrating
darkness that was Tiberius Beckett.

He moved into my home and I realized that the man had
two sides, and he showed me his true face. I liked him.
He became my obsession, as I became his. Together, we
did some bad things.

Do you want to know more about Tiberius Beckett?
Then let me tell you about my indecent villain.

Available Now!

Prologue

Kinsley

Fragile.

I feel like I'm going to fracture into a thousand pieces.

I stand silent and motionless beside my parents' graves, rain soaking me to the skin. The wind whistles around my body as I remain unresponsive to the penetrating darkness directed at me by Tiberius Beckett, my father's brother. The man stands tall in his dark suit, his piercing gaze seeming to search for something within me, as if he knows a secret I'm not even aware of. Despite the storm raging around us, his presence feels more unsettling than the howling wind.

My tears mix with the rain and flow down my cold cheeks. The priest speaks loudly and clearly, but his words blend as my mind refuses to comprehend them. I swallow hard as my mother's casket is lowered into the earth. Then that of my father follows. It is the end for them, and for me, too. Tiberius, at my father's request, has become my legal guardian. He doesn't want me, just as I do not want him. I tell myself I'll endure for the next two weeks until I turn eighteen. It's not long, but it feels like an eternity.

I pray that I survive the man with silver eyes.

But no one survives Tiberius Beckett.

Tiberius

Fragile.

Kinsley looks like the wind will blow her over any second. The girl does not trust me. She will. My fingers yearn to stretch across the space between us and take her in my arms. I am a hard man. But with Kinsley, my heart is fucking mush. She is my vulnerability. The girl has been in my head for a while now. It kills me to stand here and watch her suffer alone.

She is unaware of the danger she is in, just as she is unaware that my men are hidden around the cemetery to keep her safe. Me too. However, they know she is their priority. I can take care of myself, but Kinsley cannot. She needs me, even if she doesn't realize it yet.

The rain falls harder as my brother and his wife are now in the ground. Other mourners and the priest take their leave, while Kinsley and I remain. I stare at her. Kinsley lifts her face, her eyes finding mine. I don't look away, and neither does she. We stand there in silence as the rain soaks us both. In that moment, I know that I will do whatever it takes to keep the defiant young woman safe, even if it means revealing my true feelings.

Chapter One

Three days after the funeral, the rain continues to fall. The gardens have turned into fields of mud, and even the long driveway has puddles. My grand home looks gothic surrounded by the dark clouds and rain, but in the sun, it is beautiful. I've always found the house to be too spacious for our small family. The house once bustled with numerous servants, but that was before my time and before my father's as well. Grandfather used to tell me about the garden parties his mother hosted when he was six. Sadly, not long after that, there was a war. He said most of the servants left and took up arms for their country—mostly the men, but some of the women did too, I guess.

Sighing, I consider my predicament. Tiberius is a strange man and has the power to unnerve me. I think back to my younger years but can't really put my finger on when I started to feel that way. Maybe it had more to do with my father being unsettled around his brother than anything else. I must have picked up on his unease and let it affect me. However, Tiberius does nothing to help dispel those feelings around him. I think he enjoys it. I'm not like my father, though. I won't let the man push me around. I may have been showing weakness since my parents died, but no more. I'm not a little moth who needs nurturing. I'm nearly eighteen years old but feel older.

If I'm honest with myself, there is a slither of happiness within me that I will no longer be held prisoner in my home. My parents were afraid of something in the months leading to their deaths and had kept me home with a private tutor. I don't miss the city, but I do miss going into town, even if it is only for a cup of coffee while I watch the world go by. It's better than being locked up inside the Lake House.

I press a hand to my stomach, trying to quell the bundle of nerves that suddenly rises as I watch a large black car appear through the trees along the driveway. The wheels kick up muddy water as Tiberius brings the beast to a stop close to the front entrance. Another car, this one silver and sleek, pulls in beside the black one. The man has arrived, along with my parents' attorney.

Tiberius climbs from the driver's side of the car, while another man emerges from the passenger seat. They exchange words.

The attorney, Mr. Arnold Fielding, exits his car and runs for the front door. Tiberius takes one step and seems to be frozen to the spot. His head suddenly turns, and his gray eyes lift and find mine. Stunned, I gasp, but I refuse to look away first. My heart thumps heavily behind my breastbone. How did he know I was watching, and from where? He snaps his attention back to his passenger, a man in jeans and a tee. Unnerved, I head into the bathroom and splash cold water onto my face. I pat it dry with a fluffy towel. The mirror before me reflects my drawn expression. Dark circles are prominent beneath my eyes, the color matching my long hair.

A knock on my bedroom door draws my attention. I swallow hard, knowing there will be no escaping the next hour or so. Today is the reading of the will, followed by lunch with Tiberius. I am overjoyed.

Another knock.

"One moment," I shout.

I slide my feet into the shoes I kicked off earlier and take one last glance in the mirror. The dark color of my midi dress does nothing for my washed-out look. I open the door and catch the impatient look on the housekeeper's face.

"About time," Martha snaps before briskly turning away.

I roll my eyes and inhale, holding my breath for a few seconds before slowly exhaling. It helps center me when I know I am about to face danger. That is what Tiberius Beckett is to me—the devil himself.

And there he is.

His dark-gray eyes follow me as I move down the staircase, his body remaining still like a predator. I refuse to let him see the nerves that threaten to break me in his presence. He is the kind of man who, if you give him an inch, he will take a mile.

I come to a stop at the end of the stairs and hesitate. My father's office will be used for the reading of the will, and the thought of being locked behind closed doors with Tiberius and the attorney makes me want to run. Of course, I do nothing of the sort. I am an Elliot. I can do anything.

At that moment, Mr. Fielding appears.

"My dear, Kinsley," he says as he moves, taking my cold hands into his much larger and warmer ones. "I am sorry for your loss. Come and take a seat." He leads me into the office and sits me in a Queen Anne chair in front of the large window. The choice of seating arrangement surprises me, as the meeting table would have sufficed. Nevertheless, I accept the small cup of coffee he places in my hands.

"Thank you for your condolences. It is a very difficult time," I acknowledge, trying to act the way my mother would want me to—like a lady instead of a rebel. I lean forward and place the cup on the coffee table.

"Mr. Beckett," Mr. Fielding calls, "please take a seat beside your ward."

I cringe. I do not want to be his ward, nor do I want him sitting beside me. From his hesitation, I gather he doesn't want to sit beside me either. He takes the seat opposite, which is even worse. He won't miss anything now.

Mr. Fielding clears his throat and shoots an impatient glance toward the evil man. "Let's get started, then." He unbuttons his blazer and sits, a sheaf of papers in his hand. "Kinsley, you are aware that you are now the ward of Tiberius Beckett, at your father's request."

"For two weeks. Yes, I am aware."

My gaze lifts to the man in question. His hard face shows nothing of what he is thinking. Those dark eyes of his rove over me in a way that causes my heart to pound. The sneer on his cruel lips sets me on edge. As we are, it is the first time I have been close to the man. He looks younger than I first thought. Early thirties to what I previously labeled as early forties. His thick black hair curls over his ears. High cheekbones are marked by a scar across one of them. His rugged features give him a dangerous air, but there is a fleeting hint of vulnerability in his eyes. Have I misread them? The way they narrow on me, I think not. He hates that I've seen it. Despite his intimidating presence, I feel a flicker of curiosity about the man who now holds power over me.

A throat clears, which forces my gaze away from Tiberius. Mr. Fielding clears his throat once more. "The last will and testament is rather brief, I am afraid." He looks at me over the rim of his glasses perched on the end of his thin nose. "Your father wasn't one for time-wasting."

"Get on with it," Tiberius growls as his tattooed hands clench his thighs.

"It is a joint will with your mother." Mr. Fielding clears his throat again, which is becoming annoying.

"We hereby leave all our assets to our daughter, Kinsley Elliott. The house we also leave to our daughter—"

"What?" Tiberius questions in a quiet but deep voice as his attention snaps to the attorney. His eyes narrow. "He left the house to"—he turns and glares my way with hatred—"her?"

The papers shake in Mr. Fielding's trembling hands. "That is what he wrote."

"What is going on?" I ask, annoyed. Why would Tiberius be upset that my parents left our family home to me? It makes no sense. But then it makes no sense that I would be left as Tiberius's ward when the man had made my father nervous.

"You want to know the truth, little girl?" he sneers and stands. He shoves the coffee table out of the way and leans over me, his hands tightly gripping the arms of my chair. When he is so close that I can see silver mixed in with his dark-gray eyes, he says, "The house was supposed to be left to me. I had an agreement with your father." His eyes blaze with emotion. "I have your father's signature on the agreement between us."

I'm trying to concentrate as Tiberius is making a point, but all I can think about is the heady scent of his cologne. It seeps into my senses and gives me ideas I should not be having.

"You smell nice," I blurt.

His brows shoot up to his hairline as he tightens his jaw and takes his seat, his face on the lawyer. "The house is rightfully mine. I won't sit back and accept this," he scoffs. "Even in death, he's doing his upmost to fuck with me."

I place a trembling hand on my stomach while I fight to get my equilibrium back. His reaction confuses me. I don't want to draw attention to myself, but I must ask, "Why would you think you're entitled to this house?"

"Because," he grinds out, "the house belongs to the oldest living male relative. With Jude gone, that is now me. It's the way it has always been done."

"Why didn't I know about that?" I ask softly, feeling like my family betrayed me. "I don't understand my father. I have only ever seen you from a distance, but now I am your ward. Why?"

Tiberius frowns when his eyes land on me. "None of that matters now."

I force my gaze to the lawyer. "If Tiberius thought he was getting the house, then am I correct to assume my father made a previous will? What was in it?"

"That doesn't—"

"Tell her," Tiberius snaps.

Mr. Fielding takes a sip of the glass of water in front of him, and says, "In your father's previous will, he left the house to Tiberius Beckett and explained why. As Tiberius said, the eldest male descendant was to inherit the house."

"My father was Jude Elliott. How are you a Beckett?"

"That piece of paper in your hand will not stand up

in court when I have my lawyer file an objection." The man totally ignores me and speaks to Mr. Fielding.

A headache brews behind my temples, and I want to leave the room. I feel sorry for Mr. Fielding, who has done nothing but read my parents' wishes. Tiberius reminds me of a bull ready to charge. His nostrils flare, and his large body tightens with suppressed anger. He is a tall man who obviously takes good care of himself. The muscle he possesses is unable to hide behind the clothes he wears.

I sense the tension in the room escalating as Tiberius's anger becomes palpable. I need to diffuse the situation before it escalates further. My hands feel sweaty and my mouth is dry, but I have to say something to calm Tiberius down.

"I don't want the house. He can have it." I rush the words out and bring the two men to silence. In truth, the house is the only home I've ever known, but I always planned to leave when I turned eighteen.

"What?" Tiberius shakes his head. "What did you say?"

I swallow hard, and say, "You can have the house." I turn my gaze to Mr. Fielding. "You can arrange that, right?"

"Actually"—the older man sighs—"nothing can be done until you turn twenty-one."

Tiberius releases a string of curse words, some of which raise my eyebrows in shock. As difficult as it is to ignore his strong presence, I turn away from him and give my full attention to Mr. Fielding. I need to concentrate.

"I'm assuming there is a clause about selling the house."

"It states that you must live in the house until you turn twenty-one, after which time, you can leave and pass on ownership. However, your father stipulated that ownership could only be passed to Tiberius Beckett."

"Let me get this straight. My father left me the house, yes?" He nods. "But I have to continue living here until I turn twenty-one, at which point he expects me to hand the house over to him." I point toward the beast of a man.

"That is correct."

"Why didn't he just leave the house to him in the first place? This doesn't make any sense." I get my unsteady legs under me and stand. "What about college? How will I go if I must live here?"

"That detail we will discuss at another time," Tiberius says, calm once more. He takes out a piece of gum and moves it between his fingers. Is he trying to quit smoking?

"My father was afraid of you." It takes courage, but I manage to hold his gaze. "Why would he make me your ward?"

"I'm the only one who would have you."

"That's not quite—"

"Mr. Fielding," snaps Tiberius. "Thank you for your time this morning. I will bring my niece into your office next week to sign the documents you have for her." He ushers the lawyer from the room.

My refusal to join Tiberius for lunch has garnered his anger once more. The man takes my arm and drags me into the formal dining room, where he pushes me into a chair beside the one at the head of the table, which he takes.

"You need to eat." His large hands tighten around his cutlery. "You've lost weight since the last time I saw you."

In truth, I am hungry. The food in front of me looks more appetizing than anything Martha has prepared since my parents died.

"Hmm," I mutter as I straighten in the chair and start to eat. Tiberius watches me with a calculated look on his face as he continues eating.

The food is pleasant, which puts me at ease and leads me to ask, "Will you be moving in?"

He nods.

"Good. At least we'll get something edible."

He pauses with a fork of beef near his lips. "Explain

that comment." He places his knife and fork on the plate and sits back, his gaze unwavering.

"Since my parents died, the food hasn't been good." I sigh. "I'm not allowed in the kitchen to make my own, so it's no wonder that I've lost weight. I hate tuna, which Martha serves me on crackers for lunch daily."

"I shudder at the thought," he says. In his next breath, he shouts, "Martha!"

The woman who hates me comes dashing into the room. "Sir?"

My cheeks flush hotly, and I silently plead that he won't drop me in it with her. Tiberius narrows his eyes on my face, and his jaw twitches.

"I will be moving into the house later today, and I expect breakfast and dinner served in this room with my niece daily, unless otherwise stated. There will be no tuna and crackers." He pauses for a moment, holding her full attention. "There will also be no seafood put on the table. Ever."

Martha shoots me a look of hatred before she says, "Yes, sir."

"My niece is the owner of this house, which means she is your employer. If you value your position here, I suggest you treat her with respect. She needs to eat, not starve. Do I make myself clear?"

"Yes."

"Yes, what?"

"Yes, sir."

Tiberius snorts. "Go." He turns to me. "I have no clue what I am supposed to do with you."

"You could ignore me, and I will ignore you."

He grins, which surprises me. He has to be the most handsome man I've ever seen. "You're too pretty to be ignored, and I'm too big and loud." He frowns. "Others will be moving into the house with me. You need to stay out of their way." He points his fork in my direction. "They are dangerous men. I will only give you this warning once. You understand me?"

It's a good thing I've eaten all my food, as my appetite suddenly disappears. "I understand." My mind whirls, wondering who they are and why he has dangerous men living with him. My outlook is certainly looking better. Maybe I won't be bored anymore. Tiberius is a large man with an equally large personality.

As my eyes rove over his features, I realize I don't consider him my uncle. How could I when I've never known him? My curiosity about him is piqued, and while he seems slightly more approachable than he has been in the past, I decide to ask my questions.

"Are you married?"

His gray eyes shoot to mine. "No." He smirks. "Are you?"

"Considering I'm seventeen, I would have thought the answer to that question was obvious."

"If you ask me personal questions, then expect the

same in return." He grins, mirth dancing in his gaze. "What else do you want to know?"

"Why have we never actually met until now?" I sit back in the chair and try to appear relaxed. I certainly feel better than I did before. Maybe I just needed something proper to eat, or what I do not want to admit, company. I'm not sure how I feel about Tiberius. That's a lie. The man with silver eyes causes parts of my body to come alive. Butterflies flutter in my belly. Maybe it's the way he looks at me. I have his sole attention, and I want to keep it.

"There are things that your mother chose to keep from you. I need some time to decide whether or not I tell you what they are."

I watch him, my curiosity stronger than ever. "Would those things change anything?"

He sits forward with his hands on the table. He intertwines his fingers. "The secret Anna and Jude kept would change everything," he says in a deep voice, his eyes blazing. "One day, I may tell you."

I frown. If I'm not mistaken, I catch something within his gaze, as though he is scared to speak of it. I'm more determined than ever to discover what my parents kept from me.

"Not today?"

"Maybe not ever." He stands and tosses his napkin on his plate. "If I do tell you, just remember they are the ones who kept you in the dark." With that, he moves toward the large doorway. He pauses with his hand on the knob and glances over his shoulder. "I will be here from this evening."

"You!" Martha hisses the moment the large front door closes behind Tiberius.

To my horror, my legs tremble at the confrontation I know is seconds away. Martha has always been an evil woman. As soon as Tiberius spoke to her, I knew she would be on me the moment he left. And here she is.

"How dare you complain, you ungrateful little bitch!" Martha charges forward, and I stumble into the wall behind me. She follows and slaps me hard across the face.

Tears fill my eyes as I cradle my throbbing cheek, too stunned to react.

"You think it matters to me that you own this house?" she scoffs. "You know nothing." Her eyes glow with unleashed anger. "I would be careful of who I become friends with, Kinsley," she sneers. "Beckett is—"

I watch her closely as her mouth pulls tight. My heart pounds in my chest while I wonder how to break free of her hold. Martha has never laid a hand on me before, but now the woman before me is finally showing her true colors. I pull myself up to my full five-foot-five height and glare at the woman.

"Do not touch me again," I say, clear and precise. "Next time, I will fight back."

Her eyes narrow. "You are brave all of a sudden." She scowls and looks out of the window. "I may not like you, but if the rumors about Tiberius are true, then I fear for you." Her arm shoots out and holds me against the wall. She is stronger than she appears. "No more whispering into that man's ear about me, or you will be very sorry." With one last shove, she turns and leaves.

I gasp and give into the tears that have been threatening to fall throughout the whole confrontation. My cheek stings as I place it against the cold window and watch the dark clouds roll over the grounds. My stomach is in turmoil. I don't understand what is going on. The one fact that I do know is that I am the ward of Tiberius Beckett. Why him? I have no idea why my father did that. Although I do not trust Martha, her words have me concerned. What does she know about the man to fear for me?

Something else has become apparent. My father knew he was going to die. The changes to his will were completed three weeks before his death. The weight of my new responsibilities as Tiberius's ward settles heavily on my shoulders as I consider the implications of my father's foresight. The realization scares me.

Scared and out of my depth, I turn away from the

window. The grandeur of the dining room now seems suffocating, a stark reminder of the impending gloom that arises within me. The portrait of my father hanging on the wall seems to mock me with his knowing gaze, as if he has left behind secrets that I am now forced to uncover. The feeling of unease grows stronger, making me question everything I thought I knew about my family.

Somehow, I manage to pull myself together. I will not let Martha see how much her sharp words and slap across my face have affected me. The woman will not be working at the house for much longer if I have my way. Maybe Tiberius has his own staff that he can bring here. Anyone would be better than the bitter Martha Green.

Chapter Two

I tear off my suit and change into jeans and a tee. After fastening my biker boots, I release a frustrated growl. I don't know what the fuck to do about sweet, innocent Kinsley.

I glare out of my bedroom window, my gaze settling on the house across the lake. I open the door and step out onto the balcony. It's sparsely furnished, with just a table and two chairs, plus a comfortable chaise lounge chair. I've spent many summer nights asleep on it. The outdoors has always called to me, just like the Lake House has.

Memories always swamped me whenever I dropped in on Jude and his family. In recent years, my brother had become uneasy about those visits, which made me wonder what he might have been hiding.

As I rest on the balustrade and gaze out once more across the lake at the house, I wonder what Kinsley is up to. It's something I've wondered for a while now whenever my eyes caught on the house. Thoughts I should never have, even now. At first, it was innocent curiosity about the girl I knew my brother hadn't fathered. But over the past couple of years, I found myself unable to stay away. I've never been introduced to the girl until now. I made sure I always stopped by when I knew she wouldn't be home.

Kinsley grew up rather quickly and became a stunner. I shouldn't be obsessed with her. It's wrong. I know that what I'm feeling would be considered acceptable in the real world, if it weren't for the age difference. I'm not really her uncle. Never have been. Never will be. She doesn't know that yet.

One look at me covered in tattoos would disgust her. My brother never liked ink. Neither had my mother, which is why I have so many.

Kinsley doesn't remember, but when she was told about her parents' deaths, I showed up at the house. She was in shock, so I took charge of her. I held her while she stared into space. I held her some more when her tears finally came. I held her while she slept.

I should have stayed with her so she wasn't alone, but I was dealing with my own grief. Not only that, but I also had to deal with the cops and make arrangements for Jude and Anna. I took my grief and anger and went after the crew who had forced my brother's car off the road. His brakes had been cut, and as the crew chased after them, Jude wasn't able to slow down on the sharp bends of Snake Pass.

I saw the bodies and wish I hadn't. The only bit of luck that evening was that the car hadn't burst into flames.

One crew member was still at large. That was my fault. I lost it with the three my men and I had found. The last one died before he could give me a name. However, I did get one name from the other two. Cannon Edge.

That bastard would pay one day.

I turn my head at the sound of booted feet moving down the hallway outside my bedroom.

"Boss," Salem shouts, knocking on the door. "You in here?"

"Outside," I yell.

He strides out and comes to rest beside me, his gaze following mine. "Do you know what you're doing?"

"I don't have a fucking clue."

He snorts. "I haven't seen you this fucked up before."

I glare at my friend. "I'm not fucked up." My eyes

stray back to the Lake House. "Edge is going to come for Kinsley."

"He won't get her. Between you, me, and Jock, we've handpicked all the men who will be around the house. She will be safe."

"Tell the men they don't touch her. Make sure they know she's my family and I will personally kill anyone who causes her harm."

"Yes, boss," Salem drawls, mirth in his voice, which I ignore.

"Prick!"

"Edgar has the weasel in the basement. You wanted to talk to him."

"I want to do more than fucking talk," I snarl.

"Who is he?" I ask Edgar.

The man tied to the chair, with blood and sweat running down his face, is not familiar to me.

"Brinkley," Edgar growls. "I overheard him bragging about knowing where Jubal is hiding out. Why the fuck he'd do that is anyone's guess."

I narrow my gaze and clench my fists. "He's either stupid for flapping his jaws or doesn't know shit, which also makes him stupid."

The man spits blood on the floor. "Fuck you! I know who you are, and you and that bitch will be next."

Before the asshole can blink, I slam my fist into his face. The chair wobbles and then crashes backward.

"Where the fuck is he?"

Although the man laughs, fear sets in. I see it in his eyes and the piss stain on his jeans.

"I lied." He laughs. "I fucking lied. I don't even know who Jubal is."

I crouch beside him as I wipe my hands on a cloth. "You see, I don't believe you. With both mine and Edge's men looking for Jubal, it would be fucking idiotic to lie about knowing him." I glare at the piece of shit and force myself to stand. To Edgar, I say, "Find out what you can. Then turn him over to Edge."

"No way." Brinkley tugs against his bindings, struggling to break free. "He'll kill me."

Edgar laughs. "Beckett didn't say you have to be alive when I turn you over to Edge."

Pure fear erupts on Brinkley's face.

I walk away. Salem, who had kept to the background, says, "Something doesn't add up with that asshole."

That is what I've been thinking since Edgar brought him in.

Five minutes later, my phone beeps with a message from Edgar. I read it twice before sharing the info with Salem. "Edgar sent the location Brinkley gave him to Prez to get the murdering asshole."

"Fucking hell! Brinkley really was an idiot."

I trust Prez to find Jubal now. All I must do is wait. Something I've been doing since Jude died.

"Make sure the bikes are loaded on to the truck. I don't want to be traveling back and forth between the houses for now."

"They've already been loaded. When do you want to leave?"

"Now."

Salem heads off to round the men up while I stand outside in the fresh air. In truth, I don't want Kinsley in this world of mine, but whether I do or not, it doesn't matter anymore.

Kinsley's life is now tied to mine whether she likes it or not.

Chaptaer Three

I watch as four large black SUVs come up the driveway. My heart thuds in my chest with a mixture of fear and excitement. Tiberius said he would be back.

The moment he steps onto the gravel driveway, his head lifts, and those dark-gray eyes of his land on me. I don't move, and neither does he, until another man says something to him. I shake myself, questioning how the man can ensnare me so easily.

Men in jeans and tees climb from the vehicles. Out of the nine men I count, two are wearing dark suits.

Tiberius has changed out of his suit into black jeans and a white tee with sunglasses perched atop his head. It's certainly a different view of the man than the one I previously had. Who are the men with him? They all look dangerous and unapproachable. Surely, they're not all moving into the house.

My head turns as I hear booted feet enter the house. Tiberius gives instructions in a loud voice, and then the footsteps start upstairs. My bedroom door is locked, but that won't keep anyone out who is determined to get inside.

A moment later, there is a knock on my door. "Ms. Kinsley, your, um, uncle, would like you to come downstairs."

I frown at the door. The voice is hesitant, which is not what I expected. Suddenly, more curious than scared, I dash to the door and pull it open. My eyes shoot wide at the huge man standing before me in a lovely dark-gray suit. He is most certainly not what I expected after the voice I heard through the door.

He smirks. "Call me Jock," he says in a calm voice. "You must be Kinsley." He holds out his hand and smiles, but then his eyes narrow as he zeroes in on the side of my face that is red and bruised. "Who did that to you?" His voice deepens.

"The girl is accident prone," Martha says, appearing out of the blue.

The large man stares into my eyes, and I silently beg

him not to say anything because I know that he knows who is responsible. He turns to the woman. "Martha, isn't it? You are wanted in the kitchen." When she hovers, he adds, "Now, woman!"

I wince, which Jock notices. "She won't touch you again. Come. He's waiting for you." I nod, trying to hide my nerves as I follow Jock down the dimly lit hallway. "Don't worry too much about the men in the house. They will leave you alone."

I hesitate at the top of the stairs. "Maybe I should have changed first."

"Nonsense. You look fine." Jock smiles. My eyes travel down my white tee to where my black jeans cling to my skin. Thick socks cover my feet. I didn't bother with my biker boots today.

"Stop fidgeting," Jock says as he shoves me into my father's office—what was my father's office. The heavy door closes behind me. If I didn't know that Tiberius was already in the room, his scent would have given him away.

"You look scared," he comments.

I turn around. "It's unnerving having strange men wandering around my home."

His eyes narrow, and then he is suddenly in front of me. A large, tattooed hand holds my jaw as he turns my face to get a better look at the bruise forming there. I doubt Martha intended on leaving such a sign that she'd hit me.

Tiberius looks into my eyes. "This is because I called her out at lunch." His jaw tightens. "I'll get rid of her."

"No!" I grab hold of his wrist before I snatch my hand back. A sizzle of electricity shoots up my arm. I swallow hard. "I mean." I sigh. "I don't know what I mean."

His fingers gently smooth over the soreness of my cheek before he steps back. "That woman—"

"Boss," a dark-skinned man interrupts us. He grins when he sees me, and I don't think I've ever seen anyone with such perfect, white teeth before.

My lips twist into a smile when I realize the man is really being friendly. "Hello," I offer.

Tiberius narrows his eyes between the two of us and snaps, "Saul! I do not pay you to drool over my"—he clears his throat—"niece."

"No, sir!" Saul snaps his focus to Tiberius, who hasn't stopped glaring. "I came to tell you the truck is five minutes out."

"Okay. Get them moving once they arrive."

Saul nods and exits the room without another glance my way.

"Are the men moving in as well?" I ask the silently brooding man. I try to ignore the fact we're dressed similarly. Thank God I left my boots off; otherwise, we'd be identical.

"Yes." He enters my space, and it takes all my will power not to back down. "You will not encourage them."

It takes me a moment to understand what he is saying. When I do, my eyes widen in surprise. "He's far too old for me." I don't add that my taste in men centers on the man in front of me.

"So dramatic." He steps back and looks irritated. "Regardless, do not speak to my men."

The sound of a loud vehicle approaching breaks the silence as the wheels crunch on the driveway.

I look out the window and frown at the eighteen-wheeler. "What is in there?"

"Furniture, among other things." He pauses in the doorway. "Do you want any of the furniture from your parents' bedroom before I have it destroyed?"

"No, thank you." That is something I do not want. "However, if you wish to get rid of my father's desk, I would like that."

He nods. "Dinner will be in an hour or so."

"Why don't you step away from the window?" Jock suggests.

"I'm curious. I've seen Tiberius every now and again over the years; however, I never actually met him until the reading of the will. I mean, he was at the funeral, but we didn't speak. My father thought he was doing the right thing by making me his ward. So, I must trust in that." It doesn't stop me from admiring the fit of his jeans and tee as he moves.

"Your father knew Beckett would protect you if he asked. You will be safe here."

I turn to Jock and frown. "You call him by his family name?"

"Habit." Jock smiles. "How about a warm drink in the kitchen. I could do with a cup of coffee myself."

"Okay." I follow beside him and come to a stop. "What are they carrying upstairs?"

"A bed."

"He doesn't want to sleep in my parents' bed, so he brought his own." I glance at Jock for confirmation.

He nods.

"I suppose that makes sense." I sigh. "There are a lot of things that do not make sense to me, though. Many in fact, and I don't know where to start."

"Let's have that cup of coffee," he suggests and leads me toward the kitchen. "Problem?" he asks when I come to a sudden stop before stepping foot inside.

"I've never been allowed inside the kitchen," I whisper.

"From what I have been told, this is your house, which means this is your kitchen." He smirks and pushes his way inside. A growl comes out of his mouth when he sees Martha at the far end of the room. "You lay a hand on this girl again, and I will show you how hard a man as big as me can hit."

Oh God.

"You took the words right out of my mouth, Jock." Tiberius moves into the room. "This is your last chance, Ms. Green." His steely eyes narrow on the woman before he shoots a look I can't decipher at Jock. "Do not bring my niece over to the dark side while I'm in the office."

"Wouldn't dream of it."

Tiberius snorts and turns his attention to me. His eyes linger as he grabs an apple on his way out of the room.

Jock claps his hands. "Show's over. Now, can someone show us where we can make our coffee?"

"It's behind you. Nothing too fancy," a timid voice replies.

I turn to find a former employee. The young woman is maybe three years older than me. She's also the daughter of one of Martha's friends, and I'm sure she fears the vile woman too. "Thank you, Marie." I smile at her. "I didn't know you were working here again."

"Mr. Beckett called the old staff back." Marie moves closer. "I am sorry about your parents, Kinsley." She grabs my hand and squeezes.

"Thank you," I say, choking on the words.

I turn my attention to Jock, who's pouring two cups of coffee. He passes me a cup, then places a hand to my back and guides me back out along the hallway.

"The girl seemed nice," he says when we reach the living room.

"Marie is." I sit at one end of the sofa and inhale the rich aroma before I take a sip. "This is very good."

"I made it, so of course it is." He chuckles. "No one comes between me and my coffee."

"Did Tiberius ask you to be nice to me?"

His eyes dance. "He told me not to let you out of my sight."

"Hmm," I mutter.

I sit back and listen to the men putting the bed together upstairs. Hammering comes from the office, which I ignore. I don't want to know what other changes are taking place. Instead, I wonder about Jock. I sense the man was truly angry when he discovered I was hit. He will follow Tiberius's orders in the end, which means I can't trust him as much as I want to. It would be nice to not be so alone anymore.

I guess I will be safe from the outside world in the house. But will I be safe from Tiberius?

Available Now!

OTHER BOOKS BY AUTHOR

Hawke's Ridge

Maddox · Colton (2026)

Den Hollows

One of Six · Two of Six (2026)

Den of Filth (New MC Series 2025)

Reckless Wilder (2026)

Fifth Realm Series (Romantasy)

Quiver of Chaos · Wings & Arrows (2026)

Standalone Romantasy

Persephone Unchained

Tallulah James Mystery

Dead and a Murder or Two · Dead and the Wedding Crashers · Dead and a Deadly Deed · Dead and a Best Friend

Boston Bay Vikings

Camden · Bennett · Ethan · Sutton · Carter · Bryson · Ivan · Theo · Noah · Knox · Jericho · Roman

Boston Bay Vikings Minor League

Lake · Rhodes · Nikoli · Dario · Madden · Bradford

Single Titles

Butterflies and Darkness · Come Back to Me · Indecent Villain · Lawful · Love Stryker · Tears in the Rain · Whispers of Yesterday

Holiday Season

Holiday Kisses in the Snow · Jingle Bells

Romantic Suspense Series

Twenty Eight Days · The Next Victim (2025)

Blossom Creek

Christmas at Emelia's · A Rake in Blossom Creek · Heatwave in Blossom Creek · Secret Love in Blossom Creek · Mischief in Blossom Creek · Runaway Bride in Blossom Creek · Naughty & Nice in Blossom Creek

Bad Boy Rockers

My Brother's Girl · Past Sins · My Best Friend's Sister · Never Let Go · Saving Jace · Silent Night (Novella)

Kincaid Sisters

Meant to be Mine · You Were Always Mine · Will You be Mine

McKenzie Brothers

Playing with the Boss · A McKenzie Wedding (Novella) · Playing with Fire · Playing with Desire · Playing with Trouble · Playing with their Hearts · A McKenzie Christmas (Novella)

De La Fuente Family (McKenzie Spinoff)

Love in Montana · Love in Purgatory · Love in Bloom · Love in Country · Love in Flame · Love in Game · Love in Education

McKenzie Cousins

(McKenzie Spinoff)

Baby Makes Three · A Business Decision · Secret Kisses · Kissing Cousins · If Only · Princess & the Puck · A Bakers Delight · A Cowboy for Christmas · A Secret Affair · One Christmas · The Pregnant Professor · It Started with a Kiss

Novella's

Educate Me · One Dance · Pure

ABOUT THE AUTHOR

While Lexi is the author of the chick lit series, Tallulah James Mystery, and the fantasy/romance series, The Fifth Realm, she is also the author of over seventy novels. Based in Ireland, this British author has been writing since 2013.

Follow on social media:

Website: www.lexibuchanan.com
Email: authorlexibuchanan@gmail.com

facebook.com/lexibuchananauthor
x.com/AuthorLexi
instagram.com/authorlexib
bookbub.com/author/lexi-buchanan
amazon.com/Lexi-Buchanan/e/B009SPA94U

9 781918 152210